Earl's Red-Hot Wedding

BARBARA RUSSELL

All rights reserved.

No part of this publication may be sold, copied, distributed, reproduced or transmitted in any form or by any means, mechanical or digital, including photocopying and recording or by any information storage and retrieval system without the prior written permission of both the publisher, Oliver Heber Books and the author, Barbara Russell, except in the case of brief quotations embodied in critical articles and reviews.

PUBLISHER'S NOTE: This is a work of fiction. Names, characters, places, and incidents either are the product of the author's imagination or are used fictitiously. Any resemblance to actual persons, living or dead, business establishments, events, or locales is entirely coincidental.

COPYRIGHT 2024 © Barbara Russell

Cover art by Dar Albert at Wicked Smart Designs

Published by Oliver-Heber Books

0 9 8 7 6 5 4 3 2 1

one
On the Flying Scotsman, 1876

NOT EVEN TRAVELLING on the spectacular Flying Scotsman helped Brandon forget the responsibilities of being the youngest earl in the British Empire. Or more specifically, the youngest in a century, according to *The Times*. He felt betrayed by technology because, while he didn't understand a fig about engineering, fast trains had always distracted him from serious thoughts. Not anymore.

It was funny how he'd considered himself to be an adult man, entitled to make his own choices, before his father died and Brandon inherited the title. Now he considered himself a seventeen-year-old boy, who pretended to be someone important and was frightened of the consequences of making choices. For example, he regretted having convinced his guardian, Cowley, to let him travel alone.

A moment of peace and quiet. That was what he'd wanted. No old aristocrats giving him pieces of unrequested advice, or journalists asking him how he felt after his father had suffered from a sudden, lethal fit, or worse, eager mamas throwing their daughters at him because an earl was never too young to find a bride or a mistress. He wished Cowley were here. Selfish of him and confusing. His emotions were all over the place because he didn't feel either calm or peaceful.

In the three months he'd inherited the title and estate, he'd learned that peace and quiet were two things earls didn't enjoy often. Solicitors, politicians, and people curious to know everything about him intruded into his life. Not to mention the butler, housekeepers, and tenants who... all right. He shouldn't complain. His father had done the same job for all his life without whining, and even though Brandon wasn't ready to lead an earldom, he had the money and power to enjoy a comfortable life.

If only the creeping darkness over the Flying Scotsman didn't obstruct the view of the country; that would give him some respite. What was the point of travelling on the fastest train in the empire if he couldn't see anything? The fact that he was on his way to London to resume his responsibilities as an earl didn't thrill him.

The only good thing about the trip was a compartment all for him and the company of a forbidden book, *Carmilla*. Years ago, the book had shocked the *ton* for its sapphic love story and raised the concerned mamas of the empire to petition for its complete ban from the shelves of libraries and bookshops. Yet the book lived, thank goodness, sold by a few select bookshops that hid the real title with a fake cover. Officially, he was reading *Camille*, a harmless, perfectly appropriate novel.

It was ironic that he'd always wanted to read it, but his tutors had always forbidden it. Now that Brandon was an earl, he had the freedom to read what he wanted, but not the freedom to be *who* he wanted. He would trade all his freedom to get his father back.

The book almost slipped out of his hands when the door to his compartment slid open and an attendant swept into view.

"My lord." He bowed, wrinkling his dark-green uniform. "I'm sorry to disturb you."

For a moment, Brandon wondered who 'my lord' was. "Is something the matter?" Please not a delay because of the snow.

While he didn't look forward to arriving in London, he didn't want to sit on a motionless train in the dark.

The man bowed again. "The window in the compartment at the end of this carriage is broken, and the three passengers are quite uncomfortable due to the freezing temperature. All the other compartments are full. Would you mind letting them take these seats? The company will fully refund your ticket for the inconvenience, sir."

He did mind, actually, and was about to voice his annoyance, suggesting that he was ready to exchange compartments with the three passengers and endure the cold alone, when a pretty, dark-haired girl appeared from behind the attendant. She batted her eyelashes, and her large hazel eyes met his gaze. No, not simply hazel, but golden and emerald. It was a sign from the universe that she held a copy of *Camille*. His same edition. Same colour of the cover too! When she noticed he owned his own copy, she flashed a warm smile and a cheeky wink. A secret understanding was exchanged at their next glance. That did it. He changed his mind.

He shot up to his feet. "By all means." He was a gentleman after all, and he didn't want to be cold. "I'm happy to share the compartment."

"My lord." The attendant pulled the door fully open.

The girl smiled again, and Brandon couldn't stop himself from returning her smile.

"Thank you, my lord." She sauntered inside in a flutter of burgundy fabric, enveloped in a delicate cloud of jasmine. She was a ray of sunshine held together by velvet and satin.

A woman, who looked like an older version of the girl, and a tall man followed, and suddenly, Brandon's quiet corner had become crowded. His enthusiasm died a little. Three strangers in a confined space with him. Would he face hours of endless questions about his money, estate, dead parents, and power, or if he would attend the next Season?

What if these people were journalists and the whole 'cold

compartment affair' was a ruse to trap him into an unwanted interview?

If that was the case, he'd happily stay alone in the cold. Damn. Making decisions was his bane.

"Thank you for your hospitality." The man removed his tall hat and stretched out his hand. "I'm Mr. John Barclay and these ladies are my wife Dolores and my daughter Emily."

The ladies curtsied, which was an accomplishment, what with the train rocking quite hard.

Emily. Short and strong name. He liked it. He couldn't remember the last time he'd been in the company of a person his age. He'd been surrounded only by older people as of late. Hell, he hadn't spent time with his mates at all. No playing cricket, rowing in the Thames, or simply having fun with each other. He missed that.

He shook Mr. Barclay's hand. "You're welcome to make yourself comfortable. I'm Mr. Brandon Astley." He didn't add his title. There was a chance these people didn't know who he was. No need to say he was—

"The Earl of Hastings," Mrs. Barclay said in a lovely Spanish accent.

Dammit. Silence dropped in the narrow compartment. Only the chugging noise of the train could be heard. Emily stared at him, clenching her copy of *Carmilla* like a shield. Even Mr. Barclay stood speechless, a wrinkle on his brow.

Brandon had to be more famous than he thought, and no, it didn't please him because all the squeals of false delight and questions would start. A familiar, oppressive sensation crept over him.

He cleared his throat. "I am he. Please take a seat."

Mr. Barclay bowed his head. "I'm sorry for your loss." He didn't add 'my lord ' or 'sir', for which Brandon was grateful. "Your father was an inspiring man. I had the pleasure of meeting him on several occasions."

"Did you know my father?" he asked.

"We did business together," Mr. Barclay said. "I actually met him right before the tragedy. I still can't believe he isn't among us anymore."

Neither could he. All Hallows' Eve, a late bill in parliament, his father standing up to speak only not to say a word. *Carmilla*'s plot with its vampires was more believable.

"If we can do anything for you." Mrs. Barclay touched his hand in a move many members of the *ton* would consider too bold. Her eyes, so similar to her daughter's, shone with compassion. "Please don't hesitate to tell us. It must be awful for you to be alone at such a young age."

"If you want us to leave," Emily said, "we would understand, wouldn't we, Papa, Mama?"

They nodded.

"Anything." Mrs. Barclay seemed to be about to hug him. He wouldn't mind a motherly hug, but propriety and all that imposed a certain distance with strangers.

It was Brandon's turn to become speechless. He'd expected the usual gushing remarks about his young age or his fortune, followed by an invitation to a soirée or ball, and a stream of compliments on his figure, eyes, and bearing, which weren't remarkable. He hadn't expected concern for his well-being or respect for his pain.

"Thank you." He couldn't say more, or his voice would crack. "Please stay," he said after a pause. "It's a pleasure to have your company."

The Barclays sat in front of him with the ladies' skirts taking up most of the space.

"We should arrive in London in less than an hour," Mr. Barclay said.

Emily waved her book. "You're reading *Camille*! So am I. Fancy that." A pair of dimples graced her cheeks when she smiled.

Her brightness chased away the moment of sadness. "We have the same edition," he said.

"Predictable, isn't it?" She wiggled her eyebrows. As a banned book, there weren't many disguised editions of *Carmilla*.

"I wonder what this book is about," Mrs. Barclay said. "Emily can't stop reading it. She completely ignores me when she's immersed in that story."

"It's true." Mr. Barclay squeezed Emily's hand. "And she's quite secretive about the plot. Please tell us, Lord Hastings, what is this book about?"

"Well..." How could Brandon explain *Carmilla* was a book about a female vampire, who had a sapphic interest in the other female protagonist and did her level best to get into the woman's petticoats, without getting Emily in trouble? "It's the story of Laura, who—"

Emily touched the tip of his shoe with hers, arching a dark eyebrow in a warning or maybe a plea. She gave him the slightest shake of her head, causing her sable curls to bounce over her cheeks. The olive-golden shade of her skin made her hazel eyes look bigger, and he wasn't sure why he noticed that.

"Yes?" Mrs. Barclay prompted.

He put the book aside, thinking quickly. "Er, Laura is a nun."

"A nun?" Mrs. Barclay said at the same time as Emily coughed in her closed fist.

Brandon nodded a few times. His mother had always told him he was a terrible liar. "Laura is on her way to sainthood."

"And who's Camille?" Mr. Barclay asked.

Oh bugger. "The protagonist's friend. There's a rather, ahem, inspiring story of Laura's friendship with this lady, more experienced in... sainthood, Camille."

"What an odd story," Mr. Barclay said.

"A saint." Mrs. Barclay narrowed her eyes at Emily. "Why didn't you tell me?"

A blush crept over Emily's cheeks, and even though Brandon was the cause of her moment of embarrassment, his heart gave a kick at how pretty she looked.

She fiddled with the book. "I didn't want you to think I was ready to live in a convent. You would have sent me there in a moment."

Mrs. Barclay huffed. "Nonsense. Tell me the real reason."

He winced. Emily was a worse liar than he was. Her tone was all wrong. He ought to rescue her since the whole mess was his fault.

"Would you like to see the first-class restaurant, Miss Emily? I'd be delighted to offer you a cup of tea if your parents agree."

"Yes please. That would be wonderful." She stood up, and he rose as well. "Mama, Papa, may I go? Would you like anything?"

"No, darling. Enjoy the restaurant." Mr. Barclay waved them away.

Mrs. Barclay wasn't so ready to let them go. "Are you two going alone?"

"They're on a crowded train, darling. Let them have a little bit of fun," her husband said.

"Thank you, Papa, Mama." Emily kissed her father's and mother's cheeks and went to pull the door open.

Brandon rushed to do it for her, and their hands touched over the door handle. A shock of sensation went through him at the contact with her soft hand. Her olive skin caught the glow from the oil lamps, glittering with gold. He'd never seen a more lovely shade of gold. It matched her eyes and spread warmth through him as if she thawed a corner of his soul that had been frozen until now.

"Apologies." He opened the door for her and acknowledged the quickening of his pulse as she brushed past him.

She showed her devastatingly charming smile again. "Accepted."

two

BRANDON SHUT THE door to the compartment behind him and took a moment to collect himself before facing Emily again. He was rusty when it came to socialising with normal people. Never mind pretty girls. He'd make a fool out of himself.

"Thank you for getting me out of that predicament." Emily let out a breath once they were alone in the passageway. "That was close. And thank you for not telling Mama about *Carmilla*. She would have a fit."

"I wasn't prepared to think about a believable plot." He fiddled with the knot of his cravat. Since when had it become so tight? "Which chapter are you reading?"

"Thirteen," she said, walking towards the next carriage. "You, my lord?"

"The same. It sounds like a bad omen."

She laughed. "Indeed, my lord."

"Please call me Brandon." He held the next door open for her. "I feel ancient when people call me my lord."

She tilted her head, and a glossy curl fell over her cheek. "Then please call me Emily, or Emilia, as my mama calls me in Spanish."

"I detected the accent. Is she from Spain?"

Her smile dropped a little. "Valencia, but her ancestors were Moors. My great-great-great-grandfather moved to Andalusia in 1100." She lifted her chin as if challenging him to say something, and he had a lot to say.

"A Moor like Othello."

Her dimples appeared again. "Like Othello."

"Your mother looks as beautiful as you are... bugger me!" He clamped a hand over his mouth and froze in the middle of the passageway to the next carriage.

He couldn't believe he'd said *that*. With one sentence, he'd managed to be inappropriate towards Emily's mother, herself, and the entourage of his expensive tutors, who had taught him that a gentleman should never, ever swear in front of a lady, and least of all make comments on said lady's beauty or even worse, her mother's. What had possessed him to speak so frankly? He was supposed to hide his true thoughts behind polite conversations and general remarks about the weather. Maybe stifle a yawn or two. But a gentleman should never be so direct.

His face warmed to a boiling point. He was tempted to pull down a window and let the wind and icy snow cool him down, or better yet, he should return to his compartment. Embarrassment anchored him to the spot. They would probably have to chop his feet off to remove him from the train.

"I'm so sorry," he said through his fingers, waiting for her justified outrage to pour in, maybe even a slap.

And then she did something utterly shocking and absolutely delightful. She burst out laughing. Her warm, vigorous laugh reverberated in his chest and thawed him for good.

"Don't be sorry." Her charm dazzled him. "I like honesty, and when honesty is also a compliment, it's even better. Thank you for your kindness."

He removed his hand from his mouth, but his face was still a furnace. "What I said is true," he whispered.

She took a quick dip. "I appreciate your honesty, Brandon."

Damn, he liked the sound of his name on her lips. He liked her laughter, and he liked the fact she wasn't horrified. He drew in a breath when he offered her his arm and she took it. "May I have the pleasure of escorting you?"

"I'd be delighted."

He felt a foot taller when she took his arm. "Did you enjoy your stay in Edinburgh?"

"Yes. Papa had business there." She leaned closer. "Trading is my family's business. But we went to Edinburgh also because of the competition."

"Competition?" He stepped aside to let a couple of passengers pass.

"The Young Engineers Competitions." She lowered her voice, and her gaze lost some of its brightness. "I presented an invention of mine."

"You're an inventor? That's fantastic. Did you win?"

She moved her hand as if saying 'more or less.' "I was commended. My prototype of a parasol that can be used as a regular umbrella didn't work properly during the demonstration. I designed the device so that a second layer of waterproof fabric covers the first in case of rain, but the flap got jammed. So humiliating. I nearly poked one of the judges' eyes out when I opened the parasol."

"I'm sure the next time it'll be better, and congratulations anyway. Not everyone can say they designed something."

A lovely shade of crimson coloured her cheeks. "What about you? Why were you in Edinburgh?"

He lifted a shoulder. "Estate management, and yes, it's as dull as it sounds."

She laughed again, and he'd do anything to hear her laugh. "I don't envy you," she said in a serious tone. "Your life must have changed so quickly."

"It did. I turned seventeen two weeks ago." He wasn't sure why it was important she knew that. "My mother died from consumption many years ago. It was only Father and me. When my father died, I was planning a tour of the Continent, thinking about silly cricket matches and the places I wanted to visit. And now I run an earldom. Ridiculous, isn't it?"

"Scary more than ridiculous." She gripped his arm a little more tightly.

"I'm slowly getting used to it." He opened the last door to the restaurant.

The smell of cinnamon teased his nostrils when they stepped into the warm restaurant carriage. The glow from the lamps was reflected in the dark windows.

"Goodness." She leaned against him, and he didn't mind. "So fancy! The second-class restaurant isn't so glamorous."

Indeed. "This carriage is equipped with electric lights."

Her face brightened. "Capital!"

Chandeliers sparkled from the low ceiling, and a thick red carpet covered the aisle running between two rows of pristine tables.

He went to hold a stuffed chair for her at a small table, only to realise the chair was bolted to the floor. Great. "That's embarrassing."

She touched his arm, sending a tingle down his spine. "Do not worry."

Change of subject. "Tea?"

"Please."

After he ordered the tea and sat in front of her, he remained silent, not sure about what to say. The train gave a jolt, and they both chuckled.

"I do find trains a little scary." She twirled the teaspoon in her cup. "Especially after the terrible Shipton-on-Cherwell tragedy."

"Yes, I was wary about boarding a train, too. But the other option would be travelling up and down Britain on a carriage. And well, statistically, the chances that there's another train accident as catastrophic as that one are extremely low. In a way, I feel protected."

"By statistics?"

"It sounds odd, I know." He chuckled nervously. "I'm not even good with numbers, but I trust science."

"No, it's not odd. I'm a scientist. I understand." She regarded him from over the rim of her cup. "May I ask you something?"

"Anything." It was the first time in months that he'd had a normal conversation with a person his age. Or any age. It was refreshing.

She lowered her gaze. "How are you faring? Really. I mean, your father died so unexpectedly, and now you're doing an adult's job. I'd be terrified."

No one had ever asked him that. "I am terrified. My father was my whole family, and I didn't have the chance to say goodbye. He always had time for me, no matter how busy he was. Ironically, it was me who didn't have time for him. I was too caught up in my life, believing what I was doing was of vital importance while I should have spent more time with him."

She shivered and clenched her cup. "I'm so sorry."

"No, I'm sorry." He suppressed the instinct to take her hand. "I've upset you."

"Don't apologise. I asked the question, after all. And it must be awful for you. If I were you, I wouldn't be able to do an earl's job and change my life so radically."

"At first, I couldn't. I have to thank my warden for his help."

"I can't imagine losing my parents. They're my best friends although I can't tell them about *Carmilla*," she whispered the last words.

"You seem to be a happy family." He envied her a little.

"Because we fought to be one." Her face brightened. "My paternal grandfather didn't approve of my mother because she's from Spain and not from a particularly wealthy family. So my parents eloped," she said with a touch of pride. "They flew to Gretna Green and had a red-hot wedding."

"Why is it called that?"

"A blacksmith performs the ceremony, and at the end, he smashes his hammer against the anvil until the metal gets red-hot." She mimicked the move. "It's quite remarkable, or so my parents say."

"Your parents did the right thing." Eloping. His mother wouldn't have approved, but he understood Emily's parents' choice.

The train gave another jolt, causing the tea to spill. Bloody snow.

"Where are we?" She peered at the dark window.

"Abbots Ripton, I believe. Not far from London." Which meant he didn't have a lot of time to spend with her.

He would like to ask her where she lived in London and if, by any chance, she would agree to take a walk in the park with him. Maybe it was too cold for a walk. A cup of tea in a tearoom? A play in Drury Lane? A piano concert? If he sounded desperate, it was because he was. He craved the company of someone who didn't want to talk about the stock market, the House of Lords, or the most notable debutantes of the Season. He wanted a friend to chat about books and life with honesty, as Emily did.

"There's a blizzard out there." She wiped the frost from the glass. "It's so dark."

"Yes." He wrapped his hands around his cup, gathering the courage to ask her if she wanted to see him again. But his tongue was in a knot. Curse his shyness.

"Brandon?"

"Yes?" He swallowed past the lump in his throat.

She edged closer. "This is rather forward of me, but may I ask where you live in London? We might see each other for a cup of tea or a walk in the park? A play at the theatre if you fancy it. Anything."

He whipped his head up. Could she read his mind? Who cared? She wanted to see him again. "I—"

They were rushing past the train station in Abbots Ripton, when a thunderous bang rang out. The screech of metal grinding against metal hissed in his ears, and the world turned upside down as he and Emily were shoved out of their seats. Either the restaurant carriage had tilted, or he'd hit his head hard to enough to become dizzy. Glass smashed, porcelain cracked, and wood broke around him. He hit the floor, or maybe it was the ceiling. He couldn't tell. People screamed. The lights went out. Hot tea spilt on his leg, tearing a shout out of him. Then silence.

A throb pounded from behind his eyes as he touched the area around him, panic burning the back of his mouth. "Emily?" Moans came from every corner. "Emily!"

"I'm here." Her voice trembled with fear.

His head stopped spinning, and his vision cleared as he rubbed his eyes. The lampposts from the platform lit the devastated carriage through the snowstorm. There she was, lying a couple of feet from him.

He exhaled when he closed his hand around hers. "Are you hurt?"

"I don't think so." She gripped his fingers harder. "What happened?"

"A derailment is my guess, or a collision." The irony wasn't lost on him.

Loud voices came from outside, and flashes of light, likely from lamps and torches, flickered in and out of view.

"My parents." She stood up. Glass shards rained from her skirt. She staggered on the sloping floor.

"Wait. It might not be safe." He picked himself up, stretching out his arm to touch the wall for balance. The carriage had indeed tilted to one side.

The lights glared to life again with a sizzling buzz, revealing the chaos around them. The tables had been unhinged and upturned, and shards of porcelain and glass were scattered on the floor. A woman pressed a handkerchief stained with blood to her forehead.

"Good Lord." Emily gripped his arm, and he pulled her closer.

An attendant entered the carriage, walking askew along the inclined floor. "Ladies and gentlemen, please remain calm and stay here." Blood trickled from a cut on his brow. "There was a collision with a coal train. Some carriages are damaged, and we're assessing the situation."

"I have to go and see my parents." Emily went to walk towards the door but tripped on an upturned chair and lost her balance.

Brandon caught her before she could fall.

"Miss, please." The attendant raised his voice. "You can't leave this carriage. It's dangerous. We'll let you out as soon as possible."

Her breathing became uneven as she muttered something Brandon didn't understand. On instinct, he pulled her towards him. Shivering, she clung to him with desperation, and they held each other in a rib-cracking embrace.

"I'm sure your parents are all right. The collision shouldn't have disrupted their carriage." He brushed bits of glass from her dress. "Their carriage is far back. It's likely still straight."

She showed him her trembling hand. "I'm so scared."

"So am I." He let out a nervous chuckle to release the tension. "But we're fine, and everyone here is all right."

She nodded, resting her head on his chest. He knew she only sought comfort after the fright, and that she didn't do it consciously, but he wanted to be strong for her because inside, fear gripped him with cold tendrils. He was the last of the Hastings. What would become of his family's legacy if he died now?

Lights glowed from outside as the attendants and the station clerks gathered around the train. He leaned closer to the window and shielded his eyes from the glow. A carriage of the coal train lay on its side where the Flying Scotsman had rammed into it. The coal had heaped on the railway, and steam came out of somewhere. It seemed impossible that they were still alive. Emily shivered in his arms, and he dared to hold her closer against his chest.

A loud whistle pierced the air. It sounded closer by the minute. The station clerks shouted and scattered around. The flickering flames of their lamps became frantic. A few clerks dropped their lanterns in the hurry to leave the railway as the whistle grew louder.

"What is it?" she asked between uneven breaths.

He turned her away from the window. "I think another train is coming, but I don't see what the matter is." He barely finished saying that before another deafening crash thundered, stronger than the first, and an invisible force shoved him from every direction.

The carriage rolled upside down. Once. Twice. He lost count. Brandon coiled his arms and legs around Emily and put a hand on the top of her head, ignoring the pain as he hit the walls. The world stopped making sense as he and Emily were pushed and tossed around. The metal of the carriage screeched as if tortured. The lights went off again with a crackling noise. Emily screamed, but the sound came muffled. A piercing pang burned his back as something cold and hard cut his flesh. Then it was blissful, painless darkness.

three

EMILY'S EYELIDS HAD turned into lead because when she tried to open them, it was like lifting two boulders. Her whole body was heavy, limp, and sore. Even her thoughts slogged through her brain. What had happened?

The bright sunlight blinded her for a moment. When her vision adjusted, she glanced around. White walls, floors, and curtains. She was lying in a hospital bed. The starched bedsheets chafed her skin, and the air was thick with the smell of carbolic acid. Pain burned her right shoulder as she tried to sit up. She racked her brain. The last thing she remembered was a blood-chilling screech and the carriage rolling over itself. She'd hit the floor, or maybe the ceiling, with her shoulder, and the pain had stunned her. Brandon had protected her. He'd wrapped himself around her like a vine, never letting her go. He'd taken the brunt of the many impacts. She'd heard him groan with each blow.

"Mama?" Her voice sounded coarse to her own ears. "Papa?" she called in the quiet room.

She blinked and almost cried in agony when she propped herself up. Her right arm and shoulder were tightly bandaged, limiting her mobility, and her head throbbed. But aside from that, she was in one piece. No missing limbs or bleeding wounds, and she could move all her fingers and toes despite the pain. She took a deep breath and searched the room. Other patients rested in the narrow beds. None of them seemed to be conscious. Through the open door, she caught a glimpse of passing nurses and doctors.

"Mama?" She raised her voice.

"Emily? Are you awake?"

Her heart gave a quick kick as she recognised Brandon's voice coming from the corridor.

"Brandon?" She gritted her teeth and sat upright. Goodness, her arm ached, sending stings of pain throughout her whole body.

He entered the room, rolling the wheels of the wheelchair he sat in. But that wasn't the reason her breath hitched. His face was a mask of cuts, swellings, and dark bruises. A thick bandage wrapped around his head, and his dark-green eyes showed too much white. Even his hands were marred with marks and cuts. And his nose was so swollen she wondered how he could breathe.

"Emily." His voice cracked. "You're awake." Sheer relief filled his words. "I was so worried."

When he gently took her hand, she couldn't hold back a sob that hurt her chest.

"What happened? Where are we?" she asked among sobs.

"We're at Huntingdon County Hospital." He swallowed hard, studying her face. "You've been unconscious for three days."

"Three days?" She touched her forehead, only to find it bandaged as well. That explained her headache.

"After the Flying Scotsman rammed into the coal train, the express to Leeds hit us fully." He brushed her knuckles. "The Flying Scotsman, the express to Leeds, and the coal train got smashed together. Some miscommunication happened, and the fact the Flying Scotsman was stuck on the railway and the poor visibility did the rest. It was a disaster."

She took a moment to process the news. The loud whistle and the sensation of being rolled upside down made sense.

"You hit your shoulder and head pretty badly." He closed his eyes for a moment, his Adam's apple bobbing on a swallow. "The doctor said that if you didn't wake up in a week—" He gazed away, blinking furiously.

"I'm all right. More or less." Maybe in a few hours, she'd have a full crisis about her near-death experience, but right now she was simply glad to be alive. "And you? What happened to you?"

He clenched his jaw and wiped his eyes quickly. "A metal shard stabbed me in the back. I was lucky. The cut didn't cause any internal damage. My back hurts though. I can't walk at the moment because I can't straighten my back and... Emily..." He raised his gaze to her.

A cold sensation seeped into Emily's chest. "My parents?"

Brandon's eyes shone with unshed tears. "The express to Leeds hit our compartment."

She heard the words, but they didn't mean anything.

He folded his hands around hers, but his grip lacked strength. "I'm so sorry we have to share the same tragedy."

Her parents. "No!" She meant to scream, but only a tiny sound came out of her. "I must see them." She shoved the cover aside, not caring about revealing the thin nightgown barely covering her or the pain stabbing her shoulder. "Where are they? Where?" She made a mess of the bedsheets, and gosh, the agony punched the breath out of her. "There must be a mistake. I need to see them."

He took her wrist. "They aren't here."

She winced when she tried to leave the bed. "I must see them."

"Emily." He sounded stronger. "They aren't here," he repeated more firmly.

She collapsed on the bed under the weight of her grief, a hand clamped over her mouth. He slowly inched himself up to sit next to her, his legs trembling. He didn't say how sorry he was, and she was grateful for that.

He caressed her messy curls, brushing them from her wet

cheeks. Somehow, the kind gesture made her want to cry harder, maybe because it reminded her of something her father would do.

"I know how you feel," he whispered. "I'm here for you."

She buried her face in his chest, unconcerned by the fact that he was an earl or that she was injured, and mourned her parents.

A WEEK of crying and not sleeping hadn't helped Emily feel less confused or less in pain. The food tasted like sand, the drugs left a bitter taste in her mouth, and she'd lost any sense of time.

She'd probably exhausted her personal reservoir of tears and desperation because a void of sensation lodged in her chest, and she didn't cry anymore. Maybe it was the morphia the nurses administered to her every day. At least the pain in her shoulder and head was a dull, distant throb, a stark contrast to the very vivid pain of losing her family. The only good thing about her staying at the hospital was Brandon. He never left her side, despite the fact he had to be in a lot of pain himself. He couldn't stand for more than a minute before his legs started to tremble— something to do with the stab and the blow to his back. Yet he never complained and always had a smile for her.

In his wheelchair, he sat next to her bed, reading the newspaper. A deep frown marked his brow, and she wondered if the accident had made him older. The cuts and bruises gave him an older air. She felt ancient herself, not sixteen anymore, as if she'd lived a thousand lives.

"More bad news?" she asked, tasting the bitterness of the last dose of drugs.

His dark-bronzed hair caught the pale sunlight, glittering with a dozen different hues. So pretty. She searched for the tiniest pretty things around her all the time. It was a time well spent.

"Everyone is trying to put the blame on someone or something else for the disaster. The snow, the darkness, the antiquated brake system, the inexperienced clerks." He clicked his tongue. "I think all these things are to blame, especially the brakes."

"Who cares what the reason is? People died."

"Exactly for that reason, it's important to find the cause. We can fix a mechanical problem and train people to avoid something like that happening again, but we need to know the cause." He folded the newspaper and put it aside. "I have something for you, a present."

"A present? Where did you get me a present?" The morphia dulled even her emotions because the thought of Brandon making an effort to get her something excited her, but her heart didn't change its rhythm.

"Not really a present. I borrowed it from another patient." He took out a book from a pocket in his chair. "I can't read *Carmilla* aloud to you for obvious reasons, but this one should be funny." He showed her a copy of *The Comedy of Errors*. "If you want."

"Please."

"I shall start." He coughed in his fist.

Emily would have thought she'd forgotten how to laugh, but gradually, she found herself smiling, then chuckling as much as the bandage and the pain allowed her. Brandon was an excellent reader. He made different voices for each character and delivered the jokes like a professional actor. Finally, she felt something. Her numbness lifted. The laughter unblocked the flow of emotions that were trapped somewhere in her heart. She stopped laughing. Was she a terrible daughter for laughing now? For seeing a tiny spark of light through the darkness?

"What is it?" He put aside the book.

"I feel guilty." She twisted the bedsheet with her restless fingers. "I lived. They died. I'm laughing. They can't."

"I feel guilty too. If I had refused to let you and your family sit in my compartment, your parents would be alive."

"Don't blame yourself." She laced her fingers through his, surprised by how warm and strong they were. He seemed more alive than usual because she'd been surrounded by death if that made any sense. "I'm glad you're alive."

"I'm glad you're alive," he said.

She took both his hands without thinking. In the past week, she'd sobbed all over his chest, fallen asleep in his arms, and been held by him so many times that the physical contact with him had become both a necessity and a familiar occurrence. She was too tired to care if it was appropriate or not and wasn't ashamed of admitting she needed his comfort, deep voice, and calm to sail through her dark moments. It was selfish of her to need him so terribly. Besides, she could walk; he couldn't for now. Her injuries were less serious than his. But he was the only thing that anchored her to the earth, that made sense in a world of madness.

She brushed a brown curl from his face and traced the shape of the cut across his face. "Does it hurt?"

"Not really." He touched his swollen nose. "It's getting better. I can smell things now, which isn't great considering that here everything smells of carbolic acid or morphia."

"I smell it on myself too." She kept caressing his battered face. Each blemish was a testament to his effort to protect her. He leaned against her palm. Maybe he needed her comfort as well.

He put his hand over hers. "It's early, but I wanted to talk to you about something."

"Yes?"

"I don't mean to be forward, but…" He tucked her dressing gown— something one of the nurses had given her —to cover her properly. That was another gesture that had become intimate and familiar in a short time. "Do you have any relatives who can take care of you?"

"In Spain, there's my mother's family."

His fingers stiffened. "Do you want to move there?"

Gosh, did she want to? And leave her parents here? "I don't know. I visited my mother's relatives only once when I was a child. My father's sister, Mrs. Rose Allen, lives here though, outside

London. Father hasn't..." She took a sharp breath. "Father hadn't seen her in a while. Aunt Rose became a widow many years ago, and she's been through a lot since then. She has also never been particularly fond of my mother. That caused frequent disagreements between my father and my aunt. She might not be interested in taking me in. I don't know. I should send her a message and inform her of the bad news."

"If Mrs. Allen doesn't want to help you, I'll be more than happy to." He lifted a hopeful gaze at her, his face brightening under the bruises.

She didn't have any cuts on her face because he'd formed a protective cocoon around her with his body. He couldn't walk because he'd shielded her. His back was damaged because he'd taken the blows destined to strike her. And now he wanted to provide for her.

A lump swelled in her throat. "I didn't thank you."

"For what?"

"If you hadn't protected me, I'd probably be dead."

A corner of his mouth quirked up in a smile that carried too much sadness for a young earl. "I'm not sure. I didn't know what I was doing. I just wanted to protect you."

"You did."

"I want to do more. Will you come to London with me?" He sounded as if he begged her for a favour instead of the other way around. But he'd done too much for her. She couldn't impose upon him further.

"I should ask my aunt first."

"Of course. Of course. But my offer stands. It will always stand."

"Thank you." She kissed his ruined cheek lightly, careful not to hurt him. It was the first time she'd kissed a boy.

He flushed a deep shade of red. "Thank you."

They laughed together, but this time, she didn't feel guilty.

"Master. There you are." A tall man with a well-trimmed beard entered the room and stopped next to Brandon, breaking the moment. The man removed his tall hat. "The nurse told me to look for you here. I'm so glad to see you. I've been searching for you for days."

Brandon released her hand, and she missed his warmth immediately. "Sir, I'm glad to see you too." His voice cracked.

The man squeezed Brandon's shoulder, his eyes shining. He bowed his head to Emily. "I'm the Honourable Mr. Rudyard Cowley, Lord Astley's warden. You must be Miss Emily de la Fuente Barclay."

She gave a nod. "I am she."

"Master Brandon sent me a wire to inform me of what happened. The number of patients and the general chaos caused delays in the procedure of notifying the next of kin. I spent a few days trying to find Master before he sent me the wire." He stared fondly at Brandon, clenching his hat as if fighting the urge to hug his charge. "But I'm here now."

A moment of panic seized her. Mr. Cowley was here to take Brandon home, away from her. "Are you leaving?" she asked.

"Not without you," Brandon said at the same time as Mr. Cowley said, "We're going back to London."

Brandon turned towards him. "I'm not leaving Emily alone. She needs to contact her aunt first, and I want to be sure she's well cared for."

She didn't want to force him to do something just because she needed him. He had his own injuries and anguish to deal with. But she'd be lying if she said she wasn't happy to be with him.

Mr. Cowley produced a notebook and a pencil from his pocket. "Please, Miss Barclay, tell me everything about your aunt, and I will contact her."

Brandon smiled at her encouragingly. "I won't leave you until you make a decision, and Mr. Cowley is the best sleuth I know."

Mr. Cowley grinned. "I'll find your aunt, Miss Barclay. Do not fear."

∽

BRANDON KEPT HIS PROMISE. Despite the fact that Mr. Cowley was impatient to return to London, he stayed with Emily and kept reading to her as they waited for Aunt Rose to arrive.

Since Emily had grown stronger in the past few days, she and Brandon sat on a bench outside the hospital whenever the weather allowed it. The train accident had disrupted the quiet life of the small hospital, and even days after the tragedy, injured people kept flowing in.

Brandon winced as he shifted in his wheelchair. His blanket slipped down, and she caught it with her good hand.

"Your pain isn't going away," she said, covering him with the blanket.

"The wound is healing well, but the swelling on the small of my back is causing me problems. I have a swelling the size of a watermelon. Rather uncomfortable."

"Thank you for staying here with me."

His tense expression relaxed. "You don't need to thank me. We're friends, and if you decide to stay with your aunt, promise me you'll write and visit me in London."

That was the easiest promise she'd ever made. "I promise."

She tensed all over again when Mr. Cowley walked towards them from across the yard with a short, blonde woman at his side. Emily hadn't seen Aunt Rose in a while, but her aunt's striking features were easy to recognise.

"My lord, Miss Barclay." Mr. Cowley removed his hat. "This is Mrs. Rose Allen."

"Emily. My dear child." Aunt Rose's voice quivered as she took in her niece's appearance and bandages that wrapped her head. "Such a tragedy."

"Aunt." A knot tied in Emily's throat as Aunt Rose hugged her gently.

Her mother had never spoken an ill word against Aunt Rose,

but Emily was aware of their disputes. Aunt Rose hadn't approved of Father's choice of wife or the decision to elope. But she was family. The only family Emily had.

"My darling," Aunt Rose said. "I'm so sorry. I can't believe John is dead."

Emily sagged against her aunt, overwhelmed by a fresh wave of sadness. "I miss them so much."

"I understand." Aunt Rose wiped her eyes. "I had no idea. Mr. Cowley informed me of John and Dolores's deaths." She caressed Emily's cheek. "I'm eager to take care of you, darling. Catherine will be thrilled to have her dear cousin with her. We must be together as a family."

The offer should be a relief for Emily, but the surge of happiness she expected didn't arrive. Still, she didn't want to whine and add another problem to Brandon's already tall pile of responsibilities. He'd done too much for her. She ought to grow up as he'd done.

Brandon didn't say anything. His sad smile was a stab to her chest.

"Thank you for taking care of my niece, my lord." Aunt Rose bobbed a quick curtsy to Brandon.

Brandon bowed his head. "It was an honour, madam."

What? Were they saying goodbye? Just like that? Emily's breathing sped up.

"Master, you need to return to London." Mr. Cowley gave him a pointed look. "I employed the best physician on Harley Street to help you recover quickly. The resources of this small country hospital have been severely depleted by the accident. The physicians here can't help you, and you need proper food, care, and rest."

Good gracious. He was leaving her. She wasn't ready...

Brandon took her hand again. "Maybe we can escort Emily to her new home."

"Travelling for you is going to be uncomfortable. The trip to

London will further tax your strength. I'm sure Mrs. Allen is eager to take care of Emily as well," Mr. Cowley said.

Aunt Rose caressed Emily's head. "My lord, you don't have to worry about anything. Emily is family."

Emily squeezed her lips together not to scream. The separation from Brandon shouldn't hurt so much. They'd known each other for such a short time. But a bond had been forged between them under the contorted metal of the Flying Scotsman. She couldn't deny it. It was a bond born out of fear, desperation, and a mutual need for comfort. But in the week she'd spent crying for her parents, she would dare to say Brandon and she had become intimate friends. They'd faced death together after all. And for that reason, she didn't want to be a burden to him. He'd risked his life to protect her. Besides, while she'd lost her family, her injuries were healing quickly. His condition was worse. He needed to return to London.

"It's all right, Brandon," Emily said. Mr. Cowley arched his eyebrows at hearing her addressing an earl so casually. "We'll see each other soon, won't we?"

"Yes, we will." He brought her hand up and kissed it, ignoring the fact Aunt Rose and Mr. Cowley stood in front of them.

It was her absolute first kiss from a boy. The first time ever that a young man had kissed her. Yes, it was only her hand, but it still counted as a kiss. A shock of sensation went through her. A good type of shock. The quick, chaste kiss revived her buried emotions, reminding her that her future might be less grim than she thought.

"Until we meet again then," he whispered.

"Until we meet again." And she meant every word.

four
Ten years later

EMILY WASN'T SURE what shocked her the most— the fact that she had yet another interview for a position of governess—her fourth in a couple of weeks, which was an accomplishment —or that Lady Robinson, her probable employer, looked bored to the point that she kept stifling a yawn whenever Emily spoke about her résumé.

Emily folded her hands on her lap, keeping her back straight. "I speak Spanish and French fluently," she said. "I'm good with mathematics and Latin too. And I love children. I'm sure your daughter and I will be good friends."

"You sound very confident." Lady Robinson showed off her sophisticated London accent. "So you moved from..." She narrowed her gaze on Emily's résumé, which wasn't very long. Just one page with her essential information fluffed up a little. "Painswick. I've never heard of it."

"It's a small town." Very small. So small one needed a good magnifier and a leap of faith to find it on a map. One could cross it in thirty seconds by walking at a good pace. "On the outskirts of Northampton, madam. My aunt decided to move to London recently."

Thank goodness. London would give Emily more opportunities to find a job. Not to mention that all the chores a country house required were exhausting. The ruined skin of her hands and her constant fatigue proved that.

Lady Robinson's angelic beauty was intimidating, but her not-so-angelic smile sent a chill down Emily's spine. "I heard you were on the Flying Scotsman when the accident in Abbots Ripton happened."

Bother. What did the accident have to do with anything? "How do you know that?"

Lady Robinson's facial lines tightened. "Your last name, de la Fuente Barclay"— she pronounced 'de la Fuente' wrong, but anyway —"isn't exactly common, and your father was somewhat famous."

Emily wondered why Lady Robinson had asked that question if she already knew the answer. "Yes, I was on the Flying Scotsman."

"Such a horrible tragedy. I'm so sorry." Lady Robinson didn't sound sorry at all. "Your head was gravely injured, and you were trapped in the contorted carriage. They had to cut the metal to let you out, I reckon."

Thank goodness Emily didn't remember any details of the accident. She'd lost consciousness after the crash and woken up in bed, although the sensation of being squashed and suffocated sometimes overwhelmed her when she found herself in a confined carriage, train, or narrow space. Just the thought disturbed her.

"And before you ask how I know that," Lady Robinson said, "the information was on *The Standard*. A list of the passengers who had been seriously injured was published. Also, I contacted your aunt prior to our meeting. You wrote her name in your references. She mentioned that you become upset in tight spaces."

Great. Emily shifted on the seat. Couldn't Aunt Rose stay quiet?

Still, she failed to see what her fear of confined spaces had to do with the job. Besides, her condition certainly hadn't stopped Aunt Rose from recruiting Emily to do all sorts of chores in the house. Floor scrubbing, horse grooming— she loved that —laundry, and even repairing carriages and various contraptions— she loved that last one too —had filled Emily's days for the past years. She'd learned a lot about horses and devices, but she'd also neglected her dream of becoming an engineer. It was time she moved on, found a paid job, and left Aunt Rose. That was her plan.

"I was indeed trapped in the carriage," she said. "But with due respect, what does the accident have to do with my being a governess?"

Lady Robinson leaned back on her chair. "It would seem that your dislike for tight spaces causes you problems travelling in closed carriages, trains, and covered carts."

Emily didn't deny or confirm. Yes, covered carriages and trains were her most dreaded spaces. She'd neglected overcoming her fears too.

"Would you please enter that wardrobe?" Lady Robinson pointed at a large piece of furniture that looked like an oversized, standing coffin.

"Excuse me?"

"Just get inside the wardrobe. I'll lock you there for a few minutes and then let you out. Nothing to worry about." The lady waved a dismissive hand. "Chop, chop."

Dash it all. Emily walked over to the humongous thing. Only a few minutes. It wouldn't be that terrible. Sweat dampened the back of her neck as she focused on entering the narrow, cramped space. She fared well in rooms and every place with high ceilings and wide windows, but tiny, constricting spaces were another matter. They required a ridiculous amount of energy and focus on her part not to scream. It was a constant battle for control as if her body and mind fought against each other. She recognised the absurdity of her predicament. Nothing horrible would happen to her inside the wardrobe. On a logical level, she was aware of that.

But her body had a different reaction, not giving a toss about her cold, hard logic.

As she tried to take the first step, the movement wasn't either graceful or quick. Her legs had turned into slabs of marble. Her pulse spiked. A buzzing noise rang in her ears. Dark spots blotched her vision. No, she couldn't do it. The inside of the coffin, disguised as a wardrobe, was too dark and small. Her back muscles stiffened too as she gnashed her teeth and didn't move an inch forward. The screams of the passengers on the Flying Scotsman echoed faintly in her mind.

"Can you enter the wardrobe or not?" Lady Robinson drummed her fingers on the door of the wardrobe.

"I..." Emily's tongue seemed stuck on the roof of her mouth.

"All right, that's enough." Lady Robinson shut the door of the wardrobe with a quick slam as if to make a point. "Your irrational fear makes you useless."

She released a breath through her teeth and sagged on her chair again, taking in deep breaths. "I beg to differ. I can take alternative means of transport to closed carriages, and I have no problem staying indoors. I fail to understand what my predicament has to do with being a governess. Surely, I won't teach classes from a wardrobe."

"How can you take care of my daughter when you suffer from a condition that paralyses you?" Lady Robinson asked the question with the tone of someone who already knew the answer. Again. "What if my daughter wants to spend the afternoon in the park? You won't be able to accompany her in a carriage."

"I could take a hansom cab." She gestured in the direction of the street. "There are plenty in London. I have to tutor your daughter in literature and mathematics, not take her around for promenades in carriages."

Lady Robinson's eyebrows lowered. "I would mind your manners if I were you."

Sod manners. Emily was tired of comments about her fear,

strange accent when she spoke French, or 'Mediterranean looks.' She worked hard in Aunt Rose's house, and yes, her French had a Spanish accent, so what? Why was she good enough for chores but not for a job as a governess?

Lady Robinson folded Emily's résumé and pushed it towards her. "I'm sorry, but I can't employ someone who isn't capable of taking care of my child."

She ignored the document. "I'm perfectly able to take care of a child!"

"And I don't like your tone." Lady Robinson rose in a swish of silk. She towered over Emily a good foot. "I also heard about your Latin temperament—"

"Excuse me?" She shoved herself to her feet, her pulse thundering. The chair scraped back with a screeching noise. "I don't have any temperament, Latin or otherwise. I'm simply outraged in front of what is a spectacular injustice. Any person would react as I do."

"I was kind to you and gave you the opportunity to have this meeting to assess if the rumours I heard were founded or not. I'm sorry to say that you disappointed me, Miss Barclay. This interview is over." Lady Robinson pulled the door open. "Remove yourself from my house."

"Gladly." Emily marched outside the pompous sitting room and thudded down the stairs.

How dared Lady Robinson! Emily might have a temper, but she was tired, so very tired of being considered good only for menial tasks. She'd spent years repairing all sorts of devices and contraptions in her aunt's farmhouse. From water boilers to grandfather clocks, there wasn't a mechanical item she hadn't dismantled, studied, and reassembled... all right, not always successfully. But failure and the risk of explosion were part of the learning process, weren't they?

She didn't have a degree in engineering although a couple of universities in London eagerly admitted women. In New York City, several women had graduated as engineers, and they now had respected careers. She could do the same. The problem was that she didn't have the money for the fees, books, and in general, food and rent to sustain herself. And how could she earn it when no one wanted to hire her?

Her pace slowed along the pavement as the heaviness of yet another rejection weighed on her. Now what? Lady Robinson was the last one on Emily's short list of possible employers. At first, Emily had been thrilled to have received a few requests for an interview just two weeks after she'd arrived in London, but the excitement had been doused by the too-frequent 'no, thank you.'

Lady Clayton hadn't liked her olive skin too much— her exact words; Lady Fullerton hadn't liked Emily's passion for physics and mathematics— such odd interests; and Lady Galbraith had wanted Emily to slap her son if he did something wrong. The last one was the only interview Emily had walked away from of her own volition, well before hearing the rejection. She wasn't going to slap any child, for Pete's sake.

She strolled along the pavement crammed with young ladies ready for the upcoming Season, which was the reason Aunt Rose had moved to London. The Season wouldn't start for another three months, but the preparations were on their way. New gowns, hats, and shoes for Cousin Catherine. Not to mention the effort of making the right type of connections and exchanging calling cards with other peers. It was a full-time job for Aunt Rose and Catherine.

Young ladies laughed and chatted while admiring the windows full of expensive shops displaying beautiful ballgowns, pelisses, and silk slippers. She had never had a Season. Mother had believed that sixteen was too young to become a debutante, and Father had feared losing his daughter if Emily had started attending balls and dinner parties.

She'd lost him, instead.

What's the hurry? He'd always said. *Be my little girl forever. I won't complain.*

She wouldn't have either.

Aunt Rose had never cared about Emily's Season. All her efforts went into preparing Catherine to find her a good match, which shouldn't be difficult. With her golden hair, porcelain skin, sapphire eyes, and sweet temperament, Catherine embodied the perfect beauty that was all the rage at the moment. But getting an education was Emily's priority, and Catherine was indeed stunning. She couldn't deny it.

Maybe a position as governess was too ambitious. She could be a housekeeper. Heaven knew if she was good at housework. Aunt Rose had always expected her to earn her keep, and Emily didn't enjoy being idle. But she wanted independence, her own life, her own choices, and yes, she'd had enough of Aunt Rose's orders. At twenty-six, she was a spinster, and she'd embraced spinsterhood with nonchalance. No need to live with her aunt. Besides, Aunt Rose agreed it was time for Emily to move on.

She paused in front of a majestic house shining with its bright walls and sparkling bay windows. Brandon would live in a house like that one, in an exclusive area like that. He'd changed addresses a couple of times, and she'd lost contact with him over the years. The duties of the earldom had overwhelmed him, and his spare time had been limited. Would he remember her if they met? Would he still care about her?

After their heart-breaking goodbye at the hospital, they'd written to each other for a while. His letters had been long and detailed at first, but they'd grown more succinct and detached with time until they'd ceased to arrive altogether. She'd heard he'd travelled a lot around Europe and bought a few houses in London, likely having better things to do than corresponding with a boring girl who was a housekeeper for her own aunt in a tiny, obscure village.

She wasn't angry, maybe a little envious of all the lovely places he must have visited. Places she would never be able to see, because how could she travel to distant lands without taking a train or a closed carriage? But to this day, she missed him. They'd made a promise that day at the hospital, and he hadn't kept it. It had hurt then. It still did today. But he was an earl with responsibilities and a busy life, who had made a promise to a girl he barely knew when he'd been a boy. She couldn't blame him.

When she stepped into the hallway of Aunt Rose's townhouse, she had to push down a sob. Sad thoughts were like trains with many carriages: one pulled the other forwards. Another interview, another failure. She stood there, pondering her next move. She'd just arrived in London. It was too early to be demoralised although none of the ladies had shown any appreciation of her qualities.

Aunt Rose and Catherine would be out tonight for a ball. She would have the opportunity to spend the evening writing another list of potential employers, reading a book, and maybe dismantling the cuckoo clock in the dining room just for fun.

Quick footsteps distracted her. Catherine rushed down the stairs, her silk gown fluttering around her.

"Oh, Emily. How did it go?" she asked, grabbing her best afternoon coat from the hook on the wall.

"Not well." Emily removed her worn hat and gloves. A hole had opened on the tip of the thumb. She ought to mend it before it unravelled the whole glove.

"You don't sound surprised. Help me with the coat." Catherine turned around, her golden curls bouncing.

Emily adjusted the folds of the fine woollen coat and let it drape nicely over the bustle of Catherine's dress.

"Thank you." She waved in the direction of the upper floor. "There's one of my ballgowns on your bed."

"Mending or washing?"

"Neither." Catherine checked her reflection in the oval mirror, fixing a stray curl. "You're coming with us to tonight's ball."

Emily stopped fiddling with her worn glove. "Excuse me?"

"Mother decided you might come with us." Catherine pinched her cheeks until they flushed red. "Isn't that exciting?"

No, because there had to be a reason for the unexpected invite. "It's quite sudden."

"It is, but see, one of the ladies Lady Gardner invited had to cancel at the last minute, so there was one spare gentleman, and the invitations weren't balanced. Imagine how horrified Lady Gardner was. It was awful for her."

Emily shot her gaze towards the ceiling. "Yes, awful."

"Thus Mother told her she could bring you to balance the guests. Lady Gardner was so grateful that she promised to invite me to her estate this summer and introduce me to Lord Grosvenor who might be a good match for me. Isn't that wonderful?"

"Yes, awful... I mean wonderful." Emily handed Catherine her hat. There. She was only a pawn in Aunt Rose's match-making scheme.

"I'll see you later then." Catherine hurried out of the house, leaving the door open. Why bother closing it when there was Emily? Why bother washing her own dirty clothes— enough bitterness. Emily was already a spinster, or worse, an unemployed spinster. She didn't need the bitterness.

Honestly, she should be happy about the opportunity to go to a ball with or without Aunt Rose's scheme. But she wasn't in the mood.

She dragged herself up the stairs. The good thing was that she might meet someone who needed a governess and who didn't care about her olive skin, her southern origin, her fear of carriages, and her strange accent when she spoke French. And her Latin temper. And her passion for mechanics. Easy.

Good things happened to those who stayed positive, right?

Voices came from Aunt Rose's study. Emily paused as she recognised the family's solicitor. As of late, Mr. Payne met with Aunt Rose every other day. They would shut themselves in Aunt Rose's office and discuss for hours. The meetings had started months ago in Painswick before the relocation to London. If Aunt Rose was going through some trouble, she would have discussed it with Catherine and Emily, wouldn't she?

But Aunt Rose's finances had to be in good shape. Otherwise why move to London or buy expensive dresses for Catherine's Season? Still, the meetings were suspicious.

Emily tiptoed to a quiet corner and listened. Not that she enjoyed eavesdropping on others' conversations, but if something terrible was about to happen, she wanted to know.

"... I gather it had to be done as soon as possible," Aunt Rose said in a firm tone, "before it's too late. Not that I believe anyone would come forth for her. It's impossible." She chuckled.

The sound of documents being shuffled came.

"Yet it's a race against time, madam. You have a matter of weeks, but I reckon that no one is in the position to oppose your claims over the inheritance," Mr. Payne said.

Inheritance? That would explain Aunt Rose's sudden good fortune and uncharacteristic decision to spend a lot of money on frivolities. But who had left money to Aunt Rose? Emily hadn't heard of any dead relatives.

"Excellent," Aunt Rose said. "The chances of a wedding are very low anyway."

Well, Catherine's Season had yet to start. Her chances of finding a good match were high, but it would take a while before Aunt Rose saw a penny from her future son-in-law.

Footfalls approached, and Emily headed towards her bedroom. Aunt Rose's and Mr. Payne's voices sounded muffled once she closed the door. An inheritance and a wedding. Neither had anything to do with her.

She exhaled when she saw the gown lying on her single bed. Ballgown her foot. It was one of Catherine's worn dresses. The white fabric was still good, but the style belonged to the previous decade with its wide skirt, starched petticoats, and puffed-up sleeves. Oh well, did it matter? She would go only to even the numbers. No one would notice her. Long live the wallflower!

"Emily?" Aunt Rose never knocked before entering Emily's room.

"Aunt." She lifted the dress. She wasn't a great seamstress, but she could easily remove the puffed-up sleeves to give the dress a lighter touch.

"You're coming with us tonight." Aunt Rose gave a long, appraising look at the dress.

"Catherine told me about the horror of the uneven guests."

"I trust you to behave like a lady." Aunt Rose tilted up her chin. "Catherine's future depends on how she'll be received by the genteel society of London. The Season hasn't yet started, but every public appearance counts. Don't do anything that might compromise her chances of finding a good match."

"I have no intention of doing so, Aunt." She would enjoy the music, eat those delicious pastries that always abounded at balls, and be happy to be ignored by the gentlemen while trying to find a lady with a child who needed an education.

Aunt Rose didn't leave. "There's something else. I must ask you to stop seeking employment for now."

Emily whipped her head up. "Why?"

Aunt Rose wrinkled her nose. "Your begging for a job doesn't put us in a good light. Catherine's cousin seeking employment as a common governess? Catherine would become the gossip of the Season."

Emily tossed the gown on the bed. "What are my options then? How can I become independent if I don't find work? I believe you wish me out of your house as well."

Aunt Rose was flustered. "Good gracious, you twist my words. I wish for you to be independent, not to throw you out. I'm not asking you to never find the position you want. I'm only asking you to put your search on hold until Catherine is well-integrated into society. You can't be that selfish. Besides, your passion for tinkering may be a source of embarrassment. With all those strange devices you built, one might think you're one of those anarchists who build bombs. Besides, your devices do have the tendency to explode."

That was the most absurd thing Emily had ever heard. "I need a job now, and you promised me to let me search for it," she said without completely removing the annoyance from her voice. "And you've asked me to postpone my search quite a few times now."

"I know what I said, and I'm not going back to my word. I'm asking for a few months. That's all." Aunt Rose's request sounded reasonable, but anger caused the back of Emily's mouth to tingle. "You're part of this family and being part of a family means looking out for each other. Catherine needs us now. It's a sacrifice, yes, but we must do it for her sake. After all, there's no hurry for you to leave. You do have a roof over your head and food on your table."

Yes, but Emily also had a dream that had been put on hold for a decade. Time was slipping away through her fingers. How was she supposed to find a job if she kept stopping her search for one? Gosh, was she a vicious, horrible person, or was her rage justified? She couldn't tell anymore.

Aunt Rose caressed her cheek. "Please, darling. Only for a short while, then you'll be free to do what you want."

Not really. Maybe Emily did have a temper after all. Aunt Rose had taken care of her. She'd expected Emily to earn her keep, yes, but Emily had never starved.

"I understand your frustration." Aunt Rose took Emily's hand. "When James died..." Her voice cracked. "I was left alone with a small child. Your father helped me, bless him. He did everything he could, but I had to pull myself together and build a life of my own just as you wish to do now. You have my sympathy. I don't want Catherine to go through what I did. She deserves to be happy and never worry about living hand-to-mouth."

Yes, but what about Emily? Oh, dash it. Was she whining and

thinking only about herself? It was probably the disappointment of the day that made her so sour.

"All right," she said not without effort.

"Thank you, darling. I was sure you would understand." Aunt Rose hugged her. "I believe you're going to enjoy yourself tonight."

Emily begged to differ.

five

YEARS HAD PASSED since the Flying Scotsman accident, but Brandon's back and legs still bothered him. More than bothered him, sometimes. His physician kept saying the problem wasn't simply physical but spiritual, that Brandon's pain was connected to his fear of pain. Great. Brandon didn't know what to do with the information. In fact, knowing that his fear of pain exacerbated the pain only brought more fear. The harder he tried not to be anxious, the more anxious he became, the more pain he felt. A vicious circle that had trapped him for years.

He gritted his teeth and splashed his face with cold water. Lady Gardner's house was equipped with a modern water closet and even a proper boiler for hot water. A miracle of modern engineering, but that was as far as he would go in praising the evening.

What had possessed him to come to this ball? He should have stayed home and read one of the many legal reports accumulating on his desk or discussed with Cowley the state of his factories. But no, his friend and business partner, Matthew, had insisted that Brandon's presence was needed for their work and that Brandon had to *reconnect* with society, among other things. There was a reason why Brandon had lost contact with society though. A good one.

He had to remind himself he wasn't here just to mingle with other people, but for work as well. If he wanted to successfully push Matthew's latest invention through the endless bureaucratic sea of British official procedures, he needed friends among the aristocrats. Matthew deserved the opportunity to show everyone what he could do as the brilliant engineer he was.

Building safer brakes for the increasingly faster trains was a reality Matthew had achieved while working in one of Brandon's factories. He needed Brandon's help to have the prototype legally approved and sent to production. Because new inventions had to be tested, certified, and tested again while gathering a ridiculous amount of signed papers and documents. Bureaucracy wasn't easy to deal with, even for an earl, especially for an earl who was a hermit.

He grabbed the sink and exhaled, releasing some of the tension in his back muscles. The wish to drown himself in laudanum and forget the pain was a constant nudge at the back of his head. The sweet laudanum was a false friend; it gave pleasure one moment and sheer hell the next. Brandon had experienced both.

He was past those days. Yes, he was. He'd fought his battle against opium and won. It had taken a long time, yes, but it had been worth it. Freedom at last! Freedom and a clear mind, no nausea, no itching skin, or mood swings.

He flexed his fingers and took a deep breath. Some days, the urge grew strong and was difficult to ignore. The anxiety of taking part in a ball full of people he barely knew didn't help. In fact, it could be the trigger for his darkest of needs. No, no, no. Excuses. Only that.

"I'm stronger than that," he whispered the words with little confidence. Matthew had told him to repeat them every time he wished for the quick relief of laudanum. Brandon was supposed to say the words loudly and clearly, but a whisper was all he could manage. "I'm stronger than that." His voice sounded more confident. Yes, he believed that. "I'm stronger than that."

The tremor in his body died down, and he could breathe more easily.

Now it was time to meet London's peers and make train travel safer for thousands of people. Matthew's prototype had taken years to develop. Brandon knew nothing of physics, but he knew the law. He had to do his part, well, aside from financing Matthew's project.

He fixed his cravat and went to open the door when it swung inwards, and Lady Robinson slipped inside, enveloped in a cloud of her expensive perfume.

He stepped back as a fresh wave of anxiety rolled over him. Not *her* again! How many times could a gentleman say '*no, thank you*' before getting angry and rude and calling a lady an insufferable hag?

"I believe this is the gentlemen's room," he said.

She ignored him. "There you are, my elusive earl." She shut the door behind her and strolled towards him in a swish of silk.

"I need to leave, madam." He tried to sidestep her, but she mirrored his moves like a professional boxer.

"We haven't finished our conversation." She placed a gloved hand on his chest, and a cold shiver slithered down his back. "You're always so tense when we see each other."

He removed her hand as gently as he could. "Because you don't seem to understand a simple concept." He took her wrists when she tried to touch him again. "I'm not interested. You're a married woman, and I do not pursue married women." Or unmarried ones, for that matter.

Courting someone hadn't been his priority in the past few years. When one had to deal with chronic pain and a severe addiction to opium while still trying to do a decent job at being an earl and taking care of his tenants, other things, like matters of the heart, tended to slip out of his mind.

She stuck out her bottom lip. "How can you say that if you have never tried to pursue a married woman? And what does the fact that I'm married have to do with us?"

"There is no *us*. Goodbye." He pushed her aside and reached for the knob.

"Brandon, you misunderstood me."

"No, I don't think so."

"I'm not asking to be your mistress. I only want a night of passion with a handsome earl, and that's all." She flourished her hand in a theatrical gesture.

Pff. A night of passion. Not his cup of tea.

"I won't become one of those needy, clingy women," she said. "One night. Then we'll go separate ways. You won't have to buy me presents or see me every week."

"I'm afraid I'm still not interested." He stepped out of the water closet before she could grab him again. Now, where should he go? Straight to Matthew in the ballroom or take a breath of fresh air?

"Only one night." She hounded him. She was a persistent woman. He'd give her that.

He pinched the bridge of his nose. "Why me?"

She chuckled. "Because you're young, handsome, and so kind."

He actually hadn't expected a reply from her. The remark had been a general complaint directed at the universe rather than a proper question.

"Am I too old for you?" She sounded genuinely worried. "I'm only eight years your senior. Not an old lady."

Hellfire. "It's not your age." Was he really encouraging her? But he didn't like her to think she was an old hag in his eyes. Just a hag. "Lady Robinson, I'm flattered." He wasn't. "But I'm not that type of man. Goodbye, and enjoy your evening. I wish you all the best in your pursuit of finding... ahem... someone who..." Bother.

Where was he going with that? "Er, in finding happiness." There. That was vague enough but polite.

"Happiness? If I wanted happiness, I'd buy a diamond necklace. I want a dirty fumble under the sheets!" She scrunched up her face like a five-year-old toddler ready to throw a tantrum. Time to leave.

Before she could say anything else, he hurried down the corridor. He rounded the corner and skidded to a stop upon seeing Matthew.

"Brandon! Where have you been?" Matthew clapped his shoulder. "You're missing the best part of the ball, the champagne! There are also quite a few lovely ladies."

"I'm not interested." He was growing tired of saying it.

"I chatted with a few of them," Matthew whispered. "There are ladies waiting to dance with you."

"I seriously doubt that." He touched the small of his back.

Besides, there was only one woman he was interested in talking with. Or better, interested in apologising to. Begging her if he had to. He'd broken his promise to her, but as soon as he found her, he'd make amends. Cowley had discovered Emily had moved to London with her aunt. Brandon had to see her and apologise. He was running out of excuses on that front as well.

Matthew's smile dropped. "You're nervous and—" He fell silent as Lady Robinson strode past them with her chin up. "Madam, good evening." He bowed, and she replied with a quick nod.

Brandon scratched the back of his neck, muttering a greeting.

Matthew jabbed a thumb in her direction. "Was that Lady Antonia Robinson? She looked upset."

"Yes, that was she, and yes, she is upset," Brandon whispered. "I had a heated chat with her in the gentlemen's room of all places."

Matthew held up his hand. "Say no more. Say no more. I don't care what you do in private."

Lady Robinson paused and shot him a venomous glare that would kill a cobra before disappearing behind a corner.

Brandon had no intention of talking to her again. "I'm leaving. I've had enough of this ball."

Matthew grabbed Brandon's arm. "You can't. The ball has barely started, and I need to rub shoulders with these people. We have to convince half of them that our project is valid and a good investment before someone else presents a new brake system, and we need Lord McCarley's signature on our approval documents. You must introduce me to him."

He shook his head. "I don't think I can stay. I'm sure you'll do a great job even without me. In fact, you'll have more chances of making friends if you're alone."

"Brandon." Matthew put his hands on Brandon's shoulders.

He was one of the few people who addressed the Earl of Hastings by his Christian name and for a good reason. Matthew might be stubborn and a little commanding, but Brandon wouldn't be alive without him. Literally. He'd be dead in an opium den where no one cared about him.

"It's for a good cause," Matthew said. "And I'm a damn good engineer. We have a great project, but an engineer can't introduce himself to a lord. Lord McCarley will never sign our papers if I disrespect him. You asked him if he agreed to be introduced to me, didn't you?"

"I did."

"You and I made a deal. You promised me." Matthew gave Brandon the same pointed look as that time when Brandon had nearly slipped into his bad habit again. Matthew had used the same words: *You and I made a deal. You promised me.*

Brandon didn't want to break yet another promise. He exhaled. Right. He wasn't here to enjoy himself but to build a better, safer future for train travellers and avoid another tragedy. "I'm not going to dance though."

Matthew grinned. "Fair enough. Just drink a lot of champagne until the lights become very bright, and you should be all right."

Brandon chuckled. "Good advice."

"You'd be surprised to know that drinking a lot of champagne is often the best solution for many problems."

The moment Brandon stepped into the ballroom, he regretted it. His feet urged him to leave. His brain ordered him to return home. Only his heart whispered that his and Matthew's project would save lives. Thus he had to endure the discomfort. He didn't have to do anything aside from being polite and engaging only in those conversations that mattered to him. And he had to avoid Lady Robinson. Easy. Sheesh, his head was about to explode.

He winced at the bright lights, the loud music, and the room crowded with ladies twirling around and gentlemen talking. At least a dozen different smells teased his senses, from the ladies' perfumes to the cinnamon from the cakes on the banquet table.

Matthew handed him a glass of champagne he conjured from somewhere. "The young ladies over there are soon-to-be debutantes in the next Season. This is their very first ball, an unofficial start to the Season, in case you were wondering."

"I wasn't." He sipped the champagne and scowled. It tasted bitter, or maybe it was his anxiety that ruined everything in more ways than one. "And they look like children."

"Twenty-two. Hardly children." Matthew smiled at a passing lady, who didn't return the smile. "Do you see our man?"

Brandon released a breath. Lord McCarley was a stickler for bureaucratic procedures. Their prototype wouldn't go anywhere without his approval.

"The sooner we talk to Lord McCarley, the sooner I can leave." Brandon gazed around the room until he found the lord in question. "Come." He did his best not to drag his feet. The back injury had affected his ability to walk, but he'd be damned if he let everyone know that. As he crossed the ballroom, he hoped no one had the brilliant idea to stop him for a chat. "Lord McCarley, what a pleasure to see you here."

The lord's eyebrows rose, causing his monocle to drop. "Lord Hastings, I say! What a surprise. I had no idea you decided to come. It's good to see you. How are—"

"Yes, thank you." Brandon stretched out an arm towards Matthew. "Lord McCarley, may I introduce you to Mr. Matthew Tyrell? My associate and dear friend."

Lord McCarley shook Matthew's hand. "Mr. Tyrell. Lord Hastings spoke highly of you."

"Thank you, my lord..." Matthew said something else, but Brandon didn't listen.

He remained frozen in shock as he spotted a dark-haired beauty dressed in an out-of-fashion white dress. She stood in a corner away from the crowd, sparkling like a glossy pearl in the night. His breath hitched as the chaos of the room receded.

He had found Emily.

six

BRANDON COULDN'T BELIEVE his eyes. Emily. She was exactly as he remembered her, only more beautiful. His memories didn't do justice to the golden hues of her olive skin, her proud bearing, and her glossy sable hair. If she believed the old white dress made her less noticeable, she was sorely mistaken. She stood out like the planet Venus at dusk or a ray of sunlight in a dark room.

His pulse spiked, drumming in his ears and covering the sound of the music. There was no doubt. Emily. He was so stunned that even the anxiety diminished. The ballroom seemed to have become empty. Only she existed surrounded by a golden glow like a beacon.

Matthew's furrowed brow filled Brandon's wonderful vision, blocking the view of the goddess.

"Brandon?" He nudged him with his elbow. "What is it? A moment of panic? Do you really need to leave? Here, have more champagne." Concern tightened his voice.

"Is something the matter?" Lord McCarley asked.

Brandon ignored the offer of champagne and moved Matthew

aside to keep watching Emily. "No. I don't want to leave. Never. I want to..." He didn't know what.

No, that was a lie. He wanted to talk to her. Except he had no idea how he could explain his silence to her. Laudanum's addiction wasn't something he wanted to mention at their first meeting after years of silence. But to be fair, she'd refused his invitation to visit him in London more than once, even though he'd offered to pay for all the expenses. Maybe just another excuse on his part. He'd broken his promise. The fault of their separation weighed on his shoulders alone.

"Would you excuse us for a moment, my lord?" Matthew flashed a smile at Lord McCarley and dragged Brandon away.

As Lord McCarley scowled and scoffed, Brandon kept staring at Emily.

"What are you staring at?" Matthew searched the room, following his gaze and blocking the view again. "I don't understand. The lady in white? Quite the wallflower, I'd say, but so pretty. Her dress is old-fashioned though."

"I need to go." He put the glass... somewhere. He wasn't sure if it was a table or the tray of a passing footman. Never mind.

"Where?" Matthew put a hand on his arm.

"I must talk to her."

"What about Lord McCarley?" Matthew hissed. "We've already been rude to him."

"I must talk to her. Please." He gripped Matthew's arm. "I need this."

He understood how important their project was, but Emily... Emily mattered more. There. He said it. The moment of near-death they'd shared had forged a bond between them. Yes, he'd been with her for a little over a week, but they'd been so close, too close for the experience not to leave a mark on his soul. When he'd been sick because his craving for laudanum had been stronger than he, he'd felt at his lowest, but having broken his promise to her had hurt more. In a way, it had been as if he'd turned his back on his second chance at life.

Matthew stepped aside. "It's important for you. I can see that."

While he didn't need Matthew's permission, he was glad his friend understood. "Thank you."

"But please be quick," Matthew said.

Brandon weaved his way through the crowd of guests with his uneven gait. He might have smiled once or twice at someone greeting him. He couldn't tell. He just wanted to talk to her. Everything else didn't matter.

His leg muscles stiffened as he sped up, but he did his best not to limp. He wanted to make a good impression on her.

She half-hid between a plant and a curtain, inching back whenever someone came too close, and for a moment, he was seized by the odd impulse to sweep her off her feet and show everyone how lovely she was. She smoothed her bodice and lifted her chin. He'd forgotten how elegant she looked even when she was simply standing.

While the other ladies showed hair styled with pretty ribbons and flowers, her sable curls had been gathered in a serious hairnet. But the style suited her. It made him want to free her curls and let them fall over her bare shoulders.

He paused a few feet from her because it was like getting too close to the sun.

"Emily." His voice came out in a raspy noise that startled her. "It's me. Brandon."

Her large hazel eyes widened in recognition. She shifted her weight, focusing on his face. The glass flute in her hands almost slipped out of her grip. Her long dark eyelashes fluttered down. She was the same yet different. Gone was the softness of youth. Her cheeks were sharper than he remembered, and her lips were fuller. She was no less beautiful, only more womanly.

She brought a hand to her chest. "Brandon."

Hearing his name again in her sweet voice sent a shot of energy through him—sensations he'd forgotten.

"I'm... I couldn't ignore your presence." Obviously. He cleared his throat. He hadn't started strong. "Seeing you here is a pleasant surprise." It was a rather cold way to describe the heated feelings burning within him.

She showed a quick smile. It wasn't the radiant one he wished to see— the one he'd seen only a few times before the accident— but it had stayed with him since then. Her smile didn't fail to brighten the room though.

She smoothed her bodice again. "I'm happy to see you too. It's been so long. I didn't know you would be here."

"Me neither. I didn't want to come, but I've been away from society for a while, and my friend and business partner, Matthew, needs me, because all those barons, and I..." What was he saying? Who cared about that? He exhaled, collecting his thoughts. "How are you?"

She rubbed her hands absentmindedly. "I'm all right, thank you. How are you?"

"No, I mean it." He took a step closer to her, catching a lovely whiff of her jasmine scent. "How are you? Really? I'm not asking out of social politeness. I would like a real answer."

She lowered her gaze, which he didn't like. He wanted to see her spectacular eyes. He'd been deprived of them for too long.

A gentleman approached her, an arm stretched out. "Madam, would you care for a dance?"

"No," he gritted out. "Leave. Now."

The chap paled then flushed. The change in colour was quite startling to watch. Then he hurried away, the tails of his suit flapping around. Emily remained speechless, her mouth open.

The moment the man fled, Brandon cursed his own temper. "Hell," he muttered, pinching the bridge of his nose. "I apologise. That was inexcusable. I'm a little nervous."

He should give her a moment to recover from their sudden

meeting. In less than a minute, he'd behaved like a wild beast with the woman he'd wished to see for a decade.

"I'm sorry. Please forgive me." He bowed and went to leave, but she touched his hand briefly.

As he stopped in his tracks, half in shock, half in excitement, she withdrew her hand.

"I didn't want to dance anyway," she said. "And I'm nervous too, although you gave the gentleman a fright."

"That was the point. I haven't seen you in years, and he thought he could waltz in and take you away?" Perhaps he should shut up. Everything he said came out wrong. He'd meant to joke, but instead he sounded like a possessive, jealous husband.

"It was bad timing on his part." She flourished her sad smile again. "And yours perhaps."

He didn't know what to say or do, so he decided that being honest was the best strategy. "I've been through very difficult years," he said when she didn't add anything. Perhaps if he opened up first, she'd follow. "Dark moments."

He might be the first to take a step, but he wasn't going to tell her everything about the laudanum and how low he'd fallen before slowly climbing back up, completely changed, and not necessarily for the better.

"My injury took longer to heal than I thought," he said. "It was a real struggle."

"The stab?" she asked. Did he detect a hint of concern? He hoped so.

"No. It turned out the stab was the least of my problems. The cut healed without complications. No infection or festering. It still hurts sometimes when the weather changes, but it's nothing to worry about. It was the blow to my back that caused me more problems. My lumbar vertebrae were partially crushed." And he stopped there not to overwhelm her. She didn't need to know it'd taken years for him to walk properly again. Years of sweat, blood, pain, and gruesome exercises. And oceans of laudanum.

"You never mentioned that in your letters."

He shook his head. "It was too much. There were too many bad days."

She touched his hand again, a too-fleeting gesture for him. "I'm truly sorry to hear that."

He glanced at the spot she'd touched. "I'm glad you recovered well. Physically, at least. The memories never leave."

"They are the worst." She didn't say anything else and lowered her gaze again.

Silence thickened between them.

He wanted to hold her and ask her to forgive his silence, but sometimes silence was better than the truth. But since he couldn't do that without distressing her, he offered her his hand, about to propose a dance against his better judgement.

"Would you care to dance?"

Her lips parted and not in a good fashion. It was as if she were outraged by his offer.

Fire flickered in her gaze. "I'm afraid I can't accept your invitation."

"Just one dance to atone for my absolute lack of manners towards you."

"No, I'm sorry." She clenched her fists.

Right. He'd behaved beastly to her, and she didn't trust him. Understandable. Although ladies should never refuse an invitation to dance. "Can we go somewhere and talk? There are things that need to be said." Many things.

"I'm not sure I want to talk now. If you'll excuse me." She walked towards the glass door overlooking the garden. A gust of cold wind swept through the room as she opened the door.

He acted on impulse and followed her outside. He had to tell her the truth. "I'm sorry to have broken my promise. I wanted to keep staying in touch, but difficult things happened."

She stared at the floor. "You're an earl with many responsibilities. I understand."

The cold words cut him more deeply than the stab in the back. He'd prefer if she became angry and told the truth about how she felt. Maybe she didn't care about him after all, and all these years, he'd been worried about breaking his promise while she'd brushed off his lack of replies easily.

"If you let me explain." He stepped closer, fighting the urge to hug her.

"You don't owe me any explanations." The slight tremor going through her said otherwise. "We were children. Children make promises they can't keep."

No, that wasn't true. A tightness caught in his throat.

"And I know you travelled across Europe." She sounded bitter now.

"Me?" He let out a snort. "Rumours. I haven't left England in years." How could he have? His back tormented him.

A fierce frown creased her brow. "Then why?"

"It's not easy for me to say it, but—"

"Brandon," Matthew said from the glass door. Lord McCarley stood next to him, stroking the pommel of his walking stick.

Brandon held up a hand. "Not now, Matthew."

Lord McCarley stopped touching his walking stick. "Does the Earl of Hastings care about this project or not?"

Matthew released a breath through his teeth. "I'm starting to wonder the same."

Damn. "Please," Brandon said. Could he have a moment for himself?

"You're busy," Emily said. "Don't let me keep you."

But he wanted to be kept by her. "Emily."

She clenched her fists. "Why the hurry? You've spent many a year without bothering to write to me, and now you insist on talking. I—"

"Brandon," Matthew said at the same time as Lord McCarley said, "My lord."

"Go." Emily grabbed a fistful of her skirt. "Don't worry about me. It's something you do rather well."

Those were easily the most hurtful words she could have ever tossed at him. He didn't know how to repair the damage but admitted he hadn't played his part well.

He bowed as deeply as his back allowed. "I apologise again. I hope I will see you again. Perhaps I can call on you if you let me know where you live."

"Another time." She bobbed a shallow curtsy before hurrying towards the other side of the balcony.

Another time? What kind of answer was that? His heart gave a thunderous kick as she disappeared behind a corner. He didn't have time to process the storm of emotions within him before Matthew and Lord McCarley swept up to him.

"Lord McCarley is eager to talk to you about our application to his committee and eventually start mass production of our product," Matthew said.

Brandon nodded, craning his neck to keep staring at the point where Emily had disappeared. He had to focus. He owed it to Matthew.

"I've discussed our revolutionary invention already." Matthew raised his eyebrows.

Lord McCarley smiled. "Mr. Tyrell told me everything about the miraculous brakes he developed."

Pushing aside his thoughts of Emily required every ounce of energy, but Brandon had broken his promise to her. He couldn't break his promise to Matthew as well. He had to leave Brandon behind and become the Earl of Hastings for the time being.

He faced Lord McCarley. "Sir, you won't find a better engineer than Matthew in the entire empire."

"I'm sure you're right, Hastings." Lord McCarley brought his monocle up to his eye. "What can I do for you?"

"We'd be very grateful if you could approve our prototype,"

Brandon said. "I believe we need your signature on a tall pile of documents."

Lord McCarley's bushy eyebrows lowered. "I'm afraid I can't help you. I retired from the position of approval officer. I work as developmental surveyor."

Matthew clenched his jaw. "Who is the new officer, sir?"

"Lord Robinson." Lord McCarley gazed at the ballroom. "But he's in the Americas for business. He'll stay away for a few months. Meanwhile, Lady Robinson is the one who's making the decisions about the prototype approvals, much to the chagrin of the office clerks."

"Lady Robinson?" Brandon said in disbelief.

Lord McCarley huffed. "Why, yes. Are you one of those gentlemen who don't approve? There's nothing the other clerks can argue against Lord Robinson's decision. He formally authorised his wife to act as his substitute. All legal."

"Blimey," Brandon muttered.

"Why the long face?" Lord McCarley said. "I believe it's good news. You'll have better chances with her. She's quite open-minded about new technologies. Lord Robinson has a more conservative approach. This is a good opportunity for you."

Great. Bloody fantastic. "I had no idea."

Lord McCarley frowned. "Do you listen to gossip or not? Her appointment as prototype approval chief officer has been the scandal of the week."

Matthew studied Brandon's face as if wanting to figure out his thoughts.

Brandon exhaled. "I'm afraid the news is quite shocking for me."

More than shocking. How could he be nice and ask for a favour to the lady who had tried to ravish him in the gentlemen's room?

"Now, if you'll excuse me." Lord McCarley bowed. "I

promised my wife I would dance with her. As soon as your papers are in order, we'll have another meeting, gentlemen."

"Hell." Brandon ran a hand over his clammy face after Lord McCarley had returned to the ballroom.

"Why are you worried? How's your relationship with Lady Robinson?" Matthew asked.

"Not exactly friendly. I'd say it's a tad strained."

"Strained?"

"Abysmal."

Matthew scowled. "But she followed you to the gentlemen's room. What have you done to her?"

"Me?" He pointed a finger at himself. "Why don't you ask what *she* has done to *me*? She tried to ravish me twice, catching me off guard. She wants a tryst with me. She said exactly that. No subtleties. One night of passion with me."

Matthew tilted his head as if trying to understand a complicated concept. "I'm sorry, but why didn't you agree? It's only a fumble in the bedsheets, and she's a stunner."

Brandon threw a hand up. Of course Matthew would say that. He had the emotional sensitivity of a horse hoof. "I don't want to. Is it difficult to understand?"

Dammit, what a terrible evening. First the fiasco with Emily, and now Lady Robinson.

"You'd better get acquainted with the idea of seeing Lady Robinson again." Matthew straightened Brandon's cravat. "You're going to see her a lot."

seven

NOT EVEN THE promise of an almost sunny day and a walk in the park could soothe Emily's inner turmoil.

She hadn't expected to see Brandon at the ball last night. She hadn't expected to see him at all. Ever. The ladies at the ball had gossiped about him, saying he was known for avoiding mundane events and making sporadic appearances at the gentlemen's club. He'd caught her off guard, especially with his wish to dance with her and his honest questions. But she hadn't danced in years. She was rusty. And she'd been angry. She hadn't expected to be so angry either. The moment he'd started talking, all the frustration of the past years had flared up. How awful of her. But while he'd complained about that gentleman 'waltzing in and asking her to dance,' he'd done the same— appearing out of thin air all of a sudden, after years of nothing, and having the gall to demand to talk to her.

He'd looked so handsome, strong, and healthy that she'd been ashamed of her irrational fear of narrow, oppressive spaces, which was ridiculous. She had no trouble admitting that she couldn't travel in a closed carriage. Or step into a dark wardrobe. But at that moment in front of him, a new irrational fear had taken hold of her. Seeing Lady Robinson parading around hadn't improved her mood. And yes, he had broken his promise. And she'd been angry with him. He'd vanished from her life. He couldn't expect her to welcome him with open arms.

That morning, in the bright sunlight with the breeze shuffling her hair, her behaviour seemed silly. She should have talked to him at least and given him the opportunity to justify himself. Instead, she'd behaved like a petulant child. Besides, after their quick exchange, she hadn't seen him. He'd disappeared with those two men, and she'd spent the rest of the evening thinking about all the things she could have told him and avoiding Lady Robinson.

Goodness, the way he'd growled at the gentleman who had asked her to dance. Brandon had seemed about to punch the man. She wasn't sure how to feel about his conduct. On the one hand, his moment of possessiveness meant he still cared about her. But on the other hand, it confused her. Was she supposed to be scared or impressed, flattered or outraged? Right now, she was somewhere in the middle.

Aunt Rose and Catherine chatted about last night in excited tones. Not that Emily cared about their conversation. They'd insisted that a walk in Hyde Park after a ball was mandatory. They had to show themselves around because the lords and ladies from the ball would likely promenade in the park, making alliances, planning future events, and gossiping. Thus, here she was, thinking about the pile of dirty clothes waiting for her at home and about an earl who puzzled her.

"And the Earl of Hastings was there," Aunt Rose said, grabbing Catherine's hand and Emily's attention. "Such a handsome gentleman. Did you see him?"

She changed her mind. She cared about her aunt's conversation.

Catherine huffed, stuffing her hands in her muff. "Yes, but he didn't pay attention to anyone. He appeared and then disappeared, only to make another brief entrance before vanishing for good.

Not exactly a gentleman if you ask me. Lady Gardner didn't have the time to introduce me to him." She shot a fleeting glare at Emily. "He kept talking with that curious man... Mr. Tyrell, the most boring man I've ever met."

"Isn't he the engineer who made a small fortune by designing that medical device?" Aunt Rose asked. "He might be a good match."

Interesting. At least the medical device part.

Catherine shrugged. "I don't know, but the earl talked mostly to him with one exception."

"What exception?" Aunt Rose asked.

Catherine slowed her pace to angle towards Emily. "I saw the earl conversing with Emily for a while."

Emily didn't say anything. She and Brandon hadn't exactly talked, merely exchanged a few awkward words.

"What did you talk about?" Aunt Rose touched Emily's arm, demanding her attention.

Emily had yet to understand how she felt about having seen Brandon again. She forced her face to remain blank lest she betray herself, which would lead to more questions.

"His lordship was one of the passengers on the Flying Scotsman when the Abbots Ripton accident happened."

"I see." Catherine narrowed her eyes. "He seemed quite taken by you."

"Why would you say that?" Emily asked in a harsher tone than she meant.

"The way he looked at you was explicit enough, almost scandalous." Catherine added three 's' to *scandalous*.

"Was it?" Dash it. Had she missed that?

"Are you two good friends?" Catherine added.

"No." The answer came out without hesitation, and to be honest, she and Brandon truly might not be friends any longer. But she wanted to protect him from becoming a probable target in Catherine's hunt for a husband. The letters he'd sent Emily didn't show his full name and title, simply Mr. B. Astley. Aunt Rose was none the wiser about Emily's and Brandon's letter exchange, and thank goodness for that.

"What did you talk about then?" Good gracious. Catherine was a bloodhound.

"About recovering from our injuries. Dull and sad." That at least was true.

"What injuries?" Aunt Rose had the tone of a copper interrogating a suspect. "I didn't hear the earl had serious injuries, only a few scratches."

Drat. So much for protecting Brandon. "I'm not sure, Aunt. The earl and I were interrupted by two men. After that brief conversation, I didn't see him. That's all," she said, gritting her teeth. "And I don't wish to discuss the matter further. Thank you."

Definitely, Lady Robinson had a point about Emily's temper.

Aunt Rose muttered something about Emily being rude, and Catherine huffed.

"You shall introduce me next time." Catherine didn't seem to understand the meaning of 'I don't wish to discuss the matter further.'

"I'm not in the position to do that. Do you want to be introduced to an earl by your orphaned cousin or by Lady Gardner?"

Aunt Rose nodded her approval. "Emily is right, darling."

That should close the conversation. They walked in blissful silence for a while. She almost tripped when the laces of her boot came undone.

She stopped walking. "I have to tie my shoe," she said to no one in particular.

Tying her boot wasn't an easy task since the shoelaces were threadbare. She crouched and fumbled with the worn strings. She pressed her lips in anger as the strings thinned and threatened to snap. It was like using wet paper as shoelaces; one wrong tug and the thread would dissolve.

"Come on," she muttered. She couldn't stay crouched in the middle of the path all day. "I'm sorry, it's taking—" She gazed up and faced the trees, green grass, and strangers promenading.

Catherine and Aunt Rose were nowhere to be seen. She turned around. Many Londoners took advantage of a day without rain to wander around and show off new hats and parasols, but her aunt and cousin had vanished. Great. She didn't expect them to wait for her, but they could have told her they were leaving. Oh, well. Why was she surprised?

Never mind. She tugged and pulled until something similar to a proper knot secured her boot. She headed towards the exit closest to Aunt Rose's home, but the laces got undone again. In fact, one of the hooks holding the string had come loose. A hot flare of anger burned her chest. The laces coming undone again were an injustice of sorts. How many times did she have to tie them again only to watch them unravel? Like her life.

Bother. For what reason was she so upset anyway? She chose a quiet spot and started all over again, tugging and pulling at the stupid string harder than she should.

A shadow crept over her. "Emily. We meet again."

She nearly gasped at hearing Brandon's voice so close to her. So soon after their first meeting.

He stood in front of her, elegant in a rich-brown suit that matched the deep chestnut colour of his hair. His green eyes held her captive for a moment, and his fresh mint scent reminded her of afternoon teas and chocolate bonbons. What an odd thought.

"I'm not following you. I promise. I just happened to be here because after a ball, a promenade is mandatory, or so they say. And I saw you. Again." He offered a careful smile, but she couldn't smile back.

It was the second time he'd taken her off guard, but this time the shock didn't petrify her for long. "Twice in a row." She straightened up, but he still towered over her a good foot. Goodness, he was a tall one.

"Yes, we should stop meeting like that." He let out a nervous chuckle that she didn't return.

He removed his hat, and his glorious curls fell over his sharp jaw. She didn't remember him having such strong features and harsh lines. They suited him.

"I take a daily walk here for exercising anyway. It's good for the blood circulation, my physician says." He pointed at her boot. "Your shoelaces are untied."

She opened and closed her fingers. "I stopped here for that reason. It's taking me longer than expected to tie them since they're at least seven years old." Dash it. Why did she say that?

He dipped his head to meet her gaze. "May I help?"

"No, thank you." She plonked down onto the bench behind her and tugged at the shoelaces with too much strength. They broke with a snap to spite her. "Tarnation." She removed the ribbon around her reticule and used it to replace the laces. Her reticule would remain open, but it was better than walk with an unlaced boot. "Done. Stupid boot."

She shoved up to her feet, only to end up a few inches from him. Their chests almost touched. He was so close she could see the light copper-coloured stubble on his jaw.

Clearing his throat, he stepped back with the help of his walking stick. Not to be mean, but sometimes he moved like an old man with gout. A tendon in his neck ticked, and she wondered if it was pain or annoyance.

"You're a resourceful woman."

"I have to be," she said in a low tone. "Not everyone can buy silk and Italian leather shoes." Her worn clothes spoke for themselves about her limited finances.

He fiddled with his tall hat. "I didn't want to make you uncomfortable. I know you went through difficult years." He put his hat on. "I wish you a good day, Emily." He went to leave, but... it was wrong. She hated the hurt in his expression, and it was her fault. She could have been less saucy.

"Wait." She stooped her shoulders. He'd been kind to her. She should return the favour. "You didn't make me feel uncomfortable. Thank you for your remark."

His chest heaved with his exhale. "You're most welcome. I can leave if you want to stay alone."

She was glad he didn't comment on the poor state of her boots. "No, don't leave on my account. I'm happy to see you. Really."

A shadow crossed his face. "I apologise again for last night. I didn't mean to scare you."

"You didn't scare me, but you scared the gentleman." She smiled, and he sucked in a breath that stretched his coat across his chest.

They remained in silence for a few moments, listening to the happy voices of children romping around and the chatter of the people promenading. He stared at her with an intensity she should find unpleasant but didn't. His stare told her he'd thought of her as much as she had thought of him, that he was sorry.

"I really wanted to dance with you last night, but I realise that I was too insistent. Is that why you refused my invitation?" he asked in a deep baritone so different from the voice of the boy she remembered.

"I haven't danced in years." That was true although she didn't care about being rusty.

He regarded her from underneath his heavy-lidded eyes. "And you were angry with me."

Honesty it is. She nodded.

"You still are."

The second nod was a reluctant one. She didn't want to offend him, but he was the one who had stopped writing to her.

"I understand." He worked his jaw.

"After ten years, being angry sounds irrational." Too many things were irrational in her life. "I guess that seeing you stoked the flame of my anger."

"Emotions don't usually follow rationality."

She rubbed her forehead. "Yes, but I shouldn't have been so rude, and I ruined your evening by refusing to dance."

"To be honest, I didn't want to dance either, or better, I wanted to dance with *you*, but I don't usually attend balls, and if I do, I don't dance. Ever."

"Why?" She studied his face.

Surely, as an earl, he danced a lot. His body had changed of course. He was broad across the shoulders, taller than he'd been, and had strong, masculine features that gave a rough edge to his beauty. Only the shadows under his eyes belied his vulnerability.

"Look carefully." He paced around, beating a rhythm with his walking stick.

At first, she didn't notice anything unusual, but as he quickened his steps, he started to limp. Not exactly to limp, but he seemed to drag his feet with some jerky movements rather than lift them.

He stopped pacing, his expression guarded. "It took me years to walk again, and even now, it's not always easy. It's like my body and mind refuse to cooperate and do my bidding. It's a constant fight for—"

"Control," they said together.

This time when he smiled, she smiled too.

"I had no idea," she said. "You didn't write anything about your health problems in your letters. I thought you'd recovered fully."

"No, not fully." A corner of his mouth quirked up. "Can we start over again and promise to be honest with each other? I meant it when I said there were things I needed to tell you. Truce?" He offered her his hand to shake.

"Agreed." She stretched out her hand and shivered when he held it.

"We have a deal." He brushed her knuckles with his thumb before releasing her hand. A tiny, chaste gesture that made her spine wilt for no reason other than reminding her of his kind touch.

"I wanted to write to you and tell you how much your silence bothered me, but I never did because I didn't want you to worry," she said. "I thought you had plenty of responsibilities without worrying about me."

"I thought the same as you. It was difficult for me to admit I couldn't walk. My refusal to face the truth was my worst enemy. I underestimated the problem, focusing only on not feeling pain. Needless to say, the battle didn't end well." Anger crept into his voice, but she didn't know why he was angry.

"I'm sorry to hear that. I know how physical pain can change who we are." It was the first time she'd felt confident talking about her struggle.

"I came out of that dark moment stronger. That's a good thing, I guess." He offered her his arm. "May I escort you to wherever you're going?"

"I'd be delighted." She slid her arm over his, feeling the hard muscles under the soft fabric of his sleeve.

They were so close his warmth reached her skin and his scent enveloped her. Goodness, he was all hard muscles and sharp angles. And the way he looked at her made her feel important, elegant even. Catherine had a point. He did stare at her in awe.

"Where were you going?" he asked.

"Home. I was with my aunt and cousin, but it took me too long to tie my boot, and they left without me."

His eyebrows lowered in a menacing expression that hardened his jaw. He had the same expression as last night when the gentleman asked her to dance. "They left you here alone?" His upper lip curled up in a snarl.

She lifted a shoulder. "I don't care."

"I do. Does your aunt take good care of you?"

She didn't want to sound ungrateful or worse, whining, but she'd promised to tell him the truth. "She isn't the most nurturing person. From the moment she took me in, she made it clear I had to earn my keep and that I had to avoid whining about my misfortune, or she would have sent me to a children's home."

He drew in a breath between his teeth. "She made you work, knowing that after the accident your health was in a delicate condition?" His voice rang dangerously low.

"Chores. Housework. Nothing too heavy," she hurried to say. "I didn't mind the work. It kept me busy." While she wanted to be honest, she wouldn't let him believe her years with Aunt Rose had been a complete misery. Well, they had, but she'd been fed and clothed, and she agreed about not whining.

"Why didn't you tell me anything?" The snarl was still there.

"Same reason as before. Because you had enough on your plate, and it wasn't as horrible as it seems. Besides, my aunt did her best to raise me despite her modest resources. She isn't wealthy or hasn't been until recently."

"What do you mean?" He held her arm protectively, but he'd already proved to be the protective type. His injuries were a testament to his nature.

She focused, trying to think about the moment things had changed in Aunt Rose's house. "Something changed a few months ago. My aunt must have had a stroke of luck or an unexpected income, likely an inheritance of sorts, because she started to spend more on dresses, food, and not strictly necessary items. When I asked about the new expenses, she told me not to worry. Then we moved here to give Catherine the opportunity to have a Season. A sudden change."

A deep crease appeared between his eyebrows. "I hope you don't have to do chores anymore then."

"I still do, but I really don't mind. It's good exercise, and I like to feel useful." She showed him the callouses on her fingers.

He held them again with the same care someone would use while handling a precious jewel. Her cheeks warmed a little.

His frown deepened. "Why these cuts?"

"They are from fixing devices and other things around the house. I'm a decent tinkerer." She couldn't completely remove the hint of sadness from her tone. Sadness because she didn't have any certificates that proved her skill.

"Have you become an engineer?" He released her hands.

"No." Her enthusiasm diminished a little. "The university's fees are expensive, but I read every book on mechanical engineering I could find. And practice helped me a lot."

He didn't react with the excitement she expected. "Do you still wish to become an engineer?"

"I'm looking for a job as a governess to set aside enough money to pay the fees." She forced a cheerful voice.

His jaw tightened further. "And how is your search for employment going?"

"Not well so far, but I've barely started." She didn't want to tell him about the ladies' comments on the tone of her skin or her fears. Being honest was one thing. Baring herself completely was another.

His worried expression didn't change. "My carriage is right around the corner. I'll take you home," he said as they walked out of the park.

"Carriage?" She came to a grinding halt upon seeing his sleek dark carriage, fully closed and with thick curtains over the windows. Suffocating. Stifling. Oppressive. Just the thought of entering the constricting space made her breathe faster and turned her hands clammy. A chill slithered down her back.

"I can't," she said so low he might not have heard her.

"Is something the matter?" He held the door open for her, disregarding the footman.

"I don't travel in carriages." She pushed down her anxiety, trying not to sound hysterical. "Only open ones. I deeply dislike closed vehicles." An understatement. She was absolutely, unequivocally terrified of them. But he didn't need to know that, did he? "And it's such a beautiful day. I don't want to sit in a dark carriage." She wouldn't sit in a closed carriage even when it rained.

After a moment, he shut the door. "We'll walk then."

"But your legs..." She paused, worried she might have offended him.

"I need to exercise. The more I walk, the better my legs should be, or so my physician told me." He waved at the coachman and footman. "Meet me at... where do you live?" he asked her.

"Oldie Bell Square, number fifty-two."

"I'll see you there, Adam," he said to the coachman.

"Sir." The coachman touched his tall hat before gigging the horses into a trot.

Emily took Brandon's arm again. "It's fifteen minutes. Are you sure you want to walk?"

"I am." A bronze curl brushed the tip of his nose, and she wanted to tug at it to straighten it and see it curl again when released. "How did you travel from the country to here?"

"Aunt Rose and Catherine took the train." She shivered. "I took a landau and any vehicle with an open roof, even a cart loaded with sheep. It took me days to reach London, but I prefer feeling the gusts of wind on my face." Because closed vehicles choked her.

"I understand. I can travel on a train now, but it's always an uncomfortable trip, and the noise of metal bothers me." The shadows darkened his features again. "There are more terrifying things for me." His expression softened. "But you make me feel better. Less anxious. Maybe because only you can understand me."

She leaned against him a little. "I feel the same."

As they walked along the pavement through the crowd, her shoulders began to release the tension coiling around her body. Only then did she realise they had to be an odd sight. In his expensive suit, shiny Malacca walking stick, and silk hat, he appeared as the perfect gentleman while the hem of her skirt was frayed, and her cloak had a patch in a corner.

"People will notice us," she said, pretending to ignore the curious glances tossed her way.

He dipped his head, and she caught a glimpse of the golden specks in his irises. "Is it a problem?" he asked.

"Not for me, but for you." She waved a hand between them to emphasise the difference between their outfits.

"Me?"

"I wear worn dresses, looking like a street urchin. You wear fancy clothes."

He clicked his tongue. "I could remove them, but I'm afraid that would attract more attention."

She laughed. "I bet." Although she wouldn't mind taking a look at him.

He studied her in a clinical fashion as a physician would examine a patient. He opened his mouth but changed his mind about whatever he wanted to say.

"Tell me." She tugged at his sleeve. "What were you about to say?"

"My opinion, in case you were interested, is that you look lovely as usual even in plain clothes. And I promised to be honest."

She acknowledged the quick flutter in her chest. "Who's the gentleman who was with you at the ball?" she asked to change the subject before she blushed or worse, giggled.

His face brightened. "Mr. Matthew Tyrell. He's a brilliant engineer and my best friend. His father was one of the machinists on the Flying Scotsman. He died in the collision."

"So many people suffered. Mr. Tyrell must understand you too."

"Matthew and I became friends, brothers I'd dare say. We went through our dark moments together." He hesitated before continuing. "He devised a new type of train brakes, safer, faster, and more efficient. Our goal is to have the prototype approved before starting the production and even make them compulsory on every train. I wanted something good to come out of the tragedy." His passion radiated from him.

"That sounds wonderful."

He tilted his head. "Unfortunately, having the prototype approved and homologated is a process longer than we thought, and I've been away from society for a while. Knowing the right people matters."

"Have you been away because of your recovery?" She might be imagining things, but he seemed to become quite ashen.

"Yes." He remained silent for a while. "I'm sorry I stopped writing to you," he whispered.

Her anger was as soft as candlelight now. "It doesn't matter."

"It does. I'll make amends." He put a hand on his chest. "Please give me a chance to prove myself."

Drat. Now she felt guilty. "It's the past, and the past is gruesome. The future looks better."

"Since yesterday," he said.

She couldn't help but like his reply. "I agree." She stopped in front of her aunt's townhouse, lost in the power of his focus on her. He stared at her as if the rest of London didn't exist. "Is there something you want to tell me?"

"Actually yes." He hesitated, stroking the pommel of his walking stick. "I was wondering if... you know, my water boiler doesn't work."

It took her a moment to understand the meaning of his words. "Water boiler?"

"Yes." He frowned. "I have a modern water boiler, but it hasn't worked properly as of late. The heating technician I called fixed it, or so it'd seemed. But the device has stopped working again. I was wondering if you'd like to take a look at it."

That left her speechless. It was easily the most exciting request she'd received from a man. "I would love to. Unless it's one of those electric boilers from the Americas. They're too complicated for me."

He let out a nervous laugh. "No, nothing that fancy. I don't believe anyone in England has one of those yet. Too expensive and yes, complicated. Will you come then? I'll arrange a hansom cab for you."

"Gladly."

He brought up her hand and kissed it as he'd done years ago, and just like years ago, her heart stuttered. "I'll see you later then."

eight

WHY HAD BRANDON invited Emily to his house to repair his stupid water boiler? That hadn't been his intention at all. He'd wanted to ask her to go with him to Lord Devon's ball, but at the last moment, he'd been worried she would say no. She'd rejected his offer to dance once, and statistically speaking, the chance she would reject him again was high since she'd told him she wasn't fond of dancing. The only good thing about his unplanned invitation was that she'd seemed genuinely thrilled by the idea of repairing the boiler, and well, his boiler was indeed broken. That didn't change the fact he still wanted to invite her to the ball.

Pacing in the sitting room, he checked his pocket watch. She should be here any minute now. He stopped when a hansom cab pulled over to the kerb in front of his house and Emily climbed out of it. She tilted her head up and waved at him. Bugger it. He'd been caught staring at her from the window. He returned the hand wave.

He rushed to the hallway and adjusted the knot of his cravat that had seemingly become too tight. "I'll do it, I'll do it." He waved the footman away and waited for him to leave. For some reason, he wanted to open the door for her alone.

"Sir." Cowley's voice jolted him.

"Yes?" He peeked at the pavement. What was she doing? She was stroking the neck of the horse pulling the cab.

Cowley shifted his position. "I've called the water boiler technician again and arranged a—"

"Shush!" Brandon straightened as Emily waved at the driver and got closer. "I don't need him."

"But, sir, you complained about your boiler not heating the water." Cowley was too efficient sometimes. "It's a matter of your health. Cold water upsets your back muscles."

"It's all right, I have—"

"Why are you opening the door, sir?" Cowley asked.

The knock wasn't a surprise, but the quickening of his heart was. He flung the door open maybe with too much energy. The knob almost slipped out of his grip.

"Emily." He sounded breathless.

"Good afternoon." She entered the hallway, lovely in a dark-blue dress. It was simple and a little worn, but the colour brought out her beautiful eyes. She carried a heavy-looking leather bag.

"Good afternoon. Emily, you remember Mr. Cowley, don't you? Cowley, Miss Emily de la Fuente Barclay."

Cowley's eyebrows hit his hairline. "I remember Miss Emily very well." He bowed. "It's a pleasure to see you again, miss."

She dropped a quick curtsey. "Mr. Cowley."

"Your visit is a pleasant surprise." Cowley's mouth twitched as if he were fighting a smirk. "His Lordship didn't mention it."

She removed her gloves. "Maybe because I'm here to fix the water boiler. It seems it doesn't work properly."

Behind her, Brandon slanted a glare at Cowley, begging him not to say a word.

"I guess everything makes sense now," Cowley said.

"What, sir?" Emily asked at the same time as Brandon said,

"Thank you, Cowley. I'll see you later at dinner." He nearly dragged Emily up the stairs and into his bedroom.

"Good day, Mr. Cowley," Emily called over her shoulder.

Cowley showed a cheeky grin before vanishing with the efficiency with which he did everything.

"Give me your bag," he asked.

"No, it's all right. I'm used to carrying it."

Brandon left the door to his bedroom open as manners dictated, but he'd forgotten something. "Shall I call my housekeeper to act as a chaperone?" His oversight was disrespectful. A lady might interpret his bad manners as a lack of consideration for her. "I forgot about finding a chaperone. I apologise."

"Don't worry. I'm here as your technician."

Yes, that was a tad depressing, but he would straighten the situation soon.

"What a beautiful house." Emily removed her hat as she paced in the room. Like her gown, the gloves and hat appeared tattered.

"My parents decorated it. I didn't change anything aside from a few modern improvements like the boiler." He pointed at the water closet.

A metallic click came out of her bag every time she moved. She carried the bag with both hands so heavy the thing was.

"I must insist." He went to take the bag but ended up wrapping his hand around hers over the handle. Her skin felt soft under his fingers, and he was aware of the callouses on the palm of his hand. They both froze until she released her grip on the handle and let him take the bag.

"Thank you." She averted her gaze.

He cleared his throat. "This way." He put the bag on the floor next to the boiler. "Here it is. I had a freezing bath this morning. Quite unpleasant."

"Not good for your back, I suppose." She rolled up her sleeves.

"Not at all." He flickered his gaze over her elegant arms.

She had lovely wrists, slim and delicate. Not that he'd ever paid attention to ladies' wrists, but today seemed like a good day to start.

"Let me see." She opened her bag, revealing a set of shiny tools, screwdrivers, and other things he wouldn't be able to give a name to. "One of my neighbours in Painswick had a similar model. Usually, the problem is the main pressure valve or the pump seal. Nothing too complicated."

He nodded although he had no idea what she was talking about. He perched on the stool while she unscrewed the brass panel covering the inner mechanism of the boiler. Tubes and wheels filled the space. His knowledge of technical terms ended there.

"I have to remove these tubes to reach the valve," she said, selecting another tool.

"Yes, by all means. Is it dangerous? Do I need to do anything?"

She chuckled. "No, nothing. Some water might spill, but I'll close the water valve first." She stuck out the tip of her tongue as she worked on a particularly stubborn bolt, looking adorable.

"I envy your knowledge," he said as she removed other pieces from the device.

"It's mostly a matter of practice. I know little theory, to be honest. I read several books, but I learned mostly from trial and error. Many errors."

"I'm afraid I don't find mechanics fascinating."

"Tinkering is not for everyone." She selected another tool that looked like a mediaeval instrument of torture. "I enjoy understanding how things work. I learned by disassembling and reassembling things. A few times, I haven't been successful. But all practice is good practice."

He rested his chin on his hand and watched her wrestle against... some kind of bolt in the water boiler. "Do you need help?"

"No, thank you. Everything is under control."

Not inside him. "I usually say the very same thing to Cowley when he's angry with me because I did something he doesn't approve of."

She won whatever battle she fought against the thing. "He's very fond of you."

"As I am of him. He's like a father. He's been with my family since before I was born. He taught me how to tie my shoe and..." He shrugged. "Sorry. That must be too boring for you."

"Quite the contrary. You must have many precious memories of him. You should cherish them."

"I'd be lost without him." Literally.

Her smile disappeared. "You're lucky to have him."

"I am. I wish your relationship with your aunt were better."

"It's not as tragic as I've let you believe." Her features tensed though. "We shared some good moments, and she had a difficult life that hardened her."

But Mrs. Allen shouldn't mistreat Emily. He had to force the comment down.

Bolts and pieces of metal lay around her as she removed more mechanisms from the boiler. When the technician had come here, Brandon had been thoroughly bored by the whole affair and left the man alone to do his job after a few minutes. But now he could spend hours watching Emily work. Her expression changed according to what she was doing. It softened when a bolt yielded to her pressure, and it hardened when she had to apply more strength.

"Ha-ha!" She raised the screwdriver in triumph. "That's the problem. The pressure valve hasn't been installed properly. A sloppy job if I may say so myself."

Hmm... "Is it good news?"

"Very good. I'll fix it in a moment." She attacked the boiler with tools and determination, her cheeks red and her brow furrowed in concentration.

As much as he enjoyed her company here and appreciated how

she loved repairing things, he wanted to go to the ball with her. Sod his anxiety.

She hummed a tune as she reassembled the boiler, and he couldn't help but watch her and be bewitched by her charm. Never had watching someone work with bolts and screwdrivers been so fascinating.

"Done!" she said, wiping her hands with a cloth. "It shouldn't bother you again. No more freezing showers."

"You're my saviour." He inspected the boiler but didn't see anything different. Oh, well. "You have some dirt on your nose."

"Oh." She used the cloth, smearing the dirt across her face. "Better?"

"Not really. Allow me." He selected a clean cloth from the cabinet and wiped the offending stain from her lovely skin.

She remained still, regarding him from underneath her long eyelashes. "Better?"

"Very much." He withdrew his hand with a calm gesture at odds with the turmoil inside him. "I missed you."

"I missed you too." She stashed her tools in the bag with slow gestures.

"I'm being honest. I've never meant to treat you unkindly." He hoped his honesty came through.

She remained focused on storing her tools. "Don't be silly. You've always been very kind to me."

"Except when I stopped writing to you."

"I'm not going to lie," she said, stopping her work. "My heart broke when I realised you forgot about me."

Ouch. His heart broke as well. "I wanted to write to you, but I kept postponing it because I... wasn't myself. A day became a week, a week became a month, and before I knew it, a year had passed. The more time passed, the harder it was to pick up a pen and start writing. I have no excuses." Not exactly. He had an excuse, but addiction didn't sound like a good one. His relationship with laudanum was a difficult one to explain. He wasn't justifying himself, but the situation wasn't that simple. "I can make amends."

Her face didn't brighten as much as he expected. "I told you that you don't have to."

There was a bitter note in her voice, and he suspected she was still angry.

"But I have an offer." He stepped closer.

"What do you mean?"

"Would you like to come to a ball with me?" If she refused, he'd find something else to do with her.

She paused collecting her tools. "A ball? But you don't like to dance, and I'm not a brilliant dancer either."

"I do want to dance with you. Just you. And Lord Devon is giving a ball I must attend for business. Your presence would be much appreciated. It'd make the ball more endurable."

She focused on her tools and for a few horrible moments, the sound of the metal clinking against metal filled the silence between them. Should he insist? Ask again? Or leave her alone?

"I'd love to," she finally said.

He exhaled in relief. "I'll collect you personally if I may have the honour. No carriage. I have a brand-new landau that is the fastest vehicle in the country."

She laughed. He laughed too and caught himself thinking about when the last time he'd laughed so happily had been.

She closed her bag, a blush creeping up her cheeks. "I don't have anything to wear."

He spread his arms, refraining from telling silly jokes, like 'come naked.' "It's not a problem."

"Proper attire at a ball is a must." She returned her attention to the bag again. "I'm serious. I don't have anything decent enough. The gown you saw the other day belongs to my cousin, and it's not even recent."

On impulse, he held both her hands, throwing away every precaution. She had to understand how much he cared about her.

"May I be so bold as to offer to provide a gown for you? Just this once. I invited you after all."

Her blush intensified. "You don't have to do this."

"Please? The ball is in a few days. Offering you a ballgown is part of me making amends, and I need your presence, or I'll die of boredom, discussing the weather and pretending I enjoy cricket."

Her intense amber gaze searched him as if she wanted to be certain he was telling the truth. "It sounds tragic."

"Indeed." He brushed her knuckles with his thumbs. "Please."

"All right."

The two most beautiful words he'd ever heard.

nine

EMILY SHOULD HAVE refused the invitation. There were a million reasons not to go to another ball. She didn't have a fancy gown to start with and shouldn't accept Brandon's money to buy one. She blamed her lapse of judgement on his magnificent eyes and kind manners.

Above all, she hadn't thought about what Aunt Rose would say. Right now, her aunt wasn't saying anything. She stared at Emily as if her niece had told her she wanted to run naked across Hyde Park.

"I don't understand," Aunt Rose finally said after Emily had told her the news. "Why would the earl invite *you*?"

"You said you weren't friends." Catherine gave her a pointed look from her armchair in the sitting room. A fancy armchair, surely expensive. Aunt Rose was indeed refurbishing the house, sparing no expense.

Emily shuffled the recently pressed newspapers to keep herself busy. "The earl and I are both survivors of the Abbots Ripton disaster. I guess he feels a connection with me." He did, and so did she. But the connection was deeper than what she let transpire.

More blank stares. "You don't have anything to wear." Aunt

Rose gestured at Emily's worn dress. "And I don't have the money to buy you anything so suddenly."

Emily was about to say that Aunt Rose had spent a small fortune on clothes and furniture in the past weeks when the doorbell saved her from further explanations and an argument.

"I'll get the door." She rushed out of the room before Aunt Rose could say anything. "Allen Residence." She opened the door to an elegant, dark-haired woman. The lady's dark-green dress hugged her curves and enhanced her large dark eyes.

She swept her keen gaze over Emily as if assessing her qualities. "You must be Miss Emily de la Fuente Barclay." She spoke with an accent Emily couldn't place, but the Spanish pronunciation was excellent.

"I am she. My aunt is in the sitting room. If you'd follow me, please." She started to walk.

The woman waved a dismissive hand. "I'm not here to see your aunt. I'm here for you." She stepped inside, brushing past Emily. "I'm Mrs. Sala. Lord Astley sent me here for an emergency gown for you."

Emergency gown. She didn't know what to say, but laughing would be rude.

Mrs. Sala removed her shiny silk gloves. "Shall we start? I believe we're working on a tight schedule. Where's your room?"

Emily opened and shut her mouth without pronouncing a word.

"Yes?" Mrs. Sala said with the tone of a general waiting for a stupid private to carry out a simple order.

"Upstairs, second door."

"Upstairs, second door, lads," Mrs. Sala tossed over her shoulder. "Chop, chop."

Lads? Whom was she talking to?

Mrs. Sala flipped two fingers behind her, and a stream of people flowed in. Emily could do nothing but step aside and let the carriers bring in trunks, boxes, and crates of different sizes.

A chorus of "Morning, miss," echoed in the hallway as the lads poured inside.

"What is it?" Aunt Rose came out of the sitting room. She fell silent, watching the small crowd invade her hallway and stairs.

Mrs. Sala took Emily's elbow and led her towards the stairs. "Business, dear Mrs. Allen. I don't wish to be disturbed for the next few hours unless it's for a repast. I like my tea with lemon and one sugar cube, a nice oat biscuit if you have it, and a small tangerine. If any message for me should arrive, bring it to me immediately. That would be all. Thank you."

If Emily weren't so shocked, she'd find Aunt Rose's dropped jaw funny. She followed Mrs. Sala upstairs, admiring the lady's proud bearing.

"Don't worry, dear." Mrs. Sala patted her dark curls. "I've dealt with gown emergencies many times. I'd say they're my forte. We'll find the right gown for you, mark my words, or die trying."

That sounded extreme.

"I have plenty of ballgowns in those boxes," Mrs. Sala said. "It'll be a simple matter of finding the right dress and tweaking the fabric here and there to make the gown fit you."

"Ah, thank you." Her voice sounded strangled, but she'd be lying if she said she wasn't thrilled.

Mrs. Sala strode into Emily's small bedroom as if she owned it. Between the carriers, a couple of young women in matching blue dresses and silver chatelaines, and the boxes, there was barely enough space for Emily to squeeze in.

"Thank you, lads." Mrs. Sala clapped her hands. "You may go for now. I'll call you when I need you." She closed the door behind them and grinned. "Ladies, let's begin."

Two hours later, a pile of lovely silk gowns was heaped on Emily's bedroom that smelled of tangerine and lavender. Aunt

Rose had indeed brought a repast, more to snoop around than to make Mrs. Sala comfortable, in Emily's opinion.

She'd found at least half a dozen gowns that had stolen her heart, but Mrs. Sala wasn't convinced. Honestly, Emily would be happy with any of the beautiful gowns on her bed, but the modiste had some strong opinions on what suited Emily and what made her *disappear*— Mrs. Sala's words, not Emily's. Now the words 'or die trying' got a new meaning.

"It's all wrong." Mrs. Sala paced in the cramped room, through silk sashes and long gloves. "We must find the right tone. Tone is everything. The wrong shade of fabric, even with the right cut, would be a disaster." She plopped down onto the chair, the back of her hand on her forehead. "Oh, this challenge is harder than I thought. But I shall not desist."

The two seamstresses nodded sagely, following every Mrs. Sala's move.

"But I really like this gown." Emily selected a beautiful pale-yellow gown with pink satin roses and white muslin sleeves that looked like clouds. The dress was delicate and precious like a budding flower. She put it in front of her to check the skirt's length. "It's magnificent."

Mrs. Sala threw a hand towards the ceiling and shot up to her feet. "It doesn't suit your skin tone. You have this lovely blend of brown and gold, and we must find the right colour to bring it out!"

"Actually, I wouldn't mind to soften it or even hide it." She caressed the plush fabric. "People don't usually seem to approve of my blend of brown and gold."

"Emily!" Mrs. Sala took her shoulders with surprisingly strong fingers. "How can you say that? You shouldn't hide. People make comments because you wear the wrong colours."

She seriously doubted that, but she guessed Mrs. Sala saw the world through the lenses of her modiste job. "Madam, your gowns are all spectacular. I'll be honoured to wear any of them, and I don't—"

"Stay still!" Mrs. Sala almost shouted. She tilted her head right and left, scrutinising Emily. "Pull the curtains," she ordered without turning to her seamstresses.

They hurried to do their mistress's bidding, silent and efficient like fairies. Sunlight poured into the bedroom, flickering in and out through the clouds.

"That's it." Mrs. Sala went through another pile of gowns, muttering to herself. "Yes, yes!"

Emily was grateful for Mrs. Sala's help and Brandon's gift, but if she was going to be honest, her enthusiasm for the ballgown had doused after Mrs. Sala had rejected several lovely dresses. Mrs. Sala wouldn't find the perfect gown for Emily because it didn't exist. She was happy to wear something decent and enjoy an evening with Brandon. That was all. Besides, Brandon didn't care about the colours she wore.

"This." Mrs. Sala's gaze of triumph was almost scary. "Put this on. Quickly."

The seamstresses sprang into action, helping Emily out of the dressing gown she'd put on so she could change easily. The flutter of activity didn't let her see which gown Mrs. Sala had found and what it had to do with the curtains.

"I knew it. I knew it." Mrs. Sala and her assistants slid a beautiful emerald silk gown on Emily.

No, it wasn't emerald but a soft, ever-changing shade of green, blue, and anything in between. Tiny golden roses adorned the not-too-low neckline, and the small, see-through sleeves ended with pristine lace. Folds of the magical green fabric draped her legs and hips in a game of waves and colours. It was like wearing the sea. Every time she moved, the light glinted off the gown, sparkling with different shades of green, blue, and gold. Mrs. Sala and the seamstress worked relentlessly around Emily, tugging and pulling at the fabric gently.

"*Guarda, guarda.* Look." Mrs. Sala turned Emily towards the wall mirror after they finished adjusting the dress.

Emily's mouth hung open. The dark-haired beauty in the mirror couldn't be her. The gown hugged and exalted her curves, making her look taller and with brighter eyes. Even her lips seemed fuller, and her cheeks glowed.

"It's all about your eyes," Mrs. Sala said. "They have golden and green hues that complement your skin tone. This fabric has the right balance of green, blue, and yellow. Perfect for both your eyes and skin. The shades of the taffeta change constantly, enhancing your natural beauty."

Dash it all, but the modiste was right. What had Emily said about finding the perfect gown? She'd been wrong. Every good feature on her face and body was enhanced tenfold and brought up by the dress and the fabric. She wore a magic trick.

"Goodness." She twirled on her tiptoes. The fabric swished around her legs, glittering in the light like the shimmering of the sea.

"It just needs a little adjustment on the shoulders." Mrs. Sala used a couple of pins to gather the fabric over Emily's arms. "Nothing too difficult."

Emily would never, ever doubt the woman again. In a few hours, the modiste had transformed Emily into a mermaid!

Mrs. Sala smiled in the mirror. "Chin up, Emily. Be proud of your heritage, and people will respect you. Doubt yourself, and people will mock you. It is that simple."

She started to believe it. "This ballgown feels like a suit of armour."

"That's the whole point." Mrs. Sala nodded. "Now, where's my tea? I need another cup before we finish." She opened the door and paused. "What are you doing here?" The tone didn't sound friendly.

Emily peered into the corridor to catch a glimpse of a man's jacket.

Mr. Payne removed his hat and bowed. "Madam Sala." He cast a disinterested glance at Emily. "What a surprise to see you here."

"I'm sure it is." Mrs. Sala folded her arms over her chest. "Business is business, and for Pete's sake, stop wearing brown and that awful shade of blue together. They make you look like a giant poisonous mushroom and give me a headache."

The seamstresses nodded and muttered their approval.

Emily didn't understand much about colours, but she had to agree with Mrs. Sala, and as she'd said, she would never doubt the modiste again.

Mr. Payne narrowed his gaze. "I don't remember having asked for your opinion on my clothes."

"That's painfully obvious." Mrs. Sala repeated her dramatic gesture of touching her forehead with the back of her hand. "Out of my sight. Out of my sight. Your clothes make me want to cast up my accounts."

"Always so dramatic." Scoffing, Mr. Payne entered Aunt Rose's room and slammed the door behind him.

Mrs. Sala shut the door, a frown marring her brow. "May I ask what *that* solicitor is doing here?"

Emily focused on the magnificent gown again. "Business with my aunt. He comes here regularly as of late."

Mrs. Sala leaned against the closed door, drumming her long nails on her arms. "That man is a real Payne in the neck, let me tell you. Don't trust him."

"Don't trust him," the seamstresses repeated in chorus.

"I won't." Although she had no idea what the modiste meant.

Mrs. Sala lowered her voice. "He's known for helping people make shady deals. He's clever, mind you, which makes him even more dangerous. He bends the law as he pleases and gets away with it while ruining people's lives. A true pettifogger."

Well, nothing to do with Emily then.

ten

BRANDON SHIFTED ON the seat of his landau and glanced at Emily's door. Anyone waiting for a lady outside of her house for the first time would be nervous. Yes, it was the first time he'd invited a lady to a ball of all things. Plenty of reasons to feel nervous. And he was breaking several rules of society all at once. But he hadn't had time to find a chaperone for Emily again, and quite frankly, he didn't require one. He wanted to spend some time with her and talk. Nothing scandalous. On top of that, there was another matter nagging at the back of his mind.

He hadn't asked Emily anything about her inheritance, but her family had been a wealthy one. She should be an heiress, receive her own allowance, and not need to worry about finding a governess position or threadbare shoelaces. He was more than happy to buy her a ballgown, but he hadn't expected her to suffer from financial restrictions. All these years, his only comfort about Emily's situation was knowing that she possessed the means to lead a more than comfortable life, doing whatever she wanted with her family's fortune. Instead, she had to earn her keep and search for a job while she was treated like a servant. There was something odd in that tale.

Her aunt couldn't possibly have access to Emily's money, could she? She might have administered Emily's finances when her niece had been sixteen, but now Emily should be in full control of her money. Or maybe Emily or her aunt had squandered everything in an unfortunate venture. Or there was a legal impediment. Too many options.

He needed to investigate the matter. At least Matthew was interested in hiring Emily at his workshop after Brandon had talked to him about her. That should cheer her up. He could impose his wish to hire her on Matthew, but he respected his friend too much.

She could be an engineer's apprentice instead of a governess.

He climbed out of the landau, keeping an eye on Emily's door. The open carriage was a thing of beauty— light, glossy, and made to race down the cobbled streets of London with speed and elegance. He had little if no experience in driving, especially such a fast landau. That was why he should have asked his coachman to drive.

Why had he decided to drive it by himself? He wanted to impress Emily, that was the truth. There was also another concern. A big, masculine one. At the front of the landau, Diablo gave an impatient snort, shaking his glorious midnight mane.

He tentatively patted the horse's neck. "Good boy."

Diablo shot him a scorching, equine glare and let out a squeal that chilled the night. The message was clear: touch me again and die.

Brandon loved horses. Of course he did. He was a gentleman and an Englishman, for Pete's sake. Horses were one of the pillars of his culture, along with afternoon tea, bad weather, and worse food. But if he really had to be honest, horses made him uncomfortable. Those hooves could easily break his skull in two. And the teeth? He could bet they might chop off a finger or two. His back had never allowed him to relax on a saddle, and his tension and constant pain bothered the animals. Brandon hadn't spent much time on a saddle or a carriage in the past years unless he'd visited his physician or an opium den. Not his finest moment.

On top of that, he'd hurt himself badly, falling from the saddle years ago. Horses, and especially Diablo, sensed Brandon's fear, and the horse didn't like it.

The stallion was a fine specimen. Big body, glossy coat, and fine mane. Carriage horses were all pretty and strong.

Diablo shot him another glare. Brandon inched his hand closer to the horse's neck, daring another attempt at pacifying the beast. But no. Bad idea. Diablo was ready to kick him.

"I won't touch you," Brandon said, steering away from the proud equine. "Just take Emily and me safely to the ball, and I'll give you a sugar cube."

Diablo shook his head as if saying no. But it wasn't possible, was it?

"A carrot?"

Another no.

"An apple?"

No.

"Bugger off, you—"

"Brandon?"

He spun around at hearing Emily's voice, and a shock of stillness went through him. Heavens. She was a vision in a green dress that showed off the golden hues of her skin and the green specks in her eyes. Her hair was styled in a graceful French braid with green ribbons and pearls. Golden earrings graced her earlobes, and her rouged lips completed the lovely picture.

"Good evening." He bowed but kept his gaze on her. "By Jove, you look absolutely stunning." He'd promised to be honest, after all.

She blushed. "Mrs. Sala is an amazing modiste."

"I think the credit should go to you." He couldn't stop looking at her. She was radiant and glittering— a mermaid freshly jumped out of the sea.

"Thank you for the dress." She draped a cloak that matched the dress around her shoulders. "I have no words."

"My pleasure." He frowned when Mrs. Allen and her daughter came out of the house in their evening cloaks. What was happening?

Mrs. Allen sauntered towards him, smiling so widely he could see her wisdom teeth. "My lord." She curtsied. Her daughter did the same, all battering eyelashes and blushes.

He offered a polite bow although Mrs. Allen showed to be quite bold by introducing herself to an earl. But a gentleman never reproached a lady. "Madams."

"Thank you for escorting my niece to Lord Devon's ball." Mrs. Allen gently pushed Catherine forwards. "I believe you haven't been introduced to my daughter, Catherine."

Brandon bowed again. If he wanted, he could refuse the introduction. "It's a pleasure to meet you."

"My lord." She dropped a perfect curtsy, graceful and light, before raising her clear blue eyes to him.

She was a beauty. He couldn't deny it. But she left him cold, like the view of a sunny beach in winter. One expected to feel the warmth of the sun only to be left chilly.

"Perhaps you would dance together later," Mrs. Allen said, once again being too bold. "Catherine would be pleased. She's an excellent dancer."

Brandon couldn't summon a smile. "I would love to, but I'm afraid I don't dance." Only with Emily.

"Then why go to a ball if you don't mind my asking?" Catherine asked.

"Social events aren't always avoidable, Miss Allen, and with Emily, I'm sure the evening will be more tolerable." Now he couldn't fight a bright smile.

"I see. You and Emily are good friends, sir," Mrs. Allen said.

"Only she can understand me." He meant every word.

Mrs. Allen swept her gaze over the landau. "I don't see your chaperone, my lord."

"It's a short ride," Brandon said. "And I promise to be a gentleman."

Mrs. Allen's nostrils flared, and Catherine hid a gasp behind her gloved hand. "I'm afraid I must beg you to carefully consider the implications of your behaviour, sir. I'm not sure I can allow you to be alone with my niece."

Brandon had to bite down a comment. In a few minutes, Mrs. Allen had broken several rules. First, she'd introduced herself and her daughter without a formal intermediary. He wasn't a stickler for etiquette, but Mrs. Allen didn't hold a title, and he was an earl. But now she complained about a chaperone?

He straightened. "If Emily wishes to have a chaperone or drive to Lord Devon's house by any other means than my landau, I'd be happy to oblige. Whatever the lady chooses."

Mrs. Allen jutted out her chin. "We're heading to Lord Devon's too. Emily might join us."

Every gaze turned towards Emily. He wouldn't decide for her, but he hoped she did what she truly wanted and not what pleased her aunt. While her aunt had a point, Emily was old enough to decide for herself which risks she wanted to take. Perhaps sensing the tension in the air, Diablo expressed his opinion with another impatient snort.

Emily inched closer to the landau in a sparkle of green and gold. "Thank you, Aunt, but I'm happy to go with Lord Astley."

Yes! Brandon grinned and gave another shallow bow to the stunned women. "I will see you shortly, ladies." He put a hand on the small of his back to soothe a sore spot.

Chin up, Mrs. Allen and Catherine hurried along the pavement towards a carriage waiting for them. They muttered something he didn't catch. But who cared? No one could understand the bond between Emily and himself. He'd been deprived of her company for too long.

Emily eyed the landau. "You weren't exaggerating. The landau is fantastic, and the horse is magnificent." She stretched out a hand to caress Diablo, and he blocked her hand by taking her wrist.

"Careful. He has a temper," he whispered lest Diablo hear him.

"Like I do."

He released her hand and tensed, ready to pull Emily back should Diablo do anything funny. But the traitorous creature sighed, his tail wiggling as Emily caressed his neck with long strokes.

"What a beautiful stallion," she said with awe. "He shouldn't pull a landau but run freely. What's his name?"

"Diablo. I believe he's a Spaniard."

"Like I am, again." She beamed. "*Sangre caliente!*"

"Whatever you said, I'm sure he is that thing."

She laughed, a warm, throaty laugh that cast a spell on him. Even Diablo gave another soft sound as if asking her to laugh again.

"It means hot blood," she said. "In a good way. Someone who is passionate and full of life."

"Definitely him," he agreed. "And you."

Diablo sighed again as she scratched his neck.

"You aren't afraid of him, are you?" he asked, getting closer to Diablo.

"Afraid? Of this black prince? No."

She kissed the horse. Kissed him! A proper, smacking kiss on the forehead. Diablo helped the process by bowing his proud head. He exhaled blissfully some more, seemingly to melt under her hand. She cooed. He asked for more scratches, and she whispered something in his ear before kissing him again.

What the bloody hell was happening?

Was Brandon jealous of a horse? Yes, he had every right to be.

He was supposed to be the one she kissed. Silly of him but also not so silly.

"I had no idea you loved horses so much." He couldn't completely remove a hint of frustration from his voice.

"I spent a lot of time around horses in Painswick." She kept scratching Diablo, much to the horse's delight. "They're such clever, loving animals. The best companions. And to think there are people who are frightened by them. I don't understand how anyone could be scared of horses."

Bloody hell. "Yes, unbelievable." He scratched the back of his neck.

"Shall we?" She gave one last, lingering glance to Diablo who returned the longing with another soft sound.

Brandon helped her onto the carriage, savouring the brief contact with her gloved hand.

"There's a blanket for the cold." He handed her the thick quilt.

"Thank you." She covered her lap and left enough quilt for him. "We're ready to go. I want to see Diablo at work."

"Great. Nothing more simple. Diablo, let's go." He clicked his tongue and whipped the reins, but Diablo ignored him. The horse's pointed ears didn't even twitch. "Go, Diablo."

Nothing. The beast didn't move an inch.

"Diablo? Pretty please?"

The horse stomped a hoof on the cobbles. It had to mean *sod off*.

"Hey presto! Voilà! Hocus-pocus! Open sesame!"

Nothing. Diablo didn't even snort.

Emily rolled about with laughter, a hand on her belly. "What are you doing?" she asked among hiccups of laughter.

"Trying to convince this stubborn mule to go."

She wiped a tear from her eye. "Oh, my goodness. How did you come here?"

Brandon gestured at the immovable horse. "The groom told Diablo to go, and the stallion obeyed."

"Why doesn't he want to go?" she asked, tilting her head gracefully.

"I think you bewitched my horse, and now he's too stunned to obey me. So it's not me who is a poor coachman. Not at all. It's your fault, really," he quipped.

She threw her head back and burst out laughing again. He adored that sound. Being abused by his horse was worth it just to hear her laugh. Some ladies might find her laughter loud and crude, but he loved it exactly for that reason. Diablo could stand still all night if it meant hearing Emily laugh.

"This is a serious predicament." He feigned outrage. "How are we supposed to go to Lord Devon's house? You must call back whatever spell you cast on him."

"I will." She shuffled. "Let me try."

He handed her the reins. "All yours."

"Hocus-pocus, oh, come on." She moved towards him until her shoulder touched his, and he felt that simple touch everywhere.

"*Ándale!*" she said in a firm tone.

Diablo replied with an excited neigh.

She made a soft noise, halfway between a cooing sound and a smack of her lips. Diablo sprinted off in a gentle trot as if nothing had happened.

"That's the magic word." He shook his head. "It's true. You put a spell on him."

She chuckled again. The gusts of wind danced with her dark curls, and he forgot about Diablo and the road as he watched her driving the landau with confidence. From now on, she would be the one who drove his landau if it made her so happy. He was even grateful for Diablo. The horse obeyed Emily in everything. When she asked him to slow, he did so without hesitation. When she wanted him to turn around a corner, he almost anticipated her wish. She even overtook a slow cart with an agile move that made Diablo neigh in pleasure.

She pulled the reins in front of Lord Devon's house, her cheeks flushed and her eyes shining. "That was fun."

"Indeed." He stopped himself from brushing her curls from her cheeks.

She beamed. Her chest rose and fell under the capelet. "Diablo is an excellent horse with a very sweet temperament."

Sweet and Diablo weren't two words Brandon would necessarily use together, but all right.

eleven

BRANDON HELPED EMILY out of the carriage and up the short flight of stairs to Lord Devon's house.

A footman welcomed them, another one took their coats, and a third told them to follow him to the ballroom. An endless stream of servants. Emily smiled at everyone, receiving bright smiles in turn.

He and Emily crossed the wide hallway then walked along the corridor to the main hall from where music and chatter came. He hesitated before stepping into the ballroom. The bright lights glared at him from the chandeliers, and the crowd was twice as big as the one at Lady Gardner's party. The cold stirring of his usual anxiety began. He searched the room for Matthew, who should be there already. A friendly face would be helpful since he couldn't and wouldn't take any laudanum.

"Are you nervous?" she asked.

"A bit. But your presence gives me courage. We faced death together, after all."

She nodded and took his arm.

When the master of ceremonies announced, "Lord Brandon Astley, Earl of Hastings, and Miss Emily de la Fuente Barclay," there were glances and whispers behind the fans and gloved hands. Emily's name was whispered.

He and Emily wove through the guests among ladies curtsying and gentlemen bowing. He did his best to return the greetings despite the knot of uneasiness in his belly. He preferred dealing with Diablo to a crowd of peers. Not all faces were hostile though. He didn't miss the few longing glances thrown at Emily. He couldn't blame people for staring at her. She looked stunning. Under the lights of the chandeliers, she was resplendent— an emerald wrapped in gold and silk.

Mrs. Allen was one of those who didn't seem to appreciate Emily's dazzling beauty. She observed them from behind her fan, holding it as if ready to stab them with it.

"Isn't that Mr. Tyrell?" Emily tugged at his arm.

He exhaled when he spotted Matthew. Thank goodness. He strode towards his friend perhaps too quickly, judging by how ladies and gentlemen moved out of his way. Anyway. It was either that or letting his anxiety spike.

"There you are." Matthew beamed. His gaze lingered a little too long on Emily. "I was beginning to worry."

Brandon sucked in a deep breath once he reached his friend. "Miss Emily de la Fuente Barclay, this is Mr. Matthew Tyrell, my friend and associate." He let his admiration for her ring in his voice.

"Miss de la Fuente Barclay." Matthew bowed. "Brandon talked so much about you I feel like I know you."

She dipped in a curtsey. "Mr. Tyrell."

"How was the carriage ride?" Matthew asked. "Isn't Diablo an extraordinary male?"

"Excellent," Emily said. "Very sweet and docile."

"That's why the groom chose him." Matthew wiggled his eyebrows at Brandon.

"Sweet and docile my... foot," Brandon muttered.

He had to smile during another round of greetings, bows, and curtsies. The introductions never ended. They would take up a good chunk of the evening. And where was the champagne? He could use some Dutch courage although it upset his stomach—

Matthew poked him with an elbow and stopped his inner whining. "Lady Robinson is here."

"Lady Robinson?" Emily and Brandon said together, whipping their heads towards Matthew at the same time.

Matthew shifted his gaze from him to her. "Why, yes. Brandon and I hope to conclude business with her as there were some, er, misunderstandings between them."

Indeed. "Do you know Lady Robinson?" Brandon asked.

Emily paled. Not even the rouge could hide the change in her complexion. "I had an interview with her for a governess position. She didn't believe my dislike of closed carriages would make a good governess out of me," she whispered the last words. "She was worried about me not being able to keep her daughter safe or teach her properly."

A flare of anger raised Brandon's temperature. The good thing about anger was that it crushed his anxiety in a moment. He wasn't fond of Lady Robinson to start with. Now he positively disliked her. "She won't bother you. I promise, and we don't have to interact with her in any fashion."

"Actually, you need to talk to her," Matthew said. "You must secure an agreement quickly before another company presents a different brake system and has it approved. Meeting her here in an informal event would be perfect for a good resolution."

Hell. Brandon gnashed his teeth. He wanted a simple evening with Emily, but Matthew had a point. They couldn't avoid dealing with Lady Robinson. "I will talk to her."

"Thank you." Matthew put a hand on his chest, sagging in relief.

"Brandon told me about your new train brakes," Emily said.

"We have a very efficient prototype of a new brake system." Matthew brightened as he always did when he talked about engineering. "An improved type of vacuum brakes that reduces the stopping time to merely twenty-two seconds when the speed is fifty miles per hour," he said the last words like an actor wishing to impress the audience with a plot twist.

And it must have worked because Emily gasped in delight. "Twenty-two seconds? That's an amazing achievement. How many tonnes?"

Matthew leaned closer to her and whispered, "Two hundred and sixty-six."

Brandon had heard those numbers countless times, but they meant little to him. The only thing he understood was that they were impressive, and judging by how Emily's eyes widened, very impressive.

"I heard of a German engineer who managed thirty-six seconds with half the tonnes." She positively glowed. "Mr. Tyrell, you're a genius."

Brandon shifted his weight. Yes, Matthew was an extraordinary engineer, but he couldn't help a tiny pang of jealousy at Emily's enthusiasm.

Matthew flushed a fierce red, chuckling nervously. "I'm so glad you appreciate my work, Miss Emily." He didn't seem capable of standing still. "I believe we are colleagues."

"Are we?"

"Brandon told me you're an engineer."

She blushed as well and gripped Brandon's arm more tightly. "Not really. A self-taught one. I read every book in the *Ars Mechanica Encyclopaedia* and every other text I could find. But I don't have any formal education. Lots of practice though. I'm more of a tinkerer than an engineer. Not that I wouldn't love to be one."

"The formal education is important, but your enthusiasm is contagious," Matthew said. "I'll be happy to offer you a job in my enterprise—"

"It's actually my enterprise," Brandon said.

Matthew had the decency to blush. "Yes, well, I'm always looking for new talents, and Brandon speaks so highly of you that I'm curious to hear your ideas and see your tinkering skills at work. If you agree, of course."

"Excellent choice, Matthew." Brandon's enthusiasm was doused when Emily didn't show the excitement he expected.

"Is something the matter?" Matthew asked.

"Mr. Tyrell, you're aware of my condition, aren't you?" she said in a low voice.

"Your dislike for carriages?" Matthew exchanged a glance with Brandon. "Yes, and the offer still stands. I really don't care how you choose to travel, miss. I myself rarely travel by train these days."

Emily stood speechless, her hand nearly limp on Brandon's arm.

"Did I say something?" Matthew fiddled with his French cuffs.

"Emily?" Brandon said gently, worried Matthew might have offended her.

She slid her arm out of his, only to squeeze Matthew so tightly that there was little, if any, space at all between them. It was a quick embrace, a light squeeze of her body against his, but still a fierce hug! Matthew stilled, a daft smile on his face, and Brandon scowled. First Diablo, now Matthew. Why could Matthew and Diablo get a hug or a kiss from Emily? No, the evening wasn't going as planned.

"Forgive me, sir." Emily breathed heavily, her cheeks flushed. "I got carried away by my enthusiasm." She fanned herself. "This is the best offer I've ever received. Thank you, Mr. Tyrell. I'd be delighted to work for you. I'd be happy to do anything. Nothing is too small. Any tinkering or soldering would do." She spoke so fast Brandon could barely follow her.

He arched a brow at Matthew. "I'm sure Matthew will find you something you'll like, won't you, Matthew?" he prompted when the lucky engineer didn't say anything.

Matthew smiled widely. "Absolutely. And I'm sure Miss Barclay will be happy with us."

"Thank you." Emily seemed to float over the marble floor as she rose on her tiptoes.

Good. Brandon wouldn't give her the best dance of her life, but at least she was jubilant about the job. But he did deserve a kiss, didn't he?

Lady Robinson swept into view from behind a group of young ladies and threw him an incendiary glare. Once again, his happiness was crushed by a swift death. She shot daggers at him with her glares, slashing the air with her fan.

He exhaled. "Would you please excuse me? I need a word with Lady Robinson."

"I've already told her about our project before you arrived," Matthew said. "She's aware of what we need from her."

"Excellent." He took Emily's hand and kissed it. There. His chance to show her he was a proper gentleman and kiss her hand. "I'll see you in a moment."

She was still in shock if her slow blinking was any indication. "Yes, yes."

"Take care of Miss de la Fuente Barclay for me," he said to Matthew before weaving through the crowd towards Lady Robinson.

As worry threatened to surge, he reminded himself Lady Robinson had mistreated Emily. No time to be anxious. He ought to show his character. He walked past Mrs. Allen and Catherine who bobbed a quick curtsy. Their matching hard glares were anything but polite, which reminded him he had to ask Cowley about Emily's legal situation.

Lady Robinson beckoned him to follow her with a quick gesture of her fan. Without a word, she left the ballroom and headed to a quiet, dimly lit corner close to the garden.

"Madam," he said with yet another bow. "I believe Mr. Tyrell explained—"

"Is this some kind of joke?" She pressed her firm lips in a grim line.

"A joke? I don't understand. If you're referring to our last conversation, I still firmly believe I don't want an intimate encounter with you. I must admit though that Mr. Tyrell and I need a bureaucratic favour from you. That's what I wanted to discuss with you." He controlled his voice although the music should cover his angry tone.

She pointed her fan in the direction of the ballroom. "I'm referring to *that* woman."

"What woman?"

"Emily Barclay."

The muscles in the back of his neck contracted, and his chronic pain had nothing to do with it. He'd been polite towards Lady Robinson despite the horrible fashion in which she'd treated Emily and himself, but if she believed she could disparage Emily in front of him, she was mistaken.

"I beg your pardon?" he gritted out.

"You have the audacity to talk to me about a deal after you escorted the woman who wanted to be my governess to this ball!" She huffed. "You did it on purpose to annoy and humiliate me."

"I did *not* do such a thing. Believe it or not, the world doesn't revolve around you. Madam." It became increasingly difficult for him to keep his tone of voice polite.

She gasped, a hand on her throat. "How dare you!" She jabbed a finger at him. "I came here with the intention of forging an honest deal with you. I was even ready to apologise for my forwardness and ask nothing of you aside from your stupid documents after Mr. Tyrell talked so enthusiastically about his project. But your impudence changes everything. You came here and humiliated me in front of everyone. That was a low blow from you. And you call yourself a gentleman?"

He clenched his jaw. "There's a misunderstanding here. I didn't do anything to disrespect you. I simply invited my... friend to a ball." Friend was a cold word for the warmth he and Emily shared.

"You must be joking." She shivered with anger. "I made a proposal," she half-hissed, half-whispered, "a simple proposal that you refused only to come here, causing a scandal by accompanying a woman who wanted to be in my employ. And you have the audacity to ask me to sign your papers. The message is very clear, sir."

Oh, hell. Brandon rubbed his aching forehead. "It's not what you think. There's no message. I didn't even know Miss Barclay had met you."

"So this is all a coincidence? Am I to believe she didn't tell you anything about me?" She scoffed.

He pushed down a new flare of anger. "Not everyone is obsessed with gossip and speaking ill of other people as you are, madam."

"Ah!" Gasping, she grabbed a fistful of her skirt. "I've made up my mind. You forced me to do this. Do you want me to sign the documents for the approval of your stupid invention? Then you're going to spend a night with me. Take it or leave it. Non-negotiable. Think about your answer when you return home with that woman tonight. This offer won't stand for long." She hurried past him, a storm clad in silk and armed with a fan.

Great. Brandon exhaled through his clenched teeth. He'd destroyed Matthew's work with one conversation. Not even a conversation but a monologue from Lady Robinson. But what was he supposed to do? Ignore the insults? Honestly, he'd been more than patient with the termagant. Insulting him was one thing, but disparaging Emily was quite another. No, he wouldn't feel ashamed of his actions.

He returned to the ballroom with his back muscles stiff and contracted painfully. Emily and Matthew drank champagne in a corner, chatting and laughing. Aside from Mrs. Allen and Catherine, they were the only two guests without a noble title and the only two guests he cared about. And hellfire, Emily stood out like a jewel in the crowd. He had to thank Mrs. Sala. He fiddled with his starched collar, heading towards them, collecting himself lest Emily understand how upset he was.

"How did it go?" Matthew asked, raising his eyebrows.

Brandon coughed into his closed fist. "Not well, I'm afraid. Lady Robinson didn't..." He stopped. He didn't want Emily to think she was the reason Lady Robinson had refused to help them. Emily looked so radiant and happy he didn't want to spoil her evening. "She's a stubborn woman."

Emily lowered her glass of champagne. "It's because of me, isn't it?"

"No, not at all." Dammit. He didn't sound as confident as he should have.

Matthew narrowed his gaze. "Let me guess. Lady Robinson didn't like the fact you came here with Miss de la Fuente Barclay."

Brandon didn't say anything. Apparently, everything he did that evening didn't go as planned. He couldn't even keep a secret for a little while.

"I might talk to her if it helps," Emily said. Somehow, all her radiance dimmed. She shone less brightly.

Matthew stared at his glass as if he wanted to divine the future from the champagne. "Thank you, Miss Barclay, but I don't think Lady Robinson will change her mind. We'll have to find another solution." He shot a firing glare at Brandon.

No, Brandon wasn't going to discuss the possibility of whoring himself in front of Emily. He offered her his arm. "Would you care for a dance?"

Matthew stopped sipping his champagne. "You? Dancing?"

Emily didn't smile. "Are you sure? I can leave, so you'll have another chance at talking with Lady Robinson."

Leaving because Lady Robinson was a bully? He wouldn't allow that. "I invited you because I wanted to spend time with you.

Please?" He drew in a breath when she slid her small hand over his arm tentatively.

She handed her glass to Matthew. "Mr. Tyrell, I'll see you later."

Matthew bowed to Emily and tossed him a glance. They'd discuss a new strategy and Matthew's concerns later. For now, Brandon wanted to dance with Emily.

She shook her head. "I'm so sorry—"

"Don't." He regretted his harsh tone immediately. "Apologies. I didn't mean to sound so bitter, but this situation isn't your fault." And he wanted his bloody dance. "I'm determined to enjoy the evening with you, no matter what Lady Robinson or anyone else thinks. Do you agree with me?"

Her smile didn't reach her eyes. "I do, but what about your project?"

"Matthew and I have been working together for a while, and by that I mean he spends my money with abandon and I complain about it with equal fervour."

She laughed. Good.

"We've been through difficult situations. We'll find a way to convince Lady Robinson to sign those papers." He sounded more confident than he felt because if Lady Robinson didn't change her mind, Matthew's new brakes would never see the light of day, or in the best case, the production would be delayed by years. Not a charming possibility.

"Where are we going?" Emily asked.

"Where no one can make silly comments about us." He led her away from the ballroom and entered the conservatory. The glass house wrapped around the house and offered a spectacular view of the garden. Even better than the ballroom.

The scent of orchids and winter roses replaced that of the guests' perfumes and cologne. He found a quiet spot at the end of the passageway where they could hear the music and dance without anyone watching them. A secret waltz.

He twirled her around and bowed. "Madam."

Now her smile was a genuine one. She curtsied. "My lord."

He gently took her hand and placed it on his shoulder. "It's an honour to be dancing with you."

"It's the least I could do after Lady Robinson refused to help you because of me." She squeezed her lips. "All because I don't like travelling in closed carriages. Ridiculous. What do my travelling preferences have to do with anything?"

"I've always believed our current problems, your dislike for closed vehicles, and my chronic pain were the prices we had to pay to survive. I don't feel angry anymore about my limitations and the constant pain. We've borrowed more time and paid for it. That's all."

She stared at him with awe. "You're right. Let's dance."

He started a series of short box steps, following the music. His stiff legs produced hesitant movements with him having to pause to coordinate his paces. But she laughed again, glowing under the lights glittering from the ballroom. It was as if she were surrounded by the stars. The golden light suited her. Aware of his hesitant steps, she waited for him and followed his every move, anticipating his pauses. From the outside, they had to look like a slow, uncoordinated pair of dancers.

As the waltz progressed, they were both smiling and breathless.

"I haven't danced in years," she said as they danced along the conservatory through blossoming flowers and emerald leaves.

"Me neither." He put a hand on his sore back and rubbed it. "And my body knows it. I can walk for an hour or two without consequences, but dancing doesn't agree with me."

"It has to be painful." She stepped closer for the next series of moves, and he caught a whiff of her sweet scent.

"When your back hurts, it's difficult to find a comfortable position," he said. "You lie down, it hurts. You stand, it hurts. You sit, it hurts. Walking helps."

Compassion softened her features. "But you endured the pain so admirably."

Actually, no. He'd abused laudanum, lost himself in it, and nearly destroyed his life. He didn't want to talk about that, not tonight when she was so happy. He hated that she thought he was a hero for enduring the pain. He'd tell her the truth, but for now, as selfish as it sounded, he basked in the light of her awe.

He pulled her closer, tightening his grip on her waist. She took in a breath, and her lips parted. The world revolved around her soft breathing and red lips, and hell, he wanted to kiss her. Her skirt brushed against his legs as they danced across the conservatory. If they danced in the ballroom, they would bump into other couples because they didn't follow the music due to his slow steps. But it was just the two of them among the midnight flowers. He stopped and cupped her lovely cheek. She leaned into his palm.

"Emily..."

Voices coming from a corner broke the spell.

"... this is a disaster," a high-pitched voice said.

Emily put a hand on his arm. "My aunt," she mouthed.

"Where did Emily and the earl go?" That was Catherine. "I lost sight of them."

He remained still with Emily leaning against him.

"Let's not do anything hasty," Mrs. Allen said in an eager tone. "Payne is getting everything ready. It's a matter of days now."

"Many things can happen in a few days, Mama. And we haven't paid for all the expenses yet. We'll become the laughingstock of London if we end up in debt."

Mrs. Allen exhaled. "Don't worry. Let Emily enjoy herself. The earl isn't a problem, and we have..." Whatever Mrs. Allen meant to say, Brandon didn't hear it. The voices faded away, but rage burned the back of his mouth.

He waited for the silence to return. "What is your aunt planning?" he whispered.

She shrugged. "I have no idea. She met this solicitor, Mr.

Payne, a few times. Mrs. Sala told me he isn't an honest man, but I don't understand what you and I have to do with him and my aunt."

He would find out. Whatever happened, he was going to protect Emily. He'd done it before. He would do it again.

twelve

EMILY CLUNG TO the last magic moments of the night after she'd driven Brandon's landau home. She'd danced, drunk champagne, laughed, met a wonderful horse, and even got a job. A perfect evening. She didn't want it to end.

Brandon helped her out of her seat. The cold air pebbled her skin when she removed the carriage blanket. Something had changed in Brandon after they'd eavesdropped on Aunt Rose's conversation. He'd become edgy and even furious at times, not with her though. Was she worried? Yes, but if there was one thing she'd learned after the tragedy, it was that she would survive. Whatever Aunt Rose planned, Emily would manage to carry on. Besides, the prospect of having a job with Matthew brightened her future. Aunt Rose could do her worst. Emily would be an independent woman soon.

Brandon kissed her hand. "Thank you for the lovely night and for taming Diablo."

"He didn't need to be tamed." She glanced at the proud stallion. "How are you going to go back home?"

He scrubbed the back of his neck. "I'm not sure. The groom

assured me Diablo would obey me, but that's not obviously the case."

"Maybe you can bribe Diablo." She opened her reticule and took out an apple she'd nicked from the banquet table. "Try."

"I don't think he likes it."

"Every horse loves apples."

He glanced at the apple as if it were an exploding device. "All right." He offered the fruit to Diablo who barely turned his head towards him and cast a disinterested glance at his hand. "A peace offering."

"You're too tense. He senses it." Emily nudged him. "I sense it."

"I can't be calm when he glares at me like that," he said from a corner of his mouth, moving his lips very little.

"He isn't going to hurt you." She touched Brandon's shoulder, feeling the muscles tighten like ropes.

"Right. Let's try again, mate." Brandon winced when Diablo sniffed the apple and refused it with an outraged snort. "Bugger. Excuse me," he said, baring his teeth. "He hates me."

"No. He doesn't trust you." She took the apple and offered it to Diablo.

The horse didn't hesitate. His big lips brushed against her palm softly as he chomped on the apple.

Brandon exhaled. "I told you. He hates me."

"You're nervous around him. That's all. Once you trust him, he'll trust you." She knew everything about irrational fears. Matthew would need to know closed carriages and train terrified her. She would make a full confession at the first opportunity. She caressed Diablo's warm neck. "It's not easy overcoming our fears."

Brandon removed his hat, letting his luscious curls fall. "Emily, may I ask you something?"

"Of course."

"I would like to understand what your aunt is plotting, and

with your permission, I'll ask Cowley to investigate. He's extremely skilled at gathering information while being discreet."

She tugged at her capelet to fend off a chill. "I appreciate it, but maybe you worry too much. I'm sure my aunt would never hurt me. She might not be extremely fond of me, but we're a family. We take care of each other."

"I hope that's the case." He fiddled with his hat and glanced at Diablo finishing his apple. "And I hope Diablo will take me home. Otherwise I'll be wandering around London for the rest of my life with a horse who wants to kill me."

"So dramatic." She scratched Diablo behind his ear and kissed his neck. "I'm sure he'll obey you. Won't you, darling?" she whispered to the horse.

Brandon clicked his tongue. "Kisses, treats, and terms of endearment. Diablo can't complain."

She kissed Diablo once again. "Good night, Brandon. Thank you for everything."

"Good night." He loitered, shifting his weight.

"Is something the matter?"

"Well, I couldn't help but notice that Diablo received several kisses, Matthew a hug, and I didn't get anything." He spread his arms. "I'd say this is an injustice, considering I'm the one who pays for Diablo's... oats and whatever else he eats and for Matthew's salary. And I hope it didn't escape your notice that I danced with you tonight."

"Do you think you deserve a kiss?" she asked teasingly.

"I certainly do."

Her cheeks warmed as another laugh escaped her. She'd laughed more in the past few days with Brandon than in the past few years.

"You're right." She rose on her tiptoes, putting a hand on his chest for balance, a more intimate pose than she'd foreseen.

He held his breath and stopped fiddling, his eyes focusing on her with an intensity that made her sigh. She meant to kiss his cheek but changed her mind at the last moment and brushed his lips with hers. It was a quick touch, but her whole body burned with unfamiliar sensations. She was no maiden. Living in the country with an aunt who had given her plenty of freedom— or neglect, it depended on one's point of view —had allowed her to explore pleasure with a couple of handsome stable boys. But the quick, chaste kiss with Brandon burned her from the inside out. The shock was so powerful she remained close to him, unable to move.

He had to be in shock too, because he stared at her without blinking.

Heaven. She'd kissed an earl. Brandon. Her survivor friend. No, they were no longer friends. She'd ruined their friendship forever.

She lowered her heels. "Was it a satisfying kiss?"

He nodded.

She cleared her throat. What was she supposed to do? "I should go."

He made an odd sound, halfway between a groan and a growl.

"Good night." She removed her hand from his chest before someone spotted them.

He raised two fingers to his lips and froze again as if he needed a moment. "Good night."

She walked backwards towards her door to wave at him. He tried and failed to climb into the landau, his foot slipping over the short step.

"Hell," he said.

She paused. "Are you all right?"

He gave her a mischievous smile that made him look like a rake. "Never been better." He waved at her once he managed to sit on the box. "Home, Diablo."

The horse didn't twitch. Brandon sagged and hunched his shoulders. "Bloody mule." He pinched the bridge of his nose.

She ought to rescue him. "Please, Diablo, take your master home and be a good boy," she said in her sweetest voice.

The stallion started off with a jolt, and Brandon was pushed back. "Good night," Brandon said in a cheerful voice, waving his hat.

She waved at him before entering the house. Brandon and Diablo disappeared behind a corner, and only the tingling of her body remained as a memento of the night. She leaned against the door and touched her lips. No, the fluttery feeling in her chest wasn't friendship.

She went up the stairs, humming the tune of the waltz they'd danced together. Aunt Rose and Catherine had to be still out since their cloaks were missing from the hooks. She slowed her pace in front of Aunt Rose's personal room. Perhaps she should take a look at her aunt's documents. Brandon's worry had affected her, and if she was going to be honest, doubts started to trouble her. First, Mrs. Sala had warned her about Mr. Payne. Then Brandon had asked her permission to investigate Aunt Rose's affair, and the conversation she'd eavesdropped on completed a suspicious picture. There was enough to warrant a closer look. A quick inspection of Aunt Rose's desk would do no harm.

After removing her slippers and capelet, she inched the door open. Cold air stroked her cheeks. No one had been in the room for a while, and the maid hadn't lit the fire. Good. Aunt Rose hadn't instructed the maid to keep the room warm. She didn't plan to be here any time soon.

Emily turned on an oil lamp. Only a couple of folders and books lay on the desk. Letters, bills, and newspapers formed neat piles in a corner. She went through the folders, finding only lists of expenses. Along with the usual ones— food, coal, and wax —there were other bills, expensive ones. Catherine had renewed her whole wardrobe, which wasn't surprising. Every lady, who entered the Season, bought a new set of gowns. Even Aunt Rose had purchased new dresses, cloaks, and shoes. Lots of pounds, which raised the question of where Aunt Rose found the money. Her modest pension wasn't enough to pay for all of those items, or even the house's rent. No, not rent.

She double-checked the document. Aunt Rose wasn't renting the townhouse. She was buying it. With what money? The mysterious inheritance?

Emily closed the folder and tried the drawer, but it didn't budge. But then again, if Aunt Rose was doing something questionable, she wouldn't leave evidence around.

Noises and voices coming from downstairs jolted Emily. She turned off the lamp and rushed out of the room, her pulse spiking. She barely had time to open her door before Aunt Rose reached the landing.

"Emily, have you just arrived?" she asked.

Drat. Emily swallowed past the knot in her throat. Goodness, she wasn't made for snooping around. Her legs trembled, and her breathing grew faster. "Yes, Aunt." Her voice sounded unnaturally high-pitched.

Aunt Rose came closer, eyeing her. Likely, she noticed Emily didn't wear shoes or her capelet. "There's something I have to ask you. I'm going to be blunt. Is the earl courting you?"

She let out a nervous chuckle. "Good gracious, no. The earl isn't interested in me in that way." Was she right? Was what she felt for him only an infatuation? Her imagination was running wild. They'd danced once and shared a brief kiss. No one had talked about courting anyone.

"I beg you to be careful, darling." Aunt Rose patted her hand. "There are so many scoundrels out there. You should avoid the earl until you understand his intentions."

No, she wouldn't. "I'll be careful." She couldn't help but glance at the door to her aunt's room. She'd left it ajar in her hurry, dash it.

Aunt Rose frowned. "As I told you, after my husband died, I faced some dark years." Her gaze became distant. "He left me an allowance because he was a good man, who had worked hard, but my life was far from easy, and the allowance was indeed small, even with your father's help." She lowered her gaze. "Unfortunately, our disagreements—"

"About my mother," Emily added.

Aunt Rose nodded. "I regret them because they caused John and me to grow away from with each other."

Emily gnashed her teeth. Aunt Rose regretted her behaviour only because of the money not because she'd been wrong in her dislike of Emily's mother. "Why did you hate my mother?"

"I didn't hate her!" Aunt Rose put a hand on her chest. "She came from a different culture from your father. They were too different. That's all."

Emily couldn't suppress a scoff. "They loved each other."

"Love isn't everything," Aunt Rose continued. "I did all sorts of jobs to feed Catherine and pay for her education. Don't get me wrong. I'm not complaining. My daughter is worth every sacrifice. But I want more for her. I want her to have all the opportunities I didn't have, and I'll do anything to give her the future she deserves," she said the last words almost with violence as if challenging Emily to disagree.

"I understand." Although she didn't. A mother protecting her daughter was natural, but Emily wasn't a threat to her cousin's happiness. Why did Aunt Rose make her feel as if she were?

"Good. I hope you remember that," Aunt Rose said.

She didn't say anything, a little scared by her aunt's aggressive attitude. Although it wasn't the first time Aunt Rose had warned Emily not to embarrass or damage Catherine's reputation in any way. The last warning had a different flavour. A bitter one.

Aunt Rose touched Emily's cheek. "Good night, Emily."

Emily exhaled when she was alone in her room.

Too many emotions for one night, and not all of them were pleasant.

Brandon gritted his teeth as he performed the last leg exercise of the day. The training never got any easier, and the weights he added to his bar seemed to be as heavy as the first day he'd started. But his muscles had grown thick and strong, reducing the sharpness of the pain.

With a groan, he dropped the weights onto the floor of the training room. Sweat soaked his shirt, and his muscles ached, but he couldn't deny the powerful feeling rushing through his body. The training also eased the knot in his belly. After last night at the ball, he needed to vent his frustration.

Matthew plonked himself down on the wooden bench and handed him a towel. "It took me a lot of effort to convince Lady Robinson to have a meeting with you, and now she barely talks to me. What are we supposed to do?"

Brandon wiped the sweat from his forehead. "I'll admit I didn't handle the situation with tact, but I'm not going to debase myself, Matthew, no matter what. And Lady Robinson disparaged Emily. I couldn't remain silent." Besides, after receiving a kiss from Emily, he had no intention of pursuing any other woman. She'd bewitched him with that kiss. Diablo had his sympathy.

Matthew sipped from his flask of water. "You're overreacting. It's only a fumble, and the lady is very attractive."

Not to him. He took a sip too. "Only a fumble? If you're so dismissive of the importance of sharing your body with someone, why don't you accept the lady's offer and do it then?"

"Because she wants you." A note of resentment crept into Matthew's voice. "I'm not titled. My father was an engine driver, and my mother worked on a farm. I'm not worth her time, I guess. To her, we are too different, on the opposing sides of society."

"Ridiculous." He rubbed his sore legs. "I think we should let her calm down for a day or two before asking for a new meeting, and to hell with being too different and on the opposing sides of society."

Matthew huffed. "All she wants is an assignation. A tryst. Would calling it a French rendezvous make it sound more polite?"

"No."

Matthew lowered his eyebrows as if he had an epiphany. "Perhaps Cowley can find something about her, a secret she's ashamed of. If she goes around having fumbles with all the men she fancies, she must have secrets."

"I'm not going to blackmail her."

"But she's blackmailing you. She wants you to tup her in exchange for doing something that's supposed to be her job. *She* is despicable. Not to mention," Matthew hurried to add when Brandon opened his mouth, "that she behaved beastly towards Emily. She's no angel."

"I agree, but I won't blackmail her. I will not stoop that low. And just because she behaves horribly, it doesn't mean I have to do the same. Hell, if we reciprocated every despicable act with another despicable act, there'd only be twelve people left in London."

Matthew folded his arms over his chest. "Great. Be the damn white knight. I do wonder if you believe in our dream at all." He shoved himself up and marched towards the door.

"Matthew!" Brandon called, but his friend ignored him.

He rubbed his forehead. What Matthew said wasn't true. Brandon believed in the absolute importance of producing safer brakes. They would save lives and prevent tragedies like Abbots Ripton. But hell, he didn't want to get into Lady Robinson's petticoats. Not simply out of principle. He wanted his first time with a woman to be his choice. Matthew was experienced in matters of the heart. He had a string of lovers. Good for him. For Matthew, a fumble was the same thing as training. A physical act involving sweat and awkward positions for a short-lived reward.

But Brandon had never been with anyone, thanks to his poor health. He didn't want to start with a blackmailer. His injured back hadn't allowed him much freedom in many departments, fumbles included. He knew the technicalities of the act and that they involved a lot of hip movements, which he hadn't been capable of doing for years. Even now, he wasn't sure he could perform without screaming in pain or accidentally hurting the lady. Not exactly encouraging for him... which made him think about Emily. Would she agree to be courted by him?

"Sir." Cowley's voice interrupted his thoughts.

"Cowley." He picked himself up, his legs like rubber. "News?"

Cowley gave a solemn nod. "Rather easy to acquire, but not good, I'm afraid. Mrs. Allen is ready to take possession of Miss de la Fuente Barclay's inheritance, a hefty sum of around one hundred thousand pounds."

"Blimey." Brandon passed a hand over his face. "How can she do that? It can't be legal." Succession wasn't his legal field of expertise, he dealt with property law, but the whole affair sounded dubious.

"'Fraid so, sir. Mrs. Allen's solicitor, Mr. Payne, filed a few documents that allow Mrs. Allen, in the capacity of Miss de la Fuente Barclay's warden for the past ten years, to claim the whole of her niece's fortune."

"I don't understand."

"After the accident," Cowley said. "Miss Emily wasn't old enough to inherit. Ironically, if the sum had been less conspicuous, she would have received an allowance immediately. But one hundred thousand pounds is a different matter. Mrs. Allen was appointed to become her niece's warden for a period that went beyond Miss Emily's coming of age, due to Miss Emily's delicate state of mind after the tragic loss of her parents. That extended period is going to expire in a few days. After that, Miss Emily should receive her fortune. Except Mrs. Allen declared her niece incapable of administering her inheritance, claiming her niece is afflicted by hysteria. The money will be turned over to Mrs. Allen in Emily's stead. She should pocket it soon."

"That's absurd." Brandon clenched the towel in his fist. "Emily is perfectly sane. She doesn't suffer from hysteria."

"Alas, there are witnesses who testified that Miss Emily suffered from fits of panic and frenzies when asked to board a carriage. She screamed and fled from a carriage on multiple occasions, causing disruptions. Once, her aunt was forced to stop the train to let a screaming and kicking Miss Emily out. On top of that, it seems a couple of the devices Miss Emily designed exploded, spreading the rumour in Painswick that she has sympathies for the anarchists."

"Poppycock." Brandon rubbed his temples. Those incidents had to be a ruse concocted by Emily's aunt. Emily had never mentioned anything about panic attacks and hysteria. "What does that have to do with her money?"

"The sum is too large, sir. No judge will think that one hundred pounds should be delivered in the hands on a mentally troubled anarchist. And again, there's Mrs. Allen's word and several testimonies. I suspect that Miss Emily doesn't know anything about her fortune."

"This is thievery," Brandon gritted out. "That money belongs to Emily."

Cowley nodded. "Mrs. Allen spent a lot of pounds recently on credit. It's obvious she believes Miss Emily's money will be hers."

"How can I stop this scheme?" He paced. "I won't let that woman steal Emily's legacy."

Cowley hesitated before speaking. "There's a way. If Miss Emily gets married before her aunt is declared the only heir, she'll receive the money instead. Well, her husband will since she's been declared unfit to administer her fortune."

Brandon pressed his fingers to his chest where a flutter started. If he married Emily, he could hand her the inheritance. "But?"

"Mrs. Allen and Mrs. Payne thought of everything, it would seem." Cowley's face darkened. "Mr. Payne drew up a contract and had it legally approved by a private bill at the House of Lords. I'm afraid Miss de la Fuente Barclay won't have the opportunity to enjoy her parents' legacy unless she marries by the end of this month, which is unlikely."

"Only a few days." Certainly not enough for the banns to be read, the church made ready, and the priest employed. Mrs. Allen's words made sense.

Such a short time. The problem wasn't the money per se because he wouldn't let Emily starve or become destitute. He would provide for her anyway. But her parents' legacy belonged to her. Mrs. Allen shouldn't spend a penny of it as she pleased, and Emily should know about her rights.

And he should marry her.

thirteen

DESPITE AN ALMOST sleepless night and the hours of exercise that had left him sore, Brandon didn't feel tired. Nervous energy kept him up and about. His eagerness to warn Emily after his conversation with Cowley had turned into frustration when he'd learned Emily wasn't at home. Mrs. Allen had sent her out on some errands, and Brandon had been forced to wait for her return.

Errands. How annoying. Helping Emily was the only thing on his mind as he stood next to Matthew in the horse-riding arena.

Even Matthew had to be lost in his own thoughts, judging by how his body tensed, and after their last conversation, they hadn't talked. But Matthew had bought a new horse, a mare for Diablo, and here they were, watching her prancing around.

Brandon propped his elbows on the fence surrounding the arena. The dark mare trotted about with her proud bearing. Her muscles were well-defined, and that summed up pretty much everything he knew about the animal. He had no idea what breed she was, her age, or her health state, but he was sure Diablo would like her spirit and glossy coat, providing male horses cared about luscious coats, that is. If he were a horse, he would. Oh, bugger. He was losing his mind.

"Isn't she a dark beauty?" Matthew said, resting his chin on his fist. "You don't find ladies like her easily, strong and spirited."

Like Emily. "No, you don't. Emily is such a wonderful woman," he said, not sure Matthew heard him.

Matthew folded his arms over his chest. "She's going to be an excellent broodmare."

Brandon stiffened. "Don't talk about her like that. It's disrespectful."

"She's a bloody horse." Matthew arched his brow, turning towards him. "What are you talking about? Are you using again?"

"Don't be ridiculous."

"Don't be so enigmatic then! Whom are you talking about?"

Brandon exhaled. "Emily."

Matthew's gaze travelled skywards. "Well, yes... what?" He whipped his head towards Brandon.

"Emily's aunt means to steal money from her. She's squandering Emily's inheritance, and according to Cowley, if Emily marries in a few days, the inheritance will go to her husband." He quickly recounted Mrs. Allen's scheme. The more he thought about it, the angrier he became, especially because Mrs. Allen vastly exaggerated Emily's dislike for closed carriages for her own gain, lying about Emily. "But that's not why I want to marry her. I want to protect her and take care of her."

"I see." Matthew turned his attention to the mare. "If Emily marries soon, her aunt won't see a penny."

"Exactly. But only a few days are left. It's impossible."

"Nonsense. Gretna Green," Matthew said with simplicity. "Take Emily there, have a red-hot wedding, I'll be your witness, and done. She's your wife."

Brandon had thought about that. Mainly young couples flew to Scotland to marry without their parents' consent. Although anyone who was in a hurry and didn't want to wait for the banns to be cried could ask any blacksmith master on the other side of the border to perform the ceremony. The Scots were less complicated than the English.

"It'd mean eloping," Brandon said. "Emily's reputation matters."

"She'll become your countess," Matthew said. "Her reputation will shine like never before. Besides, since when do you care about gossip?"

"This is Emily we're talking about. Not me."

"Marry her quickly. A countess with a dowry of one hundred thousand pounds will be more than welcome in society."

Brandon followed the mare shaking her glorious mane. A trip to Scotland, and he and Emily would be married. There would be gossip, yes, but then again, Matthew was right. Emily would be a very rich countess. "All I have to do is to propose then."

"You forget the part where the lady has to agree." Matthew tossed him a glance. "You wouldn't do anything without being honest with her, would you? You're a bloody white knight." His tone dripped with sarcasm.

"Don't be sour. Emily isn't Lady Predator."

The moment he realised he might be Emily's husband for real, a weight lifted from his chest.

He wanted to take care of her above everything else. From the moment he'd left her at the hospital years ago, he'd wished to go back to her and provide for her. Now he had the chance to both save her inheritance and give her the opportunity to start a new life, realise her dream of being an engineer, and be happy.

"Funny that you mention Lady Robinson, because before you tie the knot, we need to discuss her," Matthew said, touching Brandon's arm and forcing him back to reality.

"Matthew, I swear it on my honour. I am fully committed to our project, but I'm not going to sleep with Lady Robinson." He should propose today. If they were quick, they might catch the Flying Scotsman northbound. One night of travel, and they'd be in

Edinburgh by morning. Given the pressing circumstances they were in, Emily would agree the Flying Scotsman was their best chance. Surely, she'd overcome her dislike for the train and make an exception. "Besides, I'm getting married."

"I'm sure Lady Robinson doesn't care."

"I do. And it would be disrespectful towards Emily."

"One night." Matthew gripped Brandon's arm with both hands. "One night, and we have our permits done. We can start the production in spring. It would be perfect."

"No." He shrugged himself free. "I'm not yielding to a blackmailer."

"Then let me take a closer look at her life," Matthew said through gritted teeth.

"No to that as well. I'm surprised you really mean such a thing. We're gentlemen."

"I'm a desperate gentleman." Matthew spread his arms. "I'm talking about a project that has consumed my past ten years and all my finances."

"Mine, actually."

"Semantics."

Brandon shook his head. "We'll find another way to convince her."

"Brandon, I owe this to my father." Matthew's voice cracked. "His death won't have any meaning unless I make this project a reality."

Brandon's vision darkened with the sorrow for Matthew's loss. "You're right. Let me marry Emily first. After that, I promise, I swear we'll think of something."

Matthew turned his attention to the mare, shoulders hunched. "Time is slipping by."

"Emily first. Lady Robinson afterwards. I promise." Brandon clapped Matthew's shoulder. "Will you be my best man?"

Matthew blew out a sharp breath. "I will. You know I will. But after that, you must solve the situation with Lady Robinson."

"We have a deal."

EMILY'S HEARTBEAT changed rhythm every other minute. One moment, it kicked like a trapped rabbit; the next, it slowed to a crawl. All because Brandon had told her what Cowley had found. Emily was an heiress. Her heart still ached for the loss of her parents, but somehow, their legacy made her feel closer to them.

The shock of learning that Aunt Rose had lied to her about her parents' money and meant to steal her inheritance was a dagger to her heart. If Aunt Rose had asked for financial help, Emily would have given it to her, despite the way she'd been treated. But sneaking behind her back to leave her penniless hurt her more than she'd care to admit.

She kept strolling along the gravel path in Hyde Park with Brandon at her side without paying attention to where she was going. A chilly breeze blew from the north, and dark clouds gathered in the sky, discouraging the Londoners from promenading. Even the birds remained tucked into the branches of the evergreen trees. The mostly empty park added to the sense of desolation in her heart. She'd always known that Aunt Rose wasn't particularly fond of her, but stealing her inheritance and leaving her destitute was a different thing.

"I understand it's a shock." Brandon peered at her with concern.

"I don't know if I should be happy to receive my parents' legacy or angry about my aunt's deceit." She rubbed an aching spot on her brow. "Aunt Rose told me my parents hadn't left much, and I believed her."

"You were sixteen and grieving for your parents."

"If Cowley hadn't discovered the truth, Aunt Rose would have... she will get my money, won't she?" A cold sensation washed over her. "She'll get away with theft."

Brandon tilted his head to mean 'maybe.' "There's a simple solution."

Yes, find a man, marry him right now, and then ask him to please give her what her parents had wanted her to have in the first place. The solution wasn't merely impossible but insulting. Why did she have to ask her imaginary husband to receive what belonged to her? Unfair.

"Did Cowley find a loophole? Can I claim my inheritance now?" she asked.

"Unfortunately, it wouldn't be possible. I was thinking about the most obvious, simple solution. A solution standing right in front of you. Emily." He took off his hat and pressed it against his chest. "I can't go down on my knee because if I do that, I'll need your help to stand up after today's training session." He chuckled nervously.

"Do you mean…?" It was her turn to peer at him with concern. His face was flushed, and he breathed quickly. Her brain slogged through the recent revelations because he couldn't possibly mean *that* solution.

He licked his lips, a gesture that caught her attention. "What I'm clumsily trying to say is that if you marry me now, tomorrow, or in the next few days at the very least, the inheritance will be yours. Well, mine since I'll be your husband, but I'll revert it to you of course."

Another shock of stillness went through her. "Heaven." A hundred thousand pounds and Brandon as her husband.

"I want to take care of you. And I'll do my best to make you happy."

She couldn't decide if Brandon's proposal made her happy or concerned. He was a good man, funny and kind. Her heart told her she wouldn't easily find someone as special as he was. But she was tempted to refuse his proposal exactly because she respected him. He wanted to marry her to help her out of her legal conundrum, not because he loved her. There was affection between them, yes, and even attraction— she couldn't deny it. But what if he married her and then fell in love, truly in love with someone else, and regretted having married her? What if he came to resent her for this hasty decision? What if her heart broke?

He stared at her with large eyes, seemingly holding his breath. "I hate putting pressure on you, but we don't have a lot of time. Merely days. We must act now."

"But Brandon." She held his hand, feeling the hard tendons on its back. "What if you'll hate me one day? You might meet a woman you really love, and you won't be able to be with her because of me. I don't want you to hate me."

He gripped her fingers. "I could never hate you, and I won't regret this."

"You can't be so sure."

"I've never been more sure about anything in my whole life. We respect and understand each other. We share a bond. We know each other better than anyone else. Many marriages are based on less than that, and as an earl, I have to marry, and I can't think of anyone better than you. Unless you have a suitor in mind, someone you wish to marry." The last words sounded strangled and raspy as if he tried not to growl.

She shook her head. "No, I haven't."

His shoulders stooped with the breath he released. "It's not a simple matter of money. If it were only that, I would provide for you. I don't want your aunt to take control of your legacy. She knows she has no right to. Your parents would have wanted you to receive your inheritance. It's their gift to you, their hard work, and your aunt is cheating to steal it."

That was true. A sob remained trapped in her throat as she thought about her parents, how much they'd loved each other, and how much they'd loved her. They would be horrified to know Aunt Rose stole from them. Now Aunt Rose's speech about Catherine's future acquired another meaning.

"If only she had asked..." She stifled a sob. Silly, greedy woman.

"Please marry me." He squeezed her hand. "Don't worry about me. I do want to marry you, in all honesty. I won't disappoint you."

"I know you won't. I have complete trust in you." She wouldn't find another gentleman like Brandon. She cared for him, and he cared for her. What more did she want? "And I agree to marry you."

The moment she said the words, she didn't expect the rush of happiness pouring out of him or the sense of relief sweeping through her.

"Yes!" He wrapped his arms around her and swept her off her feet.

She burst out laughing, which released the tension knotting in her belly.

"Ouch!" Wincing, he put her down and scrubbed the small of his back. "A too quick move for my back. That wasn't the most romantic proposal in history, was it?"

"I beg to differ." She caressed his cheek. "What should we do now?"

"Prepare a bag with warm clothes. Don't tell anyone you're leaving." He checked his pocket watch. "We'll catch the Flying Scotsman departing at seven o'clock from King's Cross. We'll be at the border in a few hours." He sounded excited. She wasn't. "I know it'll be difficult for you, but the train is our only option, and surely, your dislike of trains won't be too much."

All the enthusiasm drained from her, and her belly knotted all over again. "The Flying Scotsman?" Her voice quivered. Her whole body quivered.

"It's the fastest way to travel. Can you do it?"

A red-hot wedding like her parents, but...

She pressed her lips and shook her head. Her pulse thundered in her ears, turning into the whistle of a train. "I can't."

He frowned. "I dislike riding a horse. I can relate to your preferences. But surely, you see the need for speed."

She shook her head. "I lied to you."

"Lied?"

"I didn't tell the whole truth." She sucked in a breath. "I don't simply dislike trains and carriages. They frighten me. I feel like I'm choking when I'm on a train."

He knitted his eyebrows. "Is it true you had several panic attacks?"

She nodded. "Aunt Rose didn't lie about that. Well, she didn't lie about my devices exploding too. Anyway, the first years after the accident, my anxiety remained manageable, but it grew until I couldn't climb into a train without screaming bloody murder. Just the thought of climbing into a closed carriage frightens me. And I absolutely cannot ride on the Flying Scotsman again! I can't do it. Please don't make me do it. I don't want to do it." She breathed hard, and her voice rose to a hysterical high-pitch she had often produced whenever forced to take a carriage. Her vision darkened at the edges, and for a split second, the screeching noise of the contorting metal of the Flying Scotsman echoed in her ears. She almost expected to feel pain exploding in her shoulder.

"Emily." Brandon's voice came from far away.

She couldn't breathe. The world spun. Or maybe she did.

"Emily." His warm, comforting hand on her cheek pulled her back from the darkness.

"Please," she whispered.

His concerned face came into sharp focus, and the sounds of London's traffic returned. "It's all right." He brushed her cheek with his knuckles in a sweet gesture that calmed her erratic pulse. "I apologise for having suggested it. I had no idea your condition was so serious."

"I didn't tell you. I was too much of a coward." She took a deep breath that burned her throat. "I was afraid you'd think I was an idiot."

"I would never." He studied her face, worry etching his features. "We'll take an open coach."

She suppressed another shiver. "How long will it take to reach the border?"

"A few days. Three, maybe four for Gretna Green. All we need is to reach the Scottish border and get married. Then we'll send a wire from Scotland to London to inform your aunt's solicitor of our wedding."

Barely on time. If something went wrong, her inheritance would be lost. "Doesn't that blasted train bother you?"

He withdrew his hand, and she missed it immediately. "A bit, but what are the chances that I get involved in *another* train disaster? Statistically, it's less than zero."

She wasn't sure she agreed with his logic. "You said that the first time we rode the train and look what happened."

He flashed a sad smile. "True, but this time, it's really statistically impossible. I trust numbers."

She didn't, which was ironic since, between them, she was supposed to be the scientist. Fate had a disturbing sense of humour and couldn't do maths, and she didn't want to tempt it. "I'm sorry to cause all these troubles."

"No troubles at all. We have a solution, but…" He took her hand. His face darkened. "Since we're confessing each other's secrets, there's something you should know about me before we get married. Something that might change your mind about me altogether."

Oh, no. Her shoulders sagged. He had a mistress. "You have a lover, don't you?"

"Good gracious, no!" He let out a nervous chuckle. "It's something worse."

"What can be worse than a mistress? An affair with a married woman?"

"Worse." His Adam's apple bobbed on a swallow as he twisted his hat with his restless fingers. "Addiction to laudanum. Past addiction to be precise, but it was intense."

She'd heard horrible stories of people addicted to opium,

laudanum, and morphia, but she couldn't imagine him behaving like one of those violent, angry people. "What happened?"

He took his time before answering, fiddling with his hands. "The back injury was more painful than I expected, and the exercises and physical practice weren't painless either. I started using laudanum to have a respite, and I didn't stop taking it." He exhaled. "The main reason why I stopped sending you letters is because I wasn't good company. I wasn't at my best. I was either in constant pain or unconscious, a whining, pitiful disaster of a man. I'm not proud of those days. You would have hated me if you had seen me."

"I don't believe that." She held his restless hand, stopping his fiddling.

"Cowley and Matthew saved my life. They forced me out of the habit. I wasn't violent. I want you to know that. But I wasn't myself. Hallucinations tormented me. More than once, I was afraid I would die from the pain. During the period of my recuperation, I begged Matthew and Cowley to give me one last drop of laudanum more times than I'd care to count, so strong was the need for opium. I lost my dignity. I lost my friends. I can't say I have fully recovered yet."

"I beg to differ."

He pressed his lips in a grim line. "That's it. That's all I meant to say." He lifted hopeful eyes on her. "I should have told you earlier, but I was afraid of sharing my secret with you."

No, he was the bravest man she'd ever met. "I was a coward too. I haven't changed my mind about you. I didn't become addicted to laudanum, but the temptation to drink it was strong. I know what it means to deal with intense pain. I managed to resist the call of laudanum only because my fear of travelling in a carriage was stronger. If laudanum could help with that, I would take it. Your big secret doesn't scare me and doesn't make me change my mind." If anything, she admired him even more for having the courage to tell her the truth. It must have been difficult for him to speak about his addiction.

He laced his fingers through hers. "Actually, there's something else I need to tell you."

"Yes?" She perked up, worried that he wanted to confess he was one of those rakehells who waltzed their way to society from one bed to another. To each their own, but she was wary of those men who sought pleasure above everything else, and oftentimes, laudanum sought out other physical pleasures.

He opened his mouth but didn't say a word.

"You can tell me anything," she said.

"It's more difficult to talk about that than about the laudanum." He let out a bitter chuckle. "Lord. This is hard." He rubbed the bridge of his nose.

Yes, it had to be something about past romantic adventures, and she had a hunch. "You have a child somewhere from a previous lover."

His shy, boyish smile warmed her chest. "You have an obsession with my secret lovers, and it's curious that you mention that because it's somehow related."

"Oh." The piercing sting of disappointment wasn't expected. "So you do have a child. It's all right. I love children. I won't do anything to change your relationship with the child."

"No." He showed a lopsided smile. "It's..." He took a deep breath. "I don't have any children, and it wouldn't be possible because I have never, ever been with a woman."

She tilted her head. "What do you— oh." He was inexperienced. A smile of relief tried to make its way to her lips, but she pushed it down mercilessly lest he think she was making fun of him.

His expression hardened. "Between the addiction and my bad back, I didn't have time to pursue a lover."

"Why would that be a problem for me?" she asked.

"I'm not sure." He grinned. "In case you…" He shook his head. "Never mind."

"I don't care, really, unless you care about the fact I have some experience." She tensed, despite he'd never given her any reason to believe he'd judge her.

He shrugged. "You'll teach me then."

"I will." Oops. Her answer came out of her faster than her brain could process it.

He straightened, his lips parting. She straightened too. They both realised what they'd so carelessly said at the same time.

Had he asked her to become his teacher in matters of fumbles? Had she just told him she wanted to have a fumble with him once married? Yes, she had. And she was fine with that.

"Thus you, ahem, you want us to be together." He sounded incredulous.

"There's plenty of time to discuss the details." Goodness, that was a fairly vague answer.

"Yes, yes. Naturally." He found the flight of a sparrow suddenly fascinating.

She shifted her weight from one foot to another. "We're going to get married."

"We are."

"Fantastic."

"Lovely." He cleared his throat.

As long as she could manage to travel more than three hundred miles across the country in an open carriage in winter.

fourteen

EMILY HAD UNDERESTIMATED the difficulty of sneaking out of her aunt's house.

When Brandon had told her to pack a few things, not tell anyone where she was going, and leave the house quietly, she'd thought it'd be easy. But nothing was easy about eloping. She wondered if it had been the same for her parents. She wondered if they'd approve.

First, since there was no time to order a proper wedding dress, she wanted to wear Mrs. Sala's emerald gown for the ceremony. She might be having a red-hot wedding, but she would wear something stunning. Packing layers of silk in a carpet suitcase was an exercise in patience. Every time she stashed a fold of the precious fabric inside the bag, another one slid out of it as if the gown were a living devilfish. Not to mention the silk was going to be all wrinkled. The gown would need to be pressed and brushed before she wore it.

After she wrestled the magnificent dress into the bag with a few other necessities, she waited for the house to be quiet. Catherine had gone to bed a while ago, but Aunt Rose was still in her study, surely plotting in the dark. The clock on the mantelpiece informed her that Brandon would be arriving in five minutes. The plan was that he'd wait for her in a dark corner of the street so as not to raise any suspicion. Their movements needed to be perfectly timed though, because Emily didn't want to linger on the street, waiting for him. Someone might notice her and call the police. Besides, constables patrolled the streets at night as well, and a person loitering on the pavement in a rich quarter attracted too much attention.

She inched the door open and peered into the corridor. A sliver of light limned the door to Aunt Rose's study. Dash it all. Why was Aunt Rose working this late? Oh, right. Stealing her niece's inheritance had to be a complicated job. Emily's parents were paying for this house and Catherine's Season.

Emily's Spanish blood boiled. Her mother would be furious. Her father would be hurt. She wanted what belonged to her. Impatience itched along her skin until she couldn't wait any longer. She had to go now.

Holding the heavy bag with both hands, she tiptoed out of her room. Aside from the light coming from Aunt Rose's office, the corridor was dark, but she'd memorised every creaking wooden plank and crease in the carpet. She had only to be very quiet. She held her breath as she crept past Aunt Rose's door. A few steps and she'd be at the top of the stairs. Then it was a matter of staying on her toes all the way down.

The problem? Her hands were all sweaty, and her legs quivered. She'd be a terrible spy; she wouldn't last five minutes on the job. Her stomach churned and sweat dampened the back of her neck.

She closed her fingers as hard as she could around the bag handle and grimaced as carrying the bag required more strength than she had imagined. What the heck had she packed in there?

Gritting her teeth, she went down the stairs, one step at a time. All her body tensed as she balanced her weight on her toes, holding the bannister. Goodness, her temperature was rising, and not in a good way. Her breath came out in quick pants. Her hand grew stiff out of sheer anxiety, but no matter. She could deal with the anxiety. Halfway down, she grinned. So far so good.

Her clammy fingers betrayed her without warning. One moment, they were nicely holding the bag. The next, they let the bag slide out of their grip. The bag rolled down the stairs in a series of loud bangs and thuds that even the queen must have heard in Buckingham Palace. The shock petrified her as she impotently watched her belongings thudding down.

"What is it?" Aunt Rose's voice thundered down the quiet corridor. A few lights were lit. Footsteps approached.

"Mama?" Catherine said. "What's happening?"

Bother. Bother. Bother.

"Emily!" Aunt Rose stood at the top of the stairs. In her red dressing gown and with the light coming from behind her, she looked like a demon escaped from hell. "What is the meaning of this?"

No time to explain. Emily rushed down the last steps and snatched the bag from the floor.

"Where are you going?" Aunt Rose shouted.

The front door didn't budge when Emily tried the knob. Curse it. In her hurry, she'd forgotten to unlock the deadbolt.

"She's eloping!" Catherine yelled. "Stop her!"

Blasted door. Fumbling with the knob, Emily pulled the door open and ran out of the house, hugging the heavy bag. Her breath turned into mist in the chilly air, and her feet slipped on the wet cobbles. She lost her balance, but thank goodness for all those winters she'd spent ice skating. She recovered her balance quickly and hurried along the pavement. Where was Brandon? A dark landau was parked at the kerb, and she dashed towards it. She gasped when someone seized her arm and yanked her backwards.

"You aren't going anywhere!" Aunt Rose grabbed Emily by the collar of her coat, nearly choking her.

She struggled. "Let me go!"

"Come inside or I'll call the police." Aunt Rose dragged her a few feet back.

"You're stealing from me."

"You're insane, girl. Hysterical and unreliable. You can't administer your parents' inheritance."

"You're a thief!" Emily swung her bag and smashed it against her aunt's face with all the strength she could muster.

Aunt Rose cried out, releasing her grip and falling on her rear. She clamped a hand over her nose. "You doxy!"

Emily remained motionless for a moment. She had never, ever hurt anyone. Aunt Rose groaned in pain as her nose bled through her fingers.

"I'm bleeding," Aunt Rose whimpered.

Goodness. "I'm sorry!" Emily said. "I... you shouldn't have tried to steal from me, and you grabbed me and I reacted on impulse."

"Oh, my nose." Aunt Rose rocked back and forth.

"Emily!" Brandon called her.

His voice shook her from her stupor. She rushed towards the landau. Why had she apologised? Never mind.

"Emily!" Brandon ran towards her, his scarf fluttering behind him like a banner. He took her bag and helped her forwards. "Are you all right?"

Catherine was crouched next to Aunt Rose who was howling as if about to die. Come off it! Surely, it couldn't be that painful, could it?

Emily nodded, too breathless to speak. Diablo neighed happily upon seeing her, and she greeted him, scratching his withers.

"Quick." Brandon tossed her bag in the landau.

She sagged on the seat. Brandon sat next to her and urged Diablo on. The horse didn't move.

"Come on! Not now, you stubborn creature," Brandon said.

Aunt Rose picked herself up and sprinted towards them. One

had to admit she was athletic for someone who didn't exercise and who had just been hit in the face.

"Let me." Emily grabbed the reins and smacked her lips.

Diablo raced into the night like a black bolt of lightning. He was so fast Emily didn't understand what Aunt Rose screamed from the pavement. Even Catherine shook her fist towards Emily. Anyway. Too late.

A quiver shuddered through her. She had really done it. She'd escaped her aunt's house to elope.

"You've been brilliant." Brandon squeezed her hand.

"I hit my aunt. I've never hit anyone."

"She didn't want to let you go. You did the right thing."

"It feels wrong though, I mean, the violence." She winced at the memory of Aunt Rose's swelling nose.

"She'll live. Without your money."

She wasn't sure about that. If they didn't pay their creditors, Aunt Rose and Catherine might end up in prison soon, overwhelmed by their debts. Thoughts for another moment.

She, Brandon, and Diablo raced through London's empty streets until she slowed Diablo before a crossing.

"Where are we going?" she asked. "We aren't travelling to Scotland with poor Diablo, are we?"

Brandon held his hat in place with a hand. "First, Diablo is anything but poor, and second, no. I wanted him only for the first part of our journey, and he did well. I have an open couch with a driver ready to go. Cowley and Matthew will take the Flying Scotsman and be in Edinburgh tomorrow morning and wait for us."

"Great." Emily wiped the sweat from her forehead. "She almost caught me."

"Almost is the key word."

She let out a nervous chuckle, releasing the tension of the rushed escape. "What a great way to start a marriage."

"Certainty, it's not going to be boring."

∼

BRANDON WOULD DO anything to make Emily comfortable, but the more they travelled north in the open carriage, the colder the weather became. Drizzling rain soaked their hats and coats. The thick blankets weren't enough to keep his legs warm. Icy gusts snuck under his shirt, and the cold air reached his lungs with each inhale. He could barely feel his lips.

Grey clouds promised snow, and he wasn't sure he and Emily could endure a snowstorm. The coachman kept glancing at the sky as he drove along a bumpy country road that was no friend of Brandon's back. Even Emily shivered next to him. The tip of her nose reddened from the cold, and her lips had a pale hue that worried him.

"How are you?" He took her hand, feeling her cold skin through the glove.

"Cold. Very cold." She snuggled closer to him.

"We're going to stop soon. The next inn should be only a few miles ahead. We'll get warm, sleep a little, and leave before dawn."

The plan didn't sound inviting. The warmth and the sleep, yes, but he didn't look forward to sitting in the open carriage again for another cold, uncomfortable day. Also, they hadn't covered as many miles as he had hoped. Between the cold and the bumpy road, the driver hadn't been able to travel fast.

The temperature dropped further as the sun lowered beyond the horizon and the wind picked up speed. His teeth chattered, and he couldn't feel his toes anymore. Not to mention his back. Sitting for hours on end in the cold caused his muscles to ache. The constant jolts shot pain down his spine. He was one breath away from throwing up.

Snowflakes started to flutter down by the time the coachman pulled over at The Swan Inn. The yellow glow pouring from the diamond windows was a promise of comfort. A short one, that is.

He helped Emily out of the carriage, his legs trembling both from the cold and the muscle spasms. She leaned against him as they shuffled to the inn door without talking.

"So cold." Her breath turned into mist around her mouth.

"We'll get warm soon." He exhaled when he stepped into the cozy inn.

The temperature difference shocked his body with a fresh pang. The scent of spices and leek soup teased his stomach which grumbled in reply. At least the nausea from the pain was gone.

Happy chatter and the clink of mugs of mulled wine filled the pleasant atmosphere. Finally, his toes thawed, causing his skin to sting with invisible needles.

He and Emily both sighed when they sat at a scarred oakwood table and closed their hands around warm cups of tea. The snowfall intensified, and large flakes filled the view, tossed around by the wind. His back kept hurting though, and the hard wooden bench didn't help. He suppressed a groan of pain as his muscles refused to relax. They were locked into a tight knot like pretzels.

"You're in pain." She brushed his fingers, her eyebrows knitting together.

"It's all right. I've seen worse."

She shook her head. "You're pale. I'm worried."

He gathered the energy to smile, but the smile didn't reach his eyes. "It just that the cold, and the hard seat of the carriage affected my back. I'll be fine in a moment." He wouldn't, but he didn't want to worry her. After a day like today, he'd need a whole week of rest, warm baths, and gentle exercise before getting better. Instead, he faced three more days of this torture.

She frowned as she sipped her tea in silence. He didn't have the strength to converse either. Besides, the snow was another reason to worry. If it kept snowing in those thick sheets, the roads would be impassable for a small carriage tomorrow, and then what? They might catch a big coach going north, but that meant travelling in a closed vehicle without the guarantee the coach wouldn't stop because of the snow. They couldn't afford to lose a day of travel.

They were already moving too slowly without adding bad weather conditions.

The delicious leek soup and mutton stew soothed the tension in his back muscles a little, but the cold still bothered him. He and his bride-to-be had to look like a miserable pair, both quiet, pale, and forlorn. By the time they got married, his back would be as stiff and cold as a slab of marble.

He and Emily dragged their sorry selves upstairs to their bedrooms. Exhaustion rode him hard. Even Emily had to be tired because her shoulders were hunched and her eyebrows angled downward to match her frown.

He paused at the door to his bedroom. "Hope you sleep well. I'll see you in the morning." He checked his pocket watch. "In a few hours. Good night." He barely took a step before she called him.

"Brandon."

"Yes?" He put a hand on the wall for support, not wanting to show her how much his body ached.

She trapped her bottom lip between her teeth and gazed around, wringing her hands. "I thought about it. Why don't we share the bedroom?"

"Excuse me?" Not that he would mind.

"You had a horrible day because of me."

"Not because of you." He waved a hand to dismiss her concerns. "We were unlucky. The weather is particularly cold and the road particularly rough."

"But we would already be in Scotland if not for me." She inched closer, and even though he was bone-tired, her sweet scent didn't fail to tease his senses. "I think we should share the bedroom."

He didn't understand what the connection between the horrible trip and their sharing of the bedroom was, but he wasn't going to question that. "Are you sure?" That he had to ask.

She squared her shoulders and lifted her chin. "We are getting married, and your back needs care. I'm good at rubbing the muscles to soothe the pain. It's the least I can do after what you've been through for me."

Who was he to say no? Had Brandon been cold a moment ago? Now he was boiling.

"Let me fetch my bag, and no," she hurried to say when he opened his mouth to offer his help. "I'll do it. You go inside and wait for me."

"All right then." He walked into his bedroom with a hand on the wall not to lose his balance. His back muscles indeed needed a massage.

The cast iron stove spread a nice warmth, and the wooden floor and wainscoting on the walls were like a hug. Just what he needed. But Emily's presence, as she returned, raised the temperature more than the fire.

She dropped her bag in a corner. "I'll wash and get changed, then I'll rub your back."

"Right." He didn't know what else to say.

She slipped behind the screen, and he couldn't help but try to catch a glimpse of her. No such luck. The louvred panel hid her completely. Only her dark silhouette was visible. He ought to wash as well. The scent of her jasmine soap wafting in the air had him breathing faster.

Washing himself with the lukewarm water in the basin was sheer torture. Just raising his arm caused his body to burn. Even his legs grew numb. He donned a fresh nightshirt not without effort.

"Have you finished?" she asked from the other side of her screen.

He cleared his throat lest she realise how much pain he was in. "Yes."

She stepped out of the screen, and for a moment the pain vanished. She was a vision. Her long sable hair was twisted in a thick braid that reached her waist, and her dark-blue dressing gown enhanced her plush curves and the flare of her hips. All the soft curves and glowing skin suited her. His mouth grew dry. She'd soon be his wife, and he could hardly believe it.

"Lower your shirt and lie down." She rubbed her hands with a scented oil, releasing the fragrance of sweet almonds in the room.

He did as he was told, wincing again as he tugged the nightshirt down his arms. The fabric gathered around his hips, hopefully preserving his modesty and inappropriate bodily reactions. His pulse galloped when he stretched on the bed, belly down, and the position caused his back muscles to contract further.

A corner of the bed dipped when she sat on its edge. Her hip brushed his, and he couldn't have foreseen the burst of pleasure going through him. Hell, and she hadn't touched him with her hands yet.

She leaned closer to his ear. "If you're uncomfortable, you'll tell me." Her soft breath brushed against his cheek.

"I will." His voice sounded strangled and not because his face was squashed against the pillow.

She shifted her position, rubbing her hip against his again. Even if the gesture was casual, it set a fire in his veins. He stifled a gasp at the gentle touch of her fingers on his shoulders.

"You're too tense. I can feel your muscles are in a knot." She massaged his upper back, kneading his muscles with her thumbs. The oil made her fingertips slick and soothing, and her scent drove him mad. "Is it the small of your back that hurts the most?"

"Yes," he croaked out.

Her fingers paused over the scar from the stab. It wasn't much of a scar, just a thin, bumpy line dangerously close to his spine. But she stroked it with reverence.

She ran her fingertips over it. "This scar is the proof that you saved my life."

"Yes, well..." He forgot what he wanted to say.

She resumed massaging his back with gentle hands, working one tense muscle at a time.

Now and then, she pressed her thumbs to his flesh, and the

sensation was both relaxing and exciting. With each rub and touch, she chased the pain and stiffness away. He closed his eyes and let the tension of the trip leave him. Finally, his body warmed, and his muscles loosened.

"Better?" Her breath caressed his neck.

"Yes." It came out huskier than he meant. Even the exhaustion was almost gone.

She ran her hands over his shoulders, biceps, and down to the small of his back, sending pleasant shivers throughout him. It was the first time a woman had touched him like that.

Her lips brushed his cheek, or so he thought. He couldn't tell. His body was alive with sensations he hadn't experienced in a long time. His muscles relaxed, except for one inconvenient part of his body that had no business hardening. He was glad she couldn't see the erection bothering him, but he couldn't help the reaction. Her touch made him want to touch her in turn and conjured up visions of them entwined in bed. He groaned in pleasure as she massaged the muscles close to his spine. Heaven.

He cleared his throat. "Where did you learn to do this so well?"

"In the stables. I rubbed horses and jockeys." She slowed her pace, lingering on the muscles of his shoulder blades. "Not that Aunt Rose or anyone else in Painswick knows that, so I'd appreciate it if you'd keep my talent to yourself."

"Jockeys?" He turned his head towards her.

"Head down or you're going to hurt yourself." She gently positioned his head on the pillow. "There's a hippodrome close to Painswick, not for races but for practice. Riding a horse is hard on the back."

"I know everything about that," he muttered between teeth. He didn't like the idea of Emily rubbing jockey's shoulders and backs.

"You're tensing again. You must release the tension."

"Right. But you must understand." He turned again. "I'm jealous. There. I said it."

"No need to be." She lowered his head again. "Your muscles are sculpted." Was there a breathy tone in her voice? "You must spend a lot of time training."

"I have to. If I don't exercise, the muscle pain becomes unbearable."

"All the work you do is plainly clear. I have never seen a more magnificent body if you don't mind my boldness."

Magnificent? He didn't know what to say. It was the first time someone had paid him a compliment about his body. No, Lady Robinson didn't count.

Emily kissed the back of his neck, and this time, he didn't believe the gesture was casual. Her soft breasts pressed against his back, tearing a different type of groan out of him.

"I'm sorry for all the pain you endured for me," she whispered, brushing his hair from his neck.

He didn't remember the pain now. Or the jockeys. "Your kiss helps. A lot."

She laughed. "Then I shall give you another one."

He couldn't contain a deep growl when she kissed a sensitive spot on the back of his neck. Hellfire. He wasn't aware he *had* a sensitive spot on his neck. He clenched a fist over the bedsheet.

"Emily." He didn't mean to sound so animalistic, but her name came out unbidden, halfway between a prayer and an order. The worst thing was that he wasn't sure what he was ordering her to do or begging her for.

She kissed the infamous spot again, lingering with her lips on his skin. It was torture and heaven together. "Better?" she asked.

"Hell, yes." He didn't apologise for cursing. He was beyond apologising.

She gave him a light bite, and he couldn't remain still any longer. He rolled on his back, taking her with him until they swapped places. She lay on her back on the bed and he was on top of her. He'd followed his impulse, and the agile move had surprised even himself, but he shouldn't have done that.

He was about to move off her, but the look on her face wasn't one of fear or shock.

"Don't move," she ordered, and he didn't mind.

There was no mistaking the fact his erection pressed against her belly or ignoring the flush in her cheeks. In the process of swapping places, the front of her dressing gown had fallen open, and an enticing triangle of golden-bronzed skin appeared.

"And now what, my lord?" She cocked her head, smiling. "You have me at your mercy."

His mouth grew dry. And now he wanted to rip her dressing gown open and nibble her skin to know what gold tasted like. But they weren't married. Not yet. On top of that, he wasn't at his best, physically speaking. He might have made a bold move, but his body begged for sleep, and his muscles needed to stretch. Besides, he wanted to take his time with her, savouring every moment. Not to hurry up because they had to leave in a few hours. Tomorrow was another day of cold, jolts, and pain. He should wait. And soon she would be his wife.

He brushed her bottom lip with his thumb and growled when she had the audacity to bite it lightly. She was going to be the death of him.

"There's nothing I want more than to spend the night kissing you."

She pouted. "But?"

"We need rest, and you aren't my wife yet. Tomorrow won't be easy on us either."

"You're right." She caressed his shoulder. "The next few days will be horrible. We must rest."

He kissed her hand and placed it on his chest, right over his frantic heart. "Will you sleep here with me?" He brushed a dark curl from her lovely face.

"Yes." She sounded breathy, and he loved it.

He hadn't realised how badly he wanted her to say yes until she did. He wrapped his arms around her and pulled her closer, feeling her warm, soft body against his. He made sure she was covered and well-tucked in bed.

"Thank you for the massage," he said, holding her. "You brought me back to life."

"So did you." She snuggled closer to him, her eyelids drooping. She was exhausted as well.

The tension and fatigue of the day vanished as he heard her breathing slow, and he took his wedding vows then and there.

He would cherish and take care of her for the rest of his life.

fifteen

EMILY TUGGED HER deerskin gloves on and stared at the white view from the window in the inn. Snow had fallen heavily during the night, and the sky promised more to come. Icicles hung from the roof, and flakes came down between the tree branches as they swayed in the wind. Beautiful but scary at the same time.

She loved the snow. Painswick turned all white in winter, and she'd spent hours ice skating and walking through the snow with her thick boots and coat before returning home and warming herself with a cup of tea by the hearth. The white view of today was different. Even if the road got cleared, today's trip would be another uncomfortable, freezing day. She'd recovered from their first day of the journey, just barely, thanks to the lovely night she'd spent in Brandon's bed in his arms. He'd been such a gentleman... perhaps too much of a gentleman. She wasn't a wanton woman, but after seeing and touching all his sculpted muscles and feeling his hard length against her body, her skin tingled with anticipation. They'd agreed to have a fumble, after all. It didn't matter if he was inexperienced. He was so gentle and caring she trusted him with her body and heart. He wouldn't hurt her.

Alas, thoughts for another day, if they survived the freezing cold and another open carriage.

She turned around when Brandon walked over to her. He tied his woollen scarf around his neck and pulled his hat down over his face, half-hiding his concerned expression. He hadn't complained once during yesterday's ride, but his pain had been obvious in the stiffness of his contracted muscles. He sported a brave smile, but the light tremor in his legs betrayed his true feelings.

"Ready?" Even his voice sounded dejected.

Something cracked in her chest, and the instinct to protect him roared to life. So far, he'd done everything to keep her safe, injuring himself and disregarding his own well-being for her. It was her turn to do something for him. She couldn't put him through another day of cold and painful travel, especially with the uncertain weather conditions. What would happen to him if they got stuck in a country lane in the middle of a snowstorm? He couldn't trek through the snow. He'd collapse. Heck, she'd had enough of the cold as well. She was sore and tired, too. If she didn't want to take an open carriage, that left only one option. Her throat tightened.

She became dizzy at the thought of climbing into the train, *that* train, again, but she wouldn't let Brandon be in pain for another day, or worse die in the snow because of her irrational fear. Sod her aunt. Emily might lose her inheritance, but she and Brandon were risking more than money.

The way he'd held her through the night, keeping her warm and comfortable, had left an ache in her chest. When she'd woken, he'd caressed her hair and got up to light the stove so she would not feel cold.

She closed her fists, making a decision that caused her knees to weaken and her heart to race. She had to be brave. She had to do it for him. Enough of being a coward.

He peered out of the window and clicked his tongue. "More

snow. Let's hope the road is clear enough for the carriage to get through. It might start to snow again. We'd better go."

"Brandon." She put a quivering hand on his arm. "I was thinking…" She took a deep breath. She needed to be brave for him.

"Yes?" He stroked her knuckles. "What is it?" he asked when she didn't add anything.

"I want to take the train," she said in one breath, closing her fingers around his arm for support.

His lips parted in shock. "Are you sure?"

She nodded, not trusting her voice. She was sure she wanted to help him. She wasn't so sure she could handle the train. But she'd deal with that later.

"Why did you change your mind?" He cocked his head.

She couldn't remove her hand from his arm. If she did, her resolve would float away with the snow. "It's cold and painful for you. I can't put you through another day like yesterday. And if we get stuck in the snow, everything we've done so far would be for nought. We'll miss the opportunity to stop my aunt, and we'll both be sick and miserable in the best of the outcomes."

He dipped his head to meet her gaze. "If you're doing it just for me, don't worry."

"How can you say that?" She snuggled closer to him. "I do worry about you, but I want to do this for me as well. Besides, it's extremely cold for me too, and we might not make it to Scotland in time. I can see how much pain you are in. You tried to hide it yesterday, but I saw how much you were hurting. This trip is difficult for both of us." She hated being the cause of so much distress for him.

He held her hands and placed them over his chest as he'd done last night. "If you change your mind, just tell me. I'll be with you all the time."

"I know."

"You're very brave."

Her laugh sounded hysterical. "I don't think so. Desperate is more accurate. Besides, we need to return to London to catch the Flying Scotsman. We might not make it." The cursed train didn't stop anywhere between London and Edinburgh, but they hadn't travelled very far, due to the weather. She could endure another day of cold before catching the Flying Scotsman.

"No, we don't need to return to London. The snow did us a favour. As I was paying for our rooms, the innkeeper told me the snow forced the Flying Scotsman to stop at a nearby station, waiting for the railway to be clear." He gave her a pointed look. "We might need to catch another train from Edinburgh to London to return home because of the weather, but we can perform the ceremony in Edinburgh itself. I'm asking again, are you absolutely sure?"

A sickening lump crawled up her throat. "In for a penny."

His nod lacked confidence. "All right." He checked his pocket watch. "We have a few hours to spend before catching the train. Getting distracted may help with your anxiety. It works with mine."

Anything to let her mind calm. "Lovely. What would you like to do?"

He showed a lopsided smile. "I have a wonderful idea."

IN RETROSPECT, going ice skating was a terrible, undignified idea.

As absurd as it sounded, Brandon hadn't thought about his sore back when he'd proposed to go ice skating on a nearby frozen lake. He'd only thought about distracting Emily from her fear. He'd been about to withdraw his offer when her face had brightened with dozens of stars of happiness. She'd told him she loved ice skating, and he couldn't have said no. Serves him right.

So here he was, wearing a pair of heavy skater boots and trying not to fall on his arse, which would be excruciating. The view was spectacular with the frozen lake shimmering like a diamond, and the light-grey sky that held back the snow for now. Everything was covered in white. Beautiful but slippery.

Emily instead twirled around, fast in her skates and with her arms spread wide. Her skirt and coat fluttered in the cold air, making her look like a flower blossoming to challenge the winter. She even threw her head back and spun on the tips of her boots.

She whooshed past him, leaving only a trail of her jasmine scent. "Isn't it amazing?"

"Yes, yes, wonderful." He held a tight grip on a low tree branch, praying to every saint in heaven that the branch didn't snap.

She came to a graceful stop in front of him, lifting a spray of tiny ice shards. Her cheeks were deliciously reddened by the exercise. "I'm being very selfish."

"Why would you say that?" He gripped the branch harder, but the bugger threatened to break. Mother Nature was against him.

"This is dangerous and painful for you."

He shrugged. "Not as long as I don't fall. I'm quite safe at the moment."

"But you aren't enjoying yourself either." She brushed a curl of hair from her face. "We can leave."

"No." He shuffled his feet to find a stable position without releasing the tree branch. "You're enjoying yourself. Please do go on." He had the feeling she would need the memory of this happy moment a few hours from now.

"You're going to freeze if you stay here without moving. Really, we can leave."

"I want to try skating." He didn't, but she was having too much fun.

She arched a sceptical brow. "Indeed."

He stretched out a hand towards her. "Show me?"

She took his hand. "You're very brave too."

Or reckless. He wasn't sure.

Emily tugged at his arm slowly until he had to release the branch. "Gently." She held his hands and skated backwards, which he loved because he could see her face.

At each step, he worried he might lose control of his balance, but Emily grasped him with confidence, and his blades cut the ice without slipping. He and Emily inched along the ice. Or rather, she dragged him along and led the way. He followed. But he didn't lose his balance, and it was fun!

"It's like dancing," Emily said, speeding up a little, still going backwards. "Only easier."

The chilly air shuffled his hair and carried the fresh scent of pine resin and her perfume. He straightened, more confident on his feet. They skated around the lake, lifting snowflakes and dry pine needles. The gusts stroked his face as they sped up. He laughed when they went faster. The trees bordering the lake became a green and white whirlwind, swapping places with the sky.

"See? You're skating!" she said.

He pulled her closer and slowly turned her around as if waltzing. "It's fantastic."

"I told you."

Without her, he wouldn't have probably tried ice skating, but he couldn't deny the thrill of confidence and happiness making him laugh. As he spun around with Emily in his arms, for once, the world was only a glittering diamond. And right at that moment, he knew without a doubt that he would die for this woman. He would do anything to make her happy, which made him think he couldn't have found a better wife to share his life with.

She wrapped her arms around his neck and started to slow them down. Her chest pressed against his, and her plush lips were an inch from his. Their breaths mingled, turning into mist. With each inhale, their bodies drew closer, and their hearts became one.

Happiness made him giddy. "Why are you slowing? Let's make another round but faster!"

"I don't think so. You've exerted yourself enough. Your back muscles are going to hurt." She hooked her arm through this. "Really. Let's get warm, have a cup of tea, and I'll rub your back again."

He grinned. Perhaps ice skating had been the best idea he'd ever had.

sixteen

EMILY TRIED TO control her breathing, the tremor coursing through her legs, and the dizziness as she stood on the platform in the small train station. The Flying Scotsman blew out steam in front of her in all its green glory. Sunshine glinted off its shiny metallic surface, reminding her of the gaze of a predator. It was hard to believe this machine had been nothing but a heap of contorted metal the last time she'd seen it. She wondered if it carried the scars of the accident as people did. If she focused, she could still hear the sickening noise of the metal being torn apart and the people screaming. Goosebumps pebbled her skin.

She had to climb into that train for Brandon and for herself. He'd proven to her that he was ready to sacrifice his well-being to make her happy. He'd even gone ice skating with her. She had to prove to him that she'd do the same.

He touched her elbow, jolting her. "Are you sure?"

No. "Yes." She started again when the attendant rang the bell and announced the train was about to leave. So soon. She needed a bit longer— no, she didn't. Brandon was right. What were the odds of being involved in another accident? Very low, perhaps, but not a complete, definitive zero. She was disappointed in herself. Enough of being worried! Statistics aside, the idea of travelling in a tight space caused her legs to weaken.

"I'm the last person who should say this, but you know, laudanum would help. It'll make you sleepy." His gaze became distant. "Detached. You won't be scared."

"No, I want to be conscious and aware of what's happening. I think it'll be worse if I know I can't react and run if something happens."

"As you wish. I admire your courage." He offered his arm, and she hesitantly took it.

Steam coiled around her like the tail of a snake, partially hiding the metal monster. The hide-and-seek effect only enhanced the Flying Scotsman's resemblance to a predator as if it waited in the mist to lunge onto its prey. The closer she went, the faster her heart beat. Time slowed down to a crawl as she climbed the few steps to the carriage on trembling legs.

Brandon put a hand on the small of her back. "Take deep breaths. Think about something happy like ice skating."

She did as told, but the smell of coal and engine oil only brought sudden, bad memories to her. She closed her eyes, fighting the urge to run.

"I can't do this," she whispered.

"We're leaving then." Brandon turned around towards the exit.

"No, wait." She took a few deep breaths. The choking sensation clogged her throat.

He hugged her and pulled her to his chest. The moment his arms wrapped around her and formed a protective cocoon, she breathed more easily.

He rubbed her back. "Better?"

"Yes, yes." She opened her eyes and moved on, keeping her gaze on the windows.

Along the aisle, she paused in front of the compartment she'd occupied with her parents. The plush seats gleamed under the light from the lamps. She almost expected to see her parents sitting inside, smiling at her.

"Mama, Papa," she said.

Brandon squeezed her hand. "This is too much. We should leave."

"No." She bit down a sob. "I have to do this for them as well. They wouldn't want me to live in fear. Mama always said, 'Face your fear with love in your heart, and success will follow.' When she moved to England and met my father, she was mocked and despised because of her origin, not by everyone, but a few people were mean to her. She faced the scorn because she loved Papa. I've never understood what she meant by saying to face your fear with love until now." She put a hand on her chest. "I love them. I want to face my fear with the strength of this love."

Brandon kissed her cheek. "I like that. It seems better than a happy memory."

She cast a last, lingering glance at the seat once occupied by her parents before moving onwards. Still, her feet were heavy, and sweat beaded her forehead. The aisle that led to the enclosed compartments was so narrow Brandon's shoulders skimmed both walls. So tight. So oppressive. It was a trap.

Even the polished wooden floor and the plush, stuffed seats in their compartment made her want to cast up her accounts and thump the walls with her fists. She perched on the very edge of the seat, clenching her fingers around her reticule.

He gently took her hands and rubbed them. "Tell me how you feel."

"Like... I'm choking." The roof seemed to get closer to her, and the whistle of the train hissed in her ears. She squeezed her eyes shut. The train jerked forwards, and she couldn't stop a cry.

"Keep your eyes closed," he said in a sweet, soft voice. "It'll help block the memories."

She was desperate to get better and was ready to try any trick so she obeyed. Yes, not seeing the compartment helped, but the noises and smells remained.

He caressed her jaw with his thumb. "During my dark years, I learned a few things about controlling my emotions. I have to thank Matthew for that. You won't conquer your fear in a day, but you'll feel a little better if you get distracted."

"Distracted? How?" Her voice quivered. "I don't think I can read."

"I wasn't thinking about reading."

The train picked up speed. She could tell by the quick noises. Goodness. The train was so fast. How could they not crush?

"Then what were you thinking about?" she asked in a shaky voice.

"Kissing you," he said very close to her. "Would you like to try?"

"Yes." She didn't even need to ponder her reply. She waited. Why was he hesitating? She would open her eyes and— Brandon's soft lips stopped her fretting.

He kissed her. It was a slow, burning kiss that shot a bolt of energy through her. The fact that her eyes were closed and her skin was so sensitive amplified the sensation of his velvety lips on hers. The tip of his tongue traced the seam of her lips, and her pulse changed its rhythm. It still went faster than usual, but not out of fear. He caressed her cheek and scattered kisses on her jaw and neck, gentle and caring as always. With each kiss, her body became less tense.

"Don't open your eyes," he whispered.

She had no intention to. A sigh left her as he bit a delicate spot close to her ear. He was right. The distraction helped her release the anxiety knotting her belly. The noises and smells bothered her, but knowing he was close and ready to support her loosened her muscles. She breathed more easily.

He drew slow circles on her back, kissing her cheek. "Better?"

"Yes." She rested her head on his shoulder, and he wrapped his arms around her.

She didn't know how long she stayed like that, with her eyes closed and held by him, but he kept caressing her back and hair, whispering he was there for her. The steady rhythm of his heartbeat reassured her. If she focused on it, she could almost ignore the train's whistle. Her rigid muscles began to relax, and her breathing became less uneven, although she was sure that, if Brandon released her, she would start screaming bloody murder. The rocking motion of the train changed as the carriage lurched.

She snapped her eyes open. "What was that?"

He stroked her back. "Nothing. Likely a bump in the railway."

A loud screech followed. That couldn't be normal. Thick sheets of snow slapped the windows. And it had been snowing like that all night. The train would crash again. The metallic noise of the train turned into an icy laugh in her ears. The Flying Scotsman mocked her. The monster wanted to claim her life as well because it was never satisfied. It sought more souls to keep. They were going to die, squashed by the metal. The walls closed in on her. Another whistle rent the air. She was choking. Her throat constricted.

"Emily." Brandon's voice sounded distant and distorted as if coming through water.

She couldn't breathe. Her vision darkened. Something heavy oppressed her chest. Her body grew numb and limp. She couldn't move her legs to leave. She would be buried in this train, unable to escape.

"I don't want to die," she whispered or maybe shouted.

Brandon's deep voice called her with desperation. He had to be far from her because she couldn't feel his warmth anymore.

"Emily, please!"

She opened her eyes, or maybe they'd been opened all along. He carried her down the passageway on the train towards the door. The wind whistled and hissed, causing the snowflakes to whip around and hit the windows. The sky had an angry dark colour that promised a blizzard.

"What happened?" she asked, her throat burning.

"Emily." He paused, peering at her face. "You fainted. Lord, you were so pale I worried you had a fit."

She rested her head against his hard chest, inhaling a whiff of his clean scent. "I'm sorry."

"Don't apologise. Taking the train was madness. We're leaving. Enough of this." He stretched out a hand towards the plunger of the emergency brakes.

"No!" She gripped the lapels of his jacket. "Please. Don't stop the train."

He shook his head. "It's too much for you." Concern etched his features, and maybe pain as well since he held her. "I'll get you out of here immediately."

"Please." She cupped his face to get his full attention. "If I leave the train now, I will never be able to take one again. I want to stay."

He scowled, his hand inches from the plunger. "You fainted. Your pulse was very low. You aren't ready for this."

"I won't faint again." She wasn't sure about that, but she was sure she wanted to stay. "I don't want to run, and we don't have to stop. We lost two days because of me, and it's snowing. We'll never reach the border in time or worse, we'll get stuck in a storm if we travel by carriage. I'm serious. Let me try again."

He let out a long exhale. "If you feel dizzy, I'll stop this damn train, and I don't care if the company fines me." He carried her back to the compartment.

"Thank you." A tightness caught her chest when he laid her on the seat, but she didn't mention it.

He studied her with his eyebrows drawn together as if worried she might drop dead on the spot, which wasn't a possibility she could exclude. She swallowed hard when the train jerked again and the whistle hissed. Everything was fine. She could control the darkness. She gripped his hand hard, but if she hurt him, he didn't say anything.

"How is your back?" she asked.

"This seat is ten times more comfortable than the landau. I'm warm, and my muscles aren't spasming. I can't complain. But I'm worried about you."

"I'm fine. I really am." She squeezed his hand. "Perhaps you can distract me again."

"Emily, I don't think it'll work."

"Yes, yes. I need the distraction. Kiss me. Please." She gripped the lapels of his jacket again. She wanted to feel his lips and hands on her. The shock from the pleasure his kisses gave her was the perfect antidote to her fear. She could easily get lost in the sensation of him kissing her.

A corner of his mouth quirked up. "I'm eager to kiss you too, but if it's too much, you must tell me."

"Yes." The anticipation already worked against her anxiety. The knot of worry in her belly loosened a little. "Kiss me. I beg you." She regretted her words because she didn't want to be kissed only to control her fear. She wanted to be kissed because she enjoyed it.

He pulled down the curtains of the glass door and kissed her, but the kiss tasted different from the previous one. He was more cautious as if worried she might break. She must have scared him for real.

She tangled her fingers through his hair and pulled him closer. "I won't break. Kiss me harder. Make me forget where I am."

He ran his tongue over his bottom lip. "Make you forget? I'll do my best, but as you know, I don't have a lot of experience. You're the expert."

"Not really." She laughed, and it felt good. Her chest became lighter. "I'm sure you're a very good kisser."

"You'll be the judge then."

"I will."

"Is it all right if I lock the door? I don't want an attendant to come here."

She nodded. "I'm on a train. A locked door doesn't matter."

He pressed his mouth against her harder and grazed her bottom lip with his teeth. Oh, yes, that was an excellent distraction from the noises and the rolling motion. She parted her lips in an invitation he didn't refuse. He thrust his tongue into her mouth, and she welcomed him. With each lash of his tongue, her pulse slowed down and another pulse started between her legs. A pleasant shiver went down her back when he trapped her bottom lip between his teeth and sucked gently. Oh, goodness. That felt so good. Her mind focused on the slow movements of his mouth over hers.

A nagging feeling still bothered the back of her head, but somehow, it was a dull throb. She wasn't deluded. The fear would roar back to life the moment she lowered her guard. But for now, she controlled it, and it made her feel more confident. If she could keep her fear down at that moment, she could do it again.

"More," she whispered against the skin of his neck.

"More?" He scattered light kisses on her jaw. "More it is."

She moaned when he kissed her more deeply while gently cradling her head. His hard body pressed against her, and his arm coiled around her waist in a possessive gesture. She was protected by him as it had happened years ago. The kiss became a bit rough and hard when he grew too eager. But she needed exactly that roughness, wild passion, and energy. Each rough kiss and sensual bite chased away the choking sensation bothering her.

She held her breath when he tentatively moved his hand from her waist to her breast, brushing the tip with his thumb.

"I'm looking forward to our wedding night," she whispered as he rubbed her nipple through the layers of fabric. If she focused on the delicious sensation, she could almost forget where she was.

"So am I, and I confess it's getting increasingly difficult to keep my hands off you." He bit her lips again, sending a jolt of anticipation down her spine. "You drive me mad with desire."

She cupped his cheek. "You won't hear me complain."

He lowered his gaze. "Am I distracting you enough?"

She shook her head. "You should try harder."

A wicked smile twisted his lips. He slid a hand under her skirts and stroked her stockings. The thin fabric was no barrier, but the contact with the rough pads of his fingers had her panting in a moment. His gentle touch had its charm because he explored her with caution and restraint, careful about her reactions. There was something utterly thrilling about being the woman who drove him mad with desire and the way he restrained himself.

"You're so soft," he said, staring at her lips. "How do you feel?"

"Better. But you aren't distracting me enough."

"Let me make amends."

He stroked the garter on her thigh as if asking permission to proceed. She inched her legs apart, aware that an attendant might knock and demand they open the door. Somehow, the danger of being caught only added another ounce of excitement, and excitement was better than fear. He untied the garter with a pull. The cheap fabric of her stocking slid down her thigh, leaving her skin bare. He took advantage of it immediately.

She sighed again as he caressed her inner thigh. She might have more experience than he did, but no one had ever touched her with such reverence. Her previous fumbles had been pleasant enough but also quick and shallow affairs. No all-consuming longing involved. No lover had ever taken his time to touch her skin as Brandon was doing. He made her feel beautiful and desirable.

He ran his fingers over her thigh, slipping closer to the opening of her drawers. He gauged her reactions every time he stroked another new inch of her skin.

"Am I distracting you?" he whispered.

She swallowed hard. "Try harder." The words came out with

effort.

His hands and intense stare were the only things keeping her sane, and she clung to them with desperation. The train didn't exist so long as she focused on his touch and the pleasure he gave her.

For a man who was learning the art of lovemaking, he knew how to please her. He got closer to her core and hesitated. The moment of stillness made her squirm with need. She was about to beg, but he inched his hand onwards and traced the slit of her drawers.

They both groaned when his fingers were a mere inch from her opening. Instant wetness pooled between her thighs, although he hadn't touched her most aching spot yet.

He paused again. "Are you all right?"

"Yes." She panted. "Please." If she sounded desperate, it was because she was.

They remained still for a moment, lost in each other's gaze. The distraction worked because she didn't care about the movement of the train, the metal hissing, or the smell of coal. Staring at her, completely focused on her face, he finally touched her intimate, burning flesh. The shock of his careful touch caused her to arch her back and push her hips towards his fingers. All the time he'd spent stroking her culminated in this one moment. He stroked her wet folds, sliding his finger deeper in and out of her. The pad of his thumb rubbed her sensitive nub, exploring, caressing, and teasing.

"You're so wet," he whispered. "And warm."

Warm? She was boiling, and above all, she could easily ignore the nasty nagging at the back of her head. It was still there, but she was controlling it, not the other way around.

She widened her legs to give him better access. He moved his finger deeper inside her, and she sank her teeth into her bottom lip not to scream. Her inner muscles clenched around his finger in welcome, making her feel more intensely.

He explored her, never averting his gaze from her face, studying her as if wanting to impress her expressions in his memories. She wanted to squeeze her thighs together to ease the ache between them but let him explore at will instead. He added a second finger, his lips parting and his Adam's apple bobbing up and down. She grew wetter by the minute as he kept stroking her nub with his thumb. Just the way he looked at her, as if she were the most beautiful woman he'd ever seen, made her all hot and bothered. Ripples of sensations coursed through her. She fell prey to the tingling of her skin and the pleasure tightening in her lower abdomen.

He kept inching his fingers in and out of her while drawing slow circles over her sensitive bud, and she couldn't contain the overwhelming pleasure any longer. Warmth spread from the aching nub and chased away the bitter taste of fear in her mouth.

She gripped his shoulders and bit down a scream as delicious spasms took hold of her. With each shocking wave of pleasure, her fear receded, relegated to a dark corner of her mind. Still there, but kept at bay.

"Brandon." It came out all breathy and husky.

His eyes became impossibly large as he stared at her in awe. When she wheezed in the aftermath of her release, he slowly pulled his fingers out of her.

"You liked it." Surprise and adoration laced his words.

Ha! He had no idea. "More than liked it. I think I'm cured of all my fears, at least for the time being. The best distraction ever."

"I'm glad I was of help."

He smiled, but it wasn't the smug smile she'd seen on a lover who experienced a moment of triumph for his performance. It was a smile of sheer happiness for having pleasured her. He pulled down her skirt to cover her properly. Not that she cared. But what he did next got her full attention and stoked her inner fire, making her ache all over again. He rubbed his fingers, glistening with her wetness, and tasted them, running his tongue over them.

Oh, goodness. She was wet again, mesmerised by the way he licked her arousal from his fingers as if he were tasting the best thing in the world. And he kept staring at her. She wilted. What was happening? Because she had no idea. Her body had never, ever brimmed with so much desire as it did now, and right after an intense release! On a train, of all places!

She couldn't gaze away from his tongue flicking over his fingers. A wicked glint twinkled in his gaze. The scoundrel was fully aware of the effect he had on her. She felt every lash of his tongue right over her nub.

He closed his mouth around a finger and sucked. "You taste delicious. Like peaches."

She didn't know what to say. She couldn't form any words. Her brain remained stuck on the pleasure she'd experienced and on watching his mouth doing wicked things, which was good for many reasons. None of her lovers— not that there had been many of them —had ever done something so extravagant and exciting.

"When we're married," he said, licking his fingers clean, "I'll taste you properly. All of you." He ran a long gaze over her, leaving behind a path of fire on her skin.

A strangled noise was the only thing she could produce.

"Will you let me do it?" he asked.

As if she would ever say no. "Yes, yes, yes. Please." She wrapped her arms around him and hugged him. "Thank you."

He kissed her cheek. "I'll always be here for you." He kept caressing her back, letting her know with his touch as well that he would protect her no matter what.

She believed him. No doubt at all. And the certainty of his support and love was the most powerful antidote to her fear.

Perhaps her fear hadn't been banished completely. It was lurking somewhere within her, waiting for her to lower her guard and to jump at her throat. But for now, she'd conquered it, and if she'd done it once, she could do it again.

seventeen

BRANDON WAS A bundle of overly susceptible nerves, minutes before the wedding ceremony. *His* wedding ceremony. He couldn't stand still but didn't want to move at the same time not to tire himself. A nightmare.

He paced and stopped, paced and stopped. It was like being on a boat. Something must have happened to the time flow because it seemed he'd waited for the ceremony of his red-hot wedding to start for hours, but the clock on the mantelpiece told him only ten minutes had passed, which wasn't possible. Matthew and Cowley had been in Edinburgh for a couple of days already, waiting for them. Cowley remained still in a corner of the room, calm and composed as usual. Not a muscle twitched.

"Brandon, calm down," Matthew said from his stuffed chair in the office of the Blacksmith Priest.

An anvil and a heavy-looking hammer stood in the middle of the room. The ceremony involved the hammer being smashed against the anvil, symbolising the forging of a new union. Or something like that.

"Brandon," Matthew said again through clenched teeth.

"You're giving me seasickness. At least decide if you want to pace or remain still."

He blew out a breath. "I just want the ceremony done, and where's Emily?"

"She's getting ready." Matthew rose and stopped Brandon's wandering. "The ceremony will be a short affair. Don't worry." He fixed Brandon's cravat and tugged at his jacket, smoothing down a few wrinkles. "Why the hurry? Have you changed your mind about marrying her? Has she changed her mind?"

"No, I just want it done and make sure Emily receives her inheritance."

They'd barely made it on time to Edinburgh because the snow had slowed down the Flying Scotsman. He hadn't seen Emily since she went to her room at the inn to wash and change. And it was taking too bloody long.

The good thing was that she hadn't fainted again, but after the excitement of their heated kisses had passed, her anxiety had returned, and she'd been miserable and uneasy for the rest of the trip. He'd done his best to comfort her, and she'd been so brave he couldn't be prouder of her. Overall, the trip had been exhausting and excruciating for both of them.

Cowley didn't flinch at Brandon's restlessness, but his tense features belied his nervousness. "I'm so proud of you, sir." His eyes glistened with unshed tears. "You're going to build your family. Your parents would be proud of you, too."

Brandon softened. "I haven't done anything yet, but thank you, Cowley."

"You're getting married," Cowley said, straightening. "Something that a few years ago I wasn't sure would happen, if you pardon my frankness."

Yes, a few years ago, Brandon had been agonising in his bed, in the throes of withdrawal symptoms, thinking he would have died.

Cowley bowed. "I'm glad you found the strength to fight that evil potion. You've made me incredibly happy."

Emotion choked Brandon. He didn't say anything but hugged his loyal secretary. Cowley remained stiff, taking a moment to return the embrace.

"I would have never made it without you. Thank you for not giving up on me," Brandon whispered.

"Never, sir." Cowley withdrew quickly to wipe his eyes. "Never."

Bugger. Now Brandon found breathing hard. He rubbed his eyes and swallowed past the clog in his throat. "Thank you to both of you."

Matthew clapped Brandon's shoulder, breaking the spell. "You're welcome. Although I'd be grateful if you didn't let us go through anything like that nightmare again."

"I won't." He clasped Matthew's arm.

Matthew's eyes shone suspiciously, and he averted his gaze. "Don't worry about the legal aspect. I'll send a wire to your solicitor as soon as you and Emily say *yes*. No need to feel so anxious. In a matter of hours, Emily will be a rich lady."

"Yes, yes. Excellent." Brandon wasn't entirely honest with his friends.

The real reason he was in a hurry had nothing to do with Emily's inheritance or legal procedures. Well, it had, but mostly he wanted their wedding night to start as soon as possible.

Visions of her flushed cheeks and glistening lips while he'd pleasured her on the train of all places filled his mind. And hellfire, he'd tasted her. It had been a mistake, not because he regretted it— far from it, he would do it again in a heartbeat —but because from that moment on, he couldn't stop thinking about her, about removing her clothes, uncovering all that golden skin, and tasting her everywhere. He wanted to hear her moan and give her all the pleasure she could take. He wanted to be a good lover for her. Someone she was proud to call husband.

He was desperate to see her cheeks flushing again in that delightful, deep crimson tone and her eyes shining with her release.

His shaft twitched in agreement, eager to do its part. He would likely combust out of need, but he'd do anything she asked, including leashing his desire should she wish so. The journey had been exhausting. She might want to sleep and recover after the bloody ceremony.

He ran a hand through his hair. He was going mad with doubts and questions, need and desperation.

"And there he goes again," Matthew said as Brandon resumed pacing and stopping.

"You'd be nervous too if you were getting married," Cowley said in his usual serious tone.

Matthew huffed. "Marriage? Not me. I'm a free gentleman."

"Libertine is the word you're looking for," Cowley said in the tone of a teacher dealing with a particularly disappointing student. "And I would use the word gentleman loosely when it applies to you."

Matthew rolled his eyes. "At your age, do you still think libertine is an insult?"

"She's here." Brandon came to a screeching halt when the door swung inwards, and a tall, bearded man strode inside.

What a disappointment.

"The groom, I suppose. I recognise the nervousness." The man shook Brandon's hand with a firm handshake. "I'm Campbell, the blacksmith who will perform your red-hot wedding."

"Great. Shall we start?" Brandon asked.

Campbell let out a deep, throaty laugh that thundered in the room. "Not without the bride."

He resumed pacing while Campbell and Cowley talked about the fact marriage was an important step in a gentleman's life. Matthew disagreed; he thought it wasn't wise to put his signature on a license that didn't have an expiration date. Brandon didn't care one way or the other. He just wanted his bloody ceremony to be over.

Soft footfalls approached, and the scent of jasmine floated in the air. "I'm ready."

Brandon came to an abrupt stop upon hearing Emily's voice. He turned around and hitched a breath. She looked lovely in her emerald gown and with her hair twisted in a gentle updo that left a few curls falling on her shoulders. A dark shawl covered her neckline. A pity, in his opinion. He wanted to see more of her, not less. The dress showed her lovely figure and exalted her skin, although the bodice had too many buttons now that he thought about it. It'd take ages to undo them. Would she be angry if he ripped them? Mrs. Sala would mend them.

Bugger. What was he thinking? He shouldn't be so eager to have her naked and sprawled for him as he did his best to pleasure her while her pink flesh glistened with her slickness. Damn.

He was a gentleman. Yes, he was, and he'd behave as such. He ordered his body parts to calm down because he wasn't going to pant all over his bride. Not now at least. Maybe later. No, certainly later. Oh, hell.

She took his arm and rose on her tiptoes to kiss his cheek. "I'm looking forward to being alone with you," she whispered for his ears only. "So we can finish what we started on the train. It might take a while to undress me though."

Instant combustion. And just like that, all his good intentions were gone, dead, vanished. His body burst with poorly concealed need and ached in all the wrong places. She could read his mind. There was no other explanation. Surely, that was the meaning of marriage.

He could barely nod, which was a shame. He should tell her he was eager to please her in everything, that he wanted to worship her in any fashion she wished, and that he'd do anything she asked. Instead, he only managed a curt bob of his head because need tightened his throat.

"Shall we start?" Campbell asked.

"Yes," he and Emily said together.

Campbell stroked his short beard. "I think I don't need to ask you if you're here on your own good will and if you indeed wish to marry each other. You seem quite smitten if I may say so."

Matthew chuckled. "The way they look at each other says it all."

Cowley sniffed but remained composed. Perhaps a red-hot wedding wasn't what he'd wanted for his master, but Brandon was glad Cowley approved.

"Then this wedding is good and holy." Campbell coughed in his closed fist and opened the Bible. "Miss Emily Maria Pilar de la Fuente Barclay and Mr. Brandon William Edmund Astley, Earl of Hastings, we're here together in front of Mr. Matthew Tyrell, Mr. Rudyard Cowley, and myself to join Emily and Brandon in marriage."

While Campbell recited the wedding formula and repeated their names at least a dozen times, Brandon stopped listening. His mind wandered to what would happen shortly after the ceremony, how he should behave, and that finally Emily would receive her inheritance. Emily looked stunning under the lights, and her eyes glowed from within. Any trace of fatigue gone. She laced her fingers through his and smiled so radiantly he couldn't help but smile back. He wanted to sweep her off her feet and dance with her, kiss her, and make her laugh. Everything.

What did the Blacksmith Priest say? Brandon didn't have the foggiest. Besides, every time he glanced at Emily, the only thing he could hear was the quick beat of his pulse and her soft breathing.

"... and by the power invested in me, I declare you husband and wife. The red-hot marriage is done!" Campbell smashed the hammer against the anvil, the sound echoing in the room. "Right-o, carry on! You may kiss the bride."

That last one Brandon heard loud and clear. He took Emily's face and kissed her but had to force himself not to do anything else. She leaned against him and kissed him back, rising on her tiptoes. It was a chaste kiss, but it held the promise of a future for them only. A future of companionship and love. Never he would have imagined he would experience such happiness.

Matthew clapped and cheered. Cowley hid his face in his handkerchief, and Campbell hit the anvil with the hammer a few more times. Brandon released Emily reluctantly, grinning like an idiot.

"My wife," he whispered.

"My husband." She kissed him again quickly.

It might be a hastily arranged marriage of convenience, but he was happier than he'd ever been. She smiled his favourite smile, and his chest tightened with love and the deep desire to be whatever she needed.

Matthew didn't waste time. He donned his hat and flung the door open. "Congratulations. I'm going to send the wire immediately."

Brandon waved at him. "Thank you, Matthew."

"I'll make sure your room is ready at the inn, sir, madam," Cowley said.

"Thank you, Cowley."

The secretary bowed and hurried out of the room. And now Brandon could finally—

"I need your signatures." Campbell tapped him on the shoulder. "After that, you may leave."

Brandon scribbled his signature, and Emily did the same. Then it was only them. They walked out of the workshop hand in hand among the congratulations of the Blacksmith Priest. The world had shifted. Something had changed. Because Brandon had never been as hopeful and grateful as he was now. For the first time since he'd lost his parents, he knew, deep in his soul, that he could be happy, and he owed that happiness to Emily.

The pavement was slippery with snow and ice, and they laughed as they walked slowly towards the inn, slipping right and left. Worse than ice skating. He caught her in his arms when she lost her balance. She laughed harder, and he loved it. They burst out laughing together for no reason other than they were in each other's arms. Darkness crept along the cobbled streets of Edinburgh, but his heart was full of light.

He brushed a strand of hair from her flushed cheek. "Once we're in London, I want another wedding."

"Another one?" She leaned against his touch.

"With guests, a ridiculously tall wedding cake, and a banquet. And music."

"Good idea, so I can have a proper chignon." She patted her hair. "I had to do it alone and it's a mess. Wayward curls everywhere."

"I think you look beautiful." He kissed her cheek only because he didn't want to cause a scandal. Alas, even married couples should refrain from public displays of affection. Never mind. He'd be affectionate in their bedroom. Very affectionate.

A moment of nostalgia caught him off guard, and he hugged Emily with desperation as if someone would soon snatch her away from him. He didn't know where the irrational fear came from. Maybe because he'd lost his parents and then he'd nearly lost her, and this moment of sheer happiness seemed too good to be true, too surreal. It wouldn't last, and soon he'd lose everything. Every moment of joy required a payment. He was so scared that he shivered.

"Don't leave me," he whispered although he wasn't sure if he begged her or prayed to heaven to grant him this one wish.

"Brandon." She ran a hand over his back. "I know how you feel. This happiness is frightening. Too strong. Too sudden. But you won't lose me, and I won't lose you. Happiness isn't a harbinger of disaster. It doesn't have to be."

He drew in a shaky breath. "How can I be so sure?"

She rose on her tiptoes and gave him a quick peck on the lips. "Statistically, it's not possible."

He barked out a laugh.

eighteen

BRANDON WANTED ONLY to carry his new wife upstairs and spend the rest of the night with her, but he owed Matthew and Cowley a dinner and a pint of ale after they'd shown him their full support, and Emily needed to eat something after the emotions of the journey. She'd dispensed with her beautiful emerald gown for a more practical shirt and skirt. But her beauty remained radiant, even in her simple clothes.

Sitting at a table in the busy inn, Matthew raised his mug. "To marriage and conspicuous inheritances. Lady Astley, Countess of Hastings, you're a ridiculously wealthy woman now."

Emily laughed behind her napkin. "Countess. It sounds so odd."

Brandon kissed her cheek, unable to keep his hands off her for more than a minute. He didn't care what people would think. If he couldn't be alone with her now, he would kiss her cheek as much as he liked. She rested her head on his shoulder, and he kissed the top of her head.

Cowley raised his mug as well. "I propose another toast to future happiness." He glared at Matthew. "Which is more important than wealth."

"I disagree," Matthew said, raising his mug too. "It's more important to be sad and rich than sad and poor. At least if you're rich, you can drown your sorrow in expensive whiskey and cigars."

Emily laughed, and Cowley grinned.

"Is it official then?" Brandon asked. "Mrs. Allen won't get Emily's inheritance, will she?"

Matthew lifted a shoulder. "I sent the wire, and your solicitor answered right back to inform me he started the procedure. I guess it's official."

"I'll check myself later, sir," Cowley said. "Make sure there's no loose thread."

"Thank you, Cowley." He turned towards Emily. "Are you still hungry?"

"Hungry?" She put a hand on her stomach. "I'm about to explode. The Cullen skink soup was delicious. I had no idea fish could be so tasty."

Matthew fiddled with his mug, lifting and lowering it a couple of times. "I hate ruining this moment, but Cowley and I have something to tell you."

"Bad news?" Brandon's heart raced in a moment. "But you said—"

"No, not about that." Matthew took another sip of ale before glancing at the secretary.

Cowley cleared his throat. "While I was waiting for your arrival, I took the liberty of sending a wire to a judge friend of mine and asking him for an update on Mr. Payne's and Mrs. Allen's activity. They haven't been idle. After Lady Emily ran away from home, they concocted something disturbing."

"Yes?" Brandon prompted when Cowley didn't add anything else.

Cowley arched his grey eyebrows. The look he gave to Brandon was charged with fatherly love. "In Mrs. Allen's contract regarding her guardianship of Lady Astley, there's now a clause added about Lady Emily's future husband. If her husband should be found mentally unfit or die, Mrs. Allen can claim Lady Emily's money, perhaps even yours, my lord, since your estate will pass to Lady Emily in the unfortunate event of your untimely death."

"Surely, we can contest the contract. It's absurd," Brandon said. "Why haven't we already?" Could his former addiction be used against them? Bloody laudanum was a curse.

"You and the countess needed to be married first," Matthew said. "And Lady Emily needed to claim her inheritance."

"We'll get ready for the claim, sir, but meanwhile..." Cowley glanced at Emily. "I'd advise caution."

Matthew nodded. "I wouldn't put it past Mrs. Allen to try to hurt you. Now the prize has multiplied. She could get her greedy hands on your money."

Emily shifted uncomfortably in her chair. "My aunt might be willing to cheat me, but hurting Brandon?" She shook her head. "She wouldn't go that far. Her scheme was driven by her past financial difficulties. She'll see reason."

"With due respect," Matthew said, "but I'm sure you didn't expect your aunt to be capable of stealing from you either. I don't trust her. Neither should you."

Emily sighed. "That's true."

"Better safe than sorry." Matthew sipped his ale, casting a glance at Brandon from over the rim of the mug. "When you return to London, it'd be better if you stay home until we challenge the contract and change it."

"It'd be better if Lady Emily avoided any contact with her aunt as well," Cowley added.

Well, that Brandon didn't mind. If he could stay alone at home with Emily, he'd be more than happy.

BRANDON SIGHED in relief when Matthew and Cowley finally bade the newlyweds goodnight. He climbed the stairs to his bedroom, nervous with anticipation. His wedding night. He couldn't imagine a more wonderful woman than Emily— his wife. The wait had been more than worth it.

She laced her fingers through his and kissed his neck, sending a jolt through his body. "Finally," she whispered. "I was looking forward to being alone with you."

"So was I."

The noises and voices coming from the dining hall ceased when he shut the heavy door behind him. A blazing log fire roared in the hearth, and the room was suffused with warm candlelight that lit her skin with golden hues. She was a goddess of fire and gold.

"We're married," she said, pacing around the room.

He drank her in. She glowed from the inside out. Exercising control on his instincts was something he was good at. But leashing his desire for her put his skill to the test.

Sod it. He wanted her so much that unless he did something, a blood vessel in his brain would burst. He walked over to her, shedding his jacket and waistcoat. He dropped them somewhere on the floor. By the time he reached her, even his shoes were gone, discarded with a kick.

Her chest rose and fell quickly the closer he came. "Will you take me now?" she whispered.

"Yes." His voice held a dominant quality and a growl he didn't know he could produce.

She had too many layers. He ought to do something about that. Thank goodness his fingers weren't too rough when he unbuttoned her shirt. Somewhere in the corner of his mind, he registered that her clothes were too worn and tattered. He would unleash Mrs. Sala again. Emily would have a new wardrobe as soon as they returned to London, but for now, she needed only her silky skin.

He shifted his gaze from her face to her shirt, wanting to see her skin being uncovered and to watch her reactions as well. Each undone button revealed her simple cotton chemise under the corset. His instinct was to rip everything off her and kiss her wherever he wanted, but he didn't want to rush the moment either. For her only, he forced himself to go slowly. Her breathing sped up when he finished unbuttoning her shirt. He pulled the lapels apart and took a moment to admire her. The simple corset pushed her generous breasts up. Their rounded tops were visible over the edge of the undergarment, covered by a flimsy chemise. He wanted to savour this moment because that was the first time he'd undressed *his* wife, and every second was precious. He dragged her shirt off her shoulders and tossed it away with as much carefulness as his impatience allowed.

"I can do it." She went to unhook the corset, but he was having none of it. He wanted to do it himself.

"Let me. Please."

She blushed as he undid the hooks on the front. That required more focus since the little buggers fought against him. A few of them were loose, and he exposed a hole in the chemise underneath.

"It's not pretty," she said, lowering her gaze. "And it's very old."

He took her chin, interrupting his work. "You're the most beautiful woman I've ever seen. You'd look like a goddess to me even if you wore rags."

She flushed again. "That's lovely, but I'd rather prefer it if you remove any cloth between us."

"Your wish is my command." He kissed the tip of her nose.

Without the corset, the fabric of the chemise flowed down to her hips, and her breasts bounced once free from their constriction. Her dark-pink nipples were visible through the fabric, and he longed to close his mouth around them. But he wasn't finished.

He untied her skirt and petticoats with a quick yank at the strings holding them. And then she stood in front of him in her modest stockings, drawers, and chemise. Perfect.

"Goodness," he muttered. "You take my breath away."

He walked around her, wanting to see the whole of her. He paused behind her and ran a slow hand over her firm arse.

Her chest heaved. "You haven't finished."

He undid her drawers as well. They slipped down her lovely legs, baring her behind to him. She was all firm muscles and velvety skin. So perfect. He dared slide a finger between her bottom cheeks. Her reply was a little moan. He caressed her rear, feeling her shiver under his touch.

The straps of her chemise required but a caress to slip down her arms. Still standing behind her, he reached to the front of the chemise and untied the strings holding it together before removing it completely.

They both groaned when he cupped her bare breasts. They filled his palms perfectly, warm and heavy. His shaft pushed against the fabric of his trousers as he pinched her taut nipples. He wanted to see them hard and puckered before tonguing them. She panted and arched her back while he rubbed and pinched her nipples. Her soft moans were the loveliest sound he'd ever heard. He needed to kiss her now, or he'd die. Taking her by the waist, he sat her on the bed and knelt between her open legs. He took a moment to explore her with his gaze.

She thrust her breasts out in invitation, and he couldn't resist. He latched his mouth around her nipple, sucking hard.

The cry of pleasure she let out made him shiver. Her pleasure was all that mattered. He tongued the other nipple and split his attention between her breasts, pinching and rubbing their hard tips. The sounds she made were the best reward. When he was satisfied her nipples were both glistening and hard, he trailed his kisses lower, tracing her belly with his lips. She writhed and squirmed.

He paused to stare at her face. "Do you like it?"

She sank her small white teeth into her bottom lip. "Yes. Don't doubt it. If I didn't, I would tell you."

"Good." Keeping his gaze on her, he rolled her nipple between his lips.

A long moan left her as she arched her back again. He was following his instinct and her reactions. All her moans and thrusts of her hips encouraged him.

He pushed her legs further apart unapologetically and remained still to admire her beauty. She was all wet and pink. Her little nub was engorged and glistening with her juice. And the scent! Hell, her sweet, spicy scent damped the air and caused his shaft to ache. The longer he stared, the wetter she became. He dipped his head and ran his tongue over her. Her sweet taste invaded his mouth and sent a shot of pleasure to his groin. He hadn't expected her reaction to be so powerful. She heaved her hips up with a jolt, grabbing fistfuls of the bedsheets. He had to keep her hips still to kiss her as he wanted to. She moaned loudly as he dug his tongue deep inside her, tasting her sweetness and getting drunk with it. He would gladly spend the whole night pleasuring her with his tongue because all the little sounds she made filled him with satisfaction and energy.

"Brandon," she whispered his name, pushing her hips towards his mouth.

Hellfire. The way she said his name, all breathy and husky, started a painful ache in his trousers. He might find his release by hearing his name alone. The muscles of her thighs contracted and squeezed him. She moaned again.

He kept kissing her even when quick pulses started from her welcoming entrance, and she cried out his name. She tangled her fingers in his hair before going limp on the bed. He kissed his way up, pausing at her magnificent breasts again to suck her perfect nipples.

"How are you?" he asked, rubbing every inch of her body he could reach.

She sighed, her chest rising and falling quickly. "Heaven."

Mission accomplished. He brushed the messy curls from her

heated face and drank her in— her heavy eyelids, flushed cheeks, and gleaming eyes.

"You're the most beautiful thing I've ever seen." He was repeating himself, and his words weren't even original, but it was true. "The moment I saw you for the first time in my compartment, I couldn't take my eyes off you. So beautiful and sweet. Now I can't believe you're my wife. The events that brought us together might not be the most favourable ones, but I'll never complain because they allowed me to meet you. How lucky I am. I would endure the pain again to meet you."

She took his face and pulled him down for a deep, soul-searching kiss. It was the first time he'd experienced such a furious kiss. There were no rules. It was a battle of lips, teeth, and entwined tongues. The kiss had to be a spell of sorts because the more he kissed her, the more desperate he grew for her.

She coiled her legs around his waist and urged him closer. "Does this position hurt?"

What? Oh, his back. "No." Right now, someone could stab him with a red-hot blade and he would keep smiling.

She lifted her hips, rubbing them against him. "Take me, husband of mine."

Her words stole his breath. He fumbled with his trousers until they were gone with her help. Fabric swished, hands shoved clothes out of the way, and legs kicked until he was naked. A moment of indecision took him. He knew the mechanics of the act but not the nuances. He also knew how to avoid a pregnancy, and they hadn't talked about that.

"What is it?" She cupped his cheek.

"I should put on a sheath," he said. "I had no idea... I mean, I didn't come prepared, and we might become parents tonight."

"I don't want to stop." She tightened the grip of her legs around him. "We're married. I want you, all of you, and if a child arrives, I could only be happy."

Blazes. He hadn't expected the wave of sheer joy flowing through him. She wanted to have a child with him! A family.

He breathed faster. "Imagine a child with your eyes."

"And with your kindness." She rolled her hips. "Take me, Brandon. I need you inside me." She met his hips with hers again, this time skin against skin.

His shaft touched her wet entrance, and he understood what it meant to be in heaven. Propping himself up on his elbows, he slid an inch inside her and stopped, groaning deep in his throat. Incredible. Nothing could have prepared him for the glorious sensation of her velvety muscles welcoming him. He paused to savour the moment before sliding another inch forwards. His back muscles stiffened a little, but if he didn't arch his back too much, he could manage the pain. She caught a breath as he slid inside her as gently as possible. When he was completely buried in her softness, they both moaned.

"Is it all right?" he asked, giddy with happiness.

"Oh, yes." She sounded breathy and husky, and he loved it.

He shifted his hips back and forth, sliding in and out of her to find a rhythm he could sustain easily.

"Brandon," she whispered, reclining her head. "Please."

That was all he needed to speed up. She helped him by raising her hips and meeting his thrusts. He paused only to capture her nipple in his mouth and tongue it and to slide a hand between them to rub her bud.

Energy built up within him. An ache grew in his abdomen. She dug her fingers into his shoulders, urging him faster. So be it. He pumped harder and deeper, feeling her muscles tensing again. She was close. He was close.

She came with a start as his name left her lips again. The sound of her release triggered his, and he roared his pleasure. It seemed to never end. The release emptied him of tension and energy and filled him with love.

They remained quiet, holding each other and sharing their breath and heat until only the embers glowed in the hearth.

BRANDON HELD Emily in his arms as the pale light of dawn streamed through the curtains. It was the most glorious dawn of his life. The first day as Emily's husband. It was a rebirth of sorts.

He hadn't slept much, but his body was full of energy, happiness, and love. His back muscles were sore, but the pain was manageable. She stirred in his arms, murmuring something. Her dishevelled curls framed her lovely face. He couldn't resist the temptation of brushing her plush bottom lip with his thumb. Would this desire for her ever be quenched? Not possible. She would always ignite his passion.

"Good morning." She blinked her eyes open and gave a wide smile. "What time is it?"

"Dawn. We need to get ready." Unfortunately. One more reason to celebrate a second wedding with a honeymoon. They would have all the time they wanted.

Murmuring something, she snuggled closer to him and buried her face in his chest. "I don't want to go anywhere."

He stroked her hair. "Neither do I, but we must make sure your inheritance is safe."

She groaned and mumbled.

"Not inviting, I know." He caressed her cheek, jaw, and neck. "Thank you."

"For what?" Her voice came muffled since her face was pressed against his chest.

"For last night. It was the best night of my life."

She tilted her head back to stare at him. "It was beautiful. The best night of my life, too."

His heart kicked faster only because he'd given her pleasure. "Are you ready to take the train again?"

A shiver left her skin pebbled. "No, but we must return to London and end my aunt's scheme for good. Before she does something reckless."

On a day like this, he wouldn't contemplate failure, or that something ominous loomed over them. "Cowley and Matthew are overprotective of me. I don't believe, not for one second, that your aunt is going to kill me. What would she do? Hire an assassin? Ridiculous."

"I'm not sure. Last night at dinner, I would have agreed with you. But the more I think about it, the more I believe Aunt Rose would be ruthless enough to do something like that." She caressed his chest, sending tingles down his spine. "I underestimated her once. I would have never, ever believed she could steal from me. If she can do that, what other things might she be capable of?"

He kissed her forehead. "I'm sure I'll be all right, and whatever happens, we'll face it together."

nineteen

GETTING ON THE Flying Scotsman wasn't a completely pain-free affair for Emily. But after having conquered her fear once and after her wedding night, the weight pressing against her chest was lighter. Other parts of her body weren't so light though. She was deliciously sore between her legs after Brandon had taken her several times during the night. The best night she'd experienced in years. He'd been magnificent. Always careful not to hurt her. Always eager to please her. But the wonderful sensations from last night faded in front of a new trip on a train.

The whistle of the train broke her pleasant wool-gathering, shoving her back to reality with brutality. The Flying Scotsman glinted in front of her once again. The most difficult part was taking the first step to board it.

"Ready?" Brandon stroked her hand.

"Yes."

She climbed into the metal monster, gripping his arm tightly. Her pulse drummed in her ears, and a cold sensation crept along her skin, but her legs were steady.

She sat next to Brandon on the soft seat in their compartment, her head resting on his shoulder. They didn't talk, just held each other, and laced their fingers. The way he looked at her with devotion warmed her from the inside out.

"Already anxious?" he asked.

"A bit, but I'm too happy to let my fear ruin everything."

"I've never been happier in my life." He kissed her hand. "After my parents died, I found myself alone and buried in responsibilities I was too young to carry. Then there was the accident, the pain, and the laudanum. You're the best thing that has ever happened to me."

She threw her arms around his neck. "I feel the same. I've never liked staying with my aunt and cousin. I didn't mind working and earning my keep, but they've never felt like family to me."

He took her waist. "Well, now you have a family that loves you. Adores you. Would do anything for you." He kissed her lips with a soft, lingering touch that made her quiver.

A breath remained trapped in her chest. Did he mean that? Did he truly love her? Because the warm feeling of happiness fluttering in her chest could only be love. But she didn't have time to say anything as Cowley and Matthew came into view. Cowley cast concerned glances at her while Matthew shot his gaze upwards at seeing them hug. Blimey. She didn't want to have a panic attack in front of them. Fainting in front of Brandon was more tolerable.

"Oh, please. Would you mind?" Matthew entered the compartment and stashed his bag on the overhead luggage rack. "You aren't alone."

"Unfortunately," Brandon said, releasing Emily.

"Sir, madam." Cowley offered a polite bow and scowled at Matthew. "I trust you had a pleasant night."

Matthew wiggled his eyebrows. "I'm sure it was *very* pleasant."

"Matthew!" Brandon said at the same time as Cowley said, "Mr. Tyrell!"

Emily's cheeks warmed. "It was a lovely evening. Thank you for being with us."

"My pleasure, madam." Cowley sat in front of them as the attendant rang the bell to signal the train doors were closing.

She stiffened. That was it. She was trapped on the Flying Scotsman.

Seemingly reading her mind, Brandon squeezed her hand. "I'm here. Take a deep breath."

She did as told, reminding herself that she'd beaten her fear once. She could do it again. Her pulse slowed, and the rhythmic strokes of Brandon's hand helped her breathe more easily.

Matthew produced a folder from his bag. "Emily, you don't mind if I call you Emily, do you?"

The abrupt request caught her attention, which was good. "No, of course not."

Judging by how Cowley scowled, he begged to differ.

"Great." Matthew shot a challenging glare at the secretary. "I know you aren't fond of trains and closed carriages."

"No, I'm not." She suppressed a gasp as the Flying Scotsman jerked into motion. Her stomach lurched. She'd done this before. She could do it again. That was her motto.

"Distraction is the key." Matthew grinned.

Emily angled towards Brandon who flashed a lopsided smile. "Yes, a distraction sounds nice."

"That's why I brought you these." Matthew handed her a stack of documents. "Projects in the developing phase that require a new pair of eyes. I'm full of fantastic ideas."

"I'd say only ideas," Cowley said.

"Don't mind Cowley. His pessimism won't ruin my mood." Matthew poked Cowley with his elbow, but Cowley didn't flinch. "He's so pessimistic that he doesn't simply see the glass as half-empty; he also thinks the remaining half will give him cholera."

She chuckled. "Sorry, Mr. Cowley."

The older man smiled. "Not at all, madam."

The documents piqued her interest. She nearly snatched them from Matthew's hands. "What would you like me to comment on?" She flipped through the pages filled with blueprints and calculations.

"Anything. Any idea or suggestion for improvement is welcome. For example..." He selected the blueprint of a spherical contraption. "This is the model of a centrifuge machine similar to the one Prandtl patented in 1864, but on a smaller scale for medical uses." He clicked his tongue. "There's something wrong with the design, but I can't decide what. I have a prototype that doesn't work. I had to put it aside to focus on bigger projects, and now I'm at a dead end."

She trapped her bottom lip between her teeth. She wasn't an expert in understanding blueprints, but the challenge tickled her. "I'll study it. Thank you."

Brandon peeked from over her shoulder. "I wouldn't know where to start."

"That's why I have something for you." Matthew gave him a copy of *Ars Mechanica*— Mechanical Art. "It's time you learn something about the projects you support and your wife's passion. Arse Mechanical." He sniggered.

Emily and Brandon laughed, but Cowley's mouth formed a flat line.

"Now, now, Mr. Tyrell," Cowley said. "You're being silly in front of the earl and the countess."

"It'd be good for you to laugh now and then. There's scientific evidence that laughter makes you feel better and prolongs your life." Matthew clapped the older man's shoulder.

Cowley didn't smile. "I believe you wished to discuss something important with his lordship."

"Right-o! Goodness, Cowley, you're as cheerful as a graveyard in winter at midnight." Matthew tilted his head towards Brandon. "We must talk about Lady Robinson. We should discuss it in private, perhaps." He shot a fleeting glance at Emily.

"Right now?" Brandon put two fingers on his temples.

"You promised," Matthew said.

Emily raised her gaze from the blueprint. "Is she causing trouble because of me?"

"Let's have a private chat, shall we?" Matthew started to stand up, but Brandon waved him down.

"No need for privacy." He touched her hand. "Emily is my wife. Everything we need to discuss involves her as well."

Emily wanted to kiss him for his trust and loyalty. Not that she wouldn't have minded if he'd decided to speak with Matthew privately. But she appreciated his attention to her.

Matthew leaned back. "As you wish. Lady Robinson was kind enough to remind us that the date for submitting our prototype for approval is approaching and urged us to make a decision. Or rather, she wants *you* to agree to her terms."

"Which are?" Emily asked.

The air tensed in an instant. Brandon shifted on the seat. Cowley stared at the floor, and Matthew chewed a corner of his mouth.

She gazed around, wondering what the problem was. "What is it?"

"You wanted this, mate." Matthew spread his hands. "Your turn."

Cowley didn't say anything but cleared his throat politely.

Brandon scrubbed the back of his head. "Lady Robinson would like to have... an intimate rendezvous with me."

"A fumble," Matthew said unhelpfully. "A dirty, dirty fumble. For one night only," he hurried to add as if that made things better.

She lowered the document and straightened. An unfamiliar flare of sheer, undiluted fury burned in her chest. She hadn't been that angry when Lady Robinson had dismissed her after the interview. She hadn't been that angry when she'd learned about Aunt Rose's scheme. But now she wanted to slap the woman and yell at her that Brandon wasn't hers.

"An intimate rendezvous? Really. And what did you say?" Her voice sounded dangerously low to her own ears.

Brandon shook his head eagerly. "Absolutely out of the question. I refused. That's why she became vindictive. I'm a gentleman, and she isn't—"

"A lady?" she said.

He hesitated. "I was about to say she isn't my type of woman, but I guess your assessment is correct."

Emily exhaled through clenched teeth. The nerve of that woman. "What solution do you propose then?"

"My idea is to unleash Cowley—" Matthew said.

"I'm not a dog," Cowley gritted out.

"Brandon says you're a bloodhound."

"Master can say what he wants."

Matthew ignored him. "And let Cowley find something dirty about Lady Robinson so we can blackmail her."

"I won't stoop to her level." Brandon scoffed.

Matthew exhaled. "I'd be flattered if she offered me a night of passion."

"Why, would you like to spend a night with Lady Robinson?" Emily asked him.

Cowley dabbed his forehead with a handkerchief, muttering something about inappropriate conversations and explicit terms.

Matthew shrugged. "I wouldn't mind. She's beautiful, and it would be for a good cause. Besides, she isn't in love with her husband, and everyone knows he has a mistress. I'm ready to sacrifice myself for the success of our work." He pressed his fist to his chest over his heart. It didn't sound like a sacrifice at all.

Emily squeezed her lips together as the thought of Lady Robinson lusting after *her* husband bothered her. "Well, you should just ask her then."

"Ask what?" Matthew said.

"If she's happy to accept your *sacrifice*." She returned her attention to the blueprint and the measurements of the different parts. "See what happens. Without blackmail or lies. Simply negotiate the deal with a counteroffer. She might agree."

Matthew scratched his chin. "But she wants Brandon."

"But he doesn't want her, and she can't have him!" Her voice rose, thundering in the confined space of the compartment. And her fear of the train? Gone. Perhaps anger was better than distractions.

Matthew held up his hand. "Fine. I'll ask her." He sounded like he agreed only to shut her up.

"Good. Then we won't talk about Lady Robinson until you see her." She lifted her chin.

Brandon caressed her hand. "You have no reason to worry."

"I know. I'm not worried. I'm outraged." She lowered the darn document again. "But what would you do if the situation were reversed?"

His green eyes darkened in a moment. "I'd chase off whoever dared to make such a proposal to you."

She shouldn't be so thrilled to hear the possessive note in his voice, but she was. "Good." And she hadn't thought about her fear. Jealousy seemed to be a good antidote, too.

Matthew hid himself behind a book, and Cowley chose the newspaper.

She didn't know how long had passed, but focusing on the project absorbed her so completely she barely heard the noises of the train. Chatting with Matthew about the cogs and gears of the device was almost as good as being kissed and touched by Brandon. Almost. Still, her heart skipped a beat when Abbots Ripton station approached. The world seemed to slow down to a crawl as visions of her last moments with her parents flew across her mind. Her parents had died here. Had they suffered? Had it been a swift death? Her whole life had changed in that place. So many lives destroyed. So much pain.

Matthew whispered, "My papa died here." His face tightened.

His father had been one of the machinists of the Flying Scotsman that night. Poor Matthew.

Brandon held her hand as the Flying Scotsman rushed past the small country station in a matter of seconds like it didn't matter. It was odd that no trace of the tragedy was left. It was if it had never happened. She guessed the damage was inside her, Brandon, and even Matthew who didn't say anything else. He hunched his shoulders and hung his head as if waiting to leave Abbots Ripton behind and never speak of it again.

She could relate. She'd allowed her fear to rule her for too long when she should have left it behind. Her parents wouldn't want her to suffer. She would make them proud. They'd given her the means to lead a new life, and she had every intention of taking advantage of that.

Brandon kept holding her hand for the rest of the journey, and she didn't let her anxiety surge.

twenty

USING A TINY screwdriver was a study in frustration for Emily.

She could work with larger screws without problems, but the prototype of the small centrifuge required a finesse of movements she hadn't mastered yet. In all her years of tinkering, she hadn't repaired small devices like this one. Goodness, only a child would employ such a small screwdriver with success.

Scoffing, she dropped the uncooperative tool and folded her arms over her chest. She'd been fiddling with the darn device for a few days, since they'd returned from Edinburgh, but she hadn't managed to implement all the ideas she had because of the slowness of her work, and because she wasn't sure why the device didn't work. With nothing else to do, thanks to her aunt's possible threat, she had plenty of time to work on the centrifuge and get bothered.

Brandon entered the workroom, carrying a bundle of letters and his copy of *Ars Mechanica*. He'd taken the reading seriously. "How are you doing? Bored to be home all the time?"

"It's not boredom that worries me, but these tiny cogs." She shoved the screwdriver away. "It's taking me forever."

He rubbed her hand. "You need to rest your muscles. You can't stress them for hours on end. It won't work. I know from experience." His touch made her breathe a little faster.

"And you? Are you bored of being home all the time?" she asked.

"Not bored, but work is accumulating. I need to go to the House of Lords and check on my tenants. Poor Cowley is acting as my lackey, running around London. He's getting tired." He dropped the letters and the book on her worktable. "No message from your aunt or Mr. Payne, for that matter. The transfer of your inheritance is complete, but Mrs. Allen and her solicitor remain silent. I don't know if it's a good thing."

"Did you finish writing our demand?"

"Yes. Finished and filed. Your aunt should receive it today." He sighed. "And then we'll see. If she refuses to sign the document of renunciation, we'll have to drag her to court."

She grimaced. "Not an exciting option."

"Speaking of exciting options." He raised an eyebrow and pointed a finger at *Ars Mechanica*. "Is that the type of reading you're interested in?"

"Absolutely. It's fascinating. Why?"

He flipped through the pages of the heavy tome. "I found it rather... inappropriate."

"Inappropriate? Physics?"

"I'll show you." He locked the door, which intrigued her.

"What is it?"

He cleared his throat and started reading. "Chapter thirteen, *The Strength of a Piston*." He paused as if expecting a reaction from her, but she shrugged. "Where's that passage? Oh, here. *To slide the piston, especially a large and thick one, into a closely fitting tube, ample lubrication is recommended.*" He gave her another pointed look.

She giggled. "It's not... oh, you scoundrel."

He continued. "*The staff will move in and out of the tight channel in order to produce enough friction to ignite a loud, piercing sound when the temperature rises, and the steam..."*

"Oh, shush!" Laughing, she put her hand on his mouth to shut him up. "Rascal."

He kissed her hand before removing it. "Is this the type of reading engineers enjoy? I shouldn't have studied law."

She laughed. "You ruined it for me. I read that book twice and never, ever thought about those terms in that fashion. I'll never be able to read it again without thinking..."

"About what?" He took her hand again and kissed it.

"About you doing wicked things," she whispered.

He had an air of hurt innocence. "Me? Wicked? I don't think so."

"You are wicked."

He held her by the waist. "I'm wicked only for you." He sat her on top of the worktable, causing the screws and bolts to clang.

"I'm glad of that because I don't want you to be wicked with anyone but me." A little aggressive tone came out of her, and she wasn't going to apologise for that. "Especially with Lady Robinson."

"Forget about her." He nestled between her legs, bunching up her skirts. "I like it when you're jealous."

"Good." She locked her legs over his rear and dragged him closer. "Because I'm possessive."

"What a coincidence! So am I. Another thing we have in common."

"Kiss me."

He took possession of her mouth with a deep kiss that meant business. She moaned into it, running her hands over his thick arms and broad shoulders. The intense kiss didn't distract her from his hands quickly unbuttoning her dress. He'd become an expert at undressing her. Sometimes, he caught her by surprise while she worked and removed her dress before she could kiss him. She wasn't complaining; it was just an observation.

She gasped when he cupped her naked breasts and pinched her nipples hard. Her toes curled from the pleasure. He could be a little rough, and she loved it. A groan rasped out of him as he caressed her breasts.

He closed his hot mouth around her nipple and sucked hard while tweaking the other. A fire spread through her as wetness pooled between her thighs. The need shuddering through her was overwhelming. She didn't need to beg him though. He could read her mind.

Lifting his head to devour her mouth again, he undid his trousers and slid inside her with one smooth thrust. She closed her eyes, wanting to fully feel it. His shaft never failed to send a shot of energy through her, filling and stretching her to the limit. Oh, yes. His piston fit tightly into her channel and thrust in and out with long, hard shoves. No hesitation or shyness.

He became wild when they made love. His hair turned dishevelled, and a feral light filled his eyes as he stared at her with an intensity that made her shudder with longing.

"I love you," he said through gritted teeth, almost growling, while beating a punishing rhythm in and out of her.

The way he said that made her take a deep breath. Those words weren't something he said lightly. They were a solemn vow that reached her soul and didn't let it go. It was his vow to her.

She kissed him, matching his possessiveness and urging him faster. "I love you."

Their breaths mingled, and their skin touched as he mercilessly pounded inside her, and she wouldn't want it to be any different. She needed his raw passion, and he gave her exactly that. When he was alone with her like now, he had nothing of the quiet, shy earl people knew. He was a wild demon that did everything to please her.

They found their releases together. She muffled her scream, burying her face in his chest, right over his heart. But he wasn't finished. He shoved aside her skirts out of his way and pushed her legs wider apart, none-too-gently. Another gasp tore out of her when he dipped his head to dig his tongue deep inside her. Blazes. She arched her back and reclined her head as he used his lips, tongue, and fingers to pleasure her. But she'd just found her release. Surely, she couldn't have a second one so quickly, and—no, she was wrong. Energy built up from her nub, which he tormented with his tongue, and jolted through her. This time, she didn't bother muffling her scream and let it all out.

It was a good thing she was sitting on the table because her whole body went limp, boneless, wilting. Her muscles slackened. She wasn't made of flesh anymore but of pleasure.

He caught her in his arms, scattering kisses on her neck. "My wife." He roared at the word *my*.

She sagged against him. It didn't matter what Aunt Rose would do. She could unleash every legal trick she had up her sleeve. Brandon and Emily might lose everything, but she'd face a thousand threats next to him.

twenty-one

BRANDON'S PULSE RACED, but he refused to give up. He wouldn't.

"You're so brave," Emily said from behind him.

Every instinct told him to desist, but no, here he was, feeding Diablo thin slices of apple while trying to befriend the proud horse. So far, his attempts had been unsuccessful. Diablo had tried to kick Brandon with his hooves and had snapped his jaw at him. If anything, Brandon had become quick at avoiding the horse's blows.

The stallion looked at him with suspicion, flaring his nostrils in warning. Emily had told him that was normal, but he begged to differ. Besides, Diablo stomped his heavy, very dangerous hoof on the ground, and Brandon knew what that meant.

He lowered his stretched-out arm. "I'm not sure I should keep trying."

She waved him in. "Of course, you should. Go on. The key to conquering a horse's heart is to be natural and relaxed."

Natural and relaxed his arse. "Please mate. I want to be your friend."

"You're doing great!" Her smile was too-cheerful.

Diablo's nostrils flared again, and a deep frown appeared between his obsidian eyes. He stepped sideways as if searching for the right trajectory to ram his head against Brandon's chest. And Brandon had had enough.

He stepped back. "It's not working."

"Nonsense." Emily narrowed her gaze. "Didn't we agree to face our fears? I travelled on the Flying Scotsman twice. It's your turn."

He tossed the apple slices into the feeding bag of the stallion. Diablo didn't spare them the slightest bit of attention, adding insult to injury.

"I was talking metaphorically, like fear of the unknown or something similar, something that doesn't actually require risking my fingers. I didn't mean this one, specific horse."

"You're overreacting. If you stop being so nervous, Diablo will adore you." She gripped the lapels of his shirt and pulled him down for a kiss.

"I seriously doubt that." He cupped her face and paused as the housekeeper ran towards them.

Her apron flapped around. "My lord!"

He held Emily more tightly. "What's the matter?"

Mrs. Reid came to a grinding halt in front of him, breathing heavily. "Mr. Cowley. I received a message from a lad sent by the Grey Coat Hospital. Mr. Cowley had a serious accident. He's gravely injured. The doctors don't believe he's going to survive."

All the blood drained from Brandon's head. Not Cowley. He was the closest thing to a father he had. "Where's Matthew?"

Mrs. Reid shook her head. "I don't know, sir."

For a long moment, the shock petrified him. He remained rooted to the spot, his thoughts scattering. Even Diablo must have sensed the tension because he snorted.

"Brandon." Emily tugged at Brandon's hand.

"I must go." He strode towards the house. "I must be next to him." He panted.

"I'm coming with you." Emily hurried to keep up with Brandon's strides. "But what if something happens to you?"

"So what? Cowley needs me." He snatched his coat and ordered his landau ready.

The trip in the open landau was torture. It reminded him of a similar trip, when a constable had told him his father had collapsed in the House of Lords. He hadn't arrived in time to give him a last goodbye. And now Cowley.

"I shouldn't have let him take on all those responsibilities," he said, rubbing his face. "He hasn't stopped working in days."

"It's not your fault, and we don't know what happened yet."

Between the busy roads and his worry, it seemed it took forever to reach the hospital. London welcomed them with its smell of coal and boisterous crowd, chaos, and traffic. Emily held his hand, and he shamelessly clung to her strength. She was his anchor. A bitter taste burned the back of his mouth as anxiety coiled in his abdomen. He should have known that something bad would happen. He'd been carefree for so long that this moment of sheer dread deleted all his recent moments of joy. No, that was unfair to Emily. He'd be forever grateful for her presence, but his premonition after his wedding had been correct. There was no joy for him without losing something.

As soon as the coachman pulled over at the kerb, Brandon jumped out of the landau. The icy gusts from the Thames chilled him, and his legs grew stiff, but he didn't care. He helped Emily out and headed towards the hospital's gate. The closer he went, the faster his pulse thudded in his ears. They hurried towards the reception area, rushing past sobbing people and white-coated doctors.

"Mr. Cowley," he said to the nurse behind the desk. "Where is he?"

She opened her mouth, but a man in a white coat cut her off.

"Lord Astley?" the man asked, moving closer. "Mr. Cowley—"

"Yes. Where is he? How's faring?" He searched around, expecting to see the older man smiling stiffly at him.

The doctor pointed to the other side of the hall. "Follow me."

He did as told, clenching Emily's hand. The man led them along a wide corridor lined with doors, and down a flight of stairs. It looked like an unused, old wing of the hospital.

Emily exchanged a glance with him. He didn't know what to say. Perhaps Cowley was in a special wing of the hospital.

The doctor entered a sort of storeroom. Debris littered the floor, and the sounds of a heavy machine came muffled from the upper floor. Lord, were they going to the morgue? Had Cowley died? Brandon's sight darkened at the edges at the thought of losing his closest friend.

Not Cowley. Please.

"Where are you taking us?" Emily came to an abrupt stop at the landing, causing him to stop as well. "I refuse to take another step until you tell us where Cowley is."

Her sharp and annoyed tone brought Brandon back to reality. He rubbed his aching brow. She was right. There was something wrong with the medic and the room.

"Cowley isn't here." The doctor cracked his knuckles, advancing towards them.

Brandon shielded Emily from the man. "What do you want?"

"Nothing personal, mate. Only business." The man threw a punch at Brandon's stomach. It was so quick he had barely time to shove Emily out of the way.

She staggered back and hit the brick wall behind her. The pain stunned him for a moment, but he was used to feeling pain. No surprise.

He pushed the pain down and raised his fists. "Emily, run!" He couldn't see if she was doing as told because the man lunged again.

"We have money," Emily said. "Take it and leave us alone!"

"Run!" Brandon repeated.

The thug aimed his meaty fist at Brandon's nose. "I don't want your money."

Brandon parried the blow and returned the favour. But the man did quick footwork and stepped behind him.

Oh, no. The man wanted to hurt Emily. She screamed for help.

"Emily!" Brandon spun, but the thug shadowed his moves and deliberately smashed his fist against Brandon's lower back. Once. Twice. Thrice.

Instant, excruciating agony. Brandon could deal with pain but not with *that* type of pain. He cried out, involuntarily freezing as his muscles locked in reaction to the blows. His knees buckled, and he ended up kneeling on the dirty floor. Another blow brought tears to his eyes. He lost count of how many times the man punched the small of his back.

The pain was so intense Brandon couldn't breathe, see, or hear. Dark blotches danced in front of him, and a buzzing noise filled his ears. Another blow had him nearly pass out. He caught a glimpse of Emily flinging herself to the thug, but he didn't have the energy to yell at her to leave.

She screamed for help again. Her scream was so loud it cut through the buzzing in his ears. The thug raised a hand to strike her, and a sudden flare of strength roared inside Brandon.

"Don't touch my wife!" He stood up and tackled the man, bringing him down with the force of his wrath.

Ignoring the pain flaming throughout his body, he rained punches on the man's face. Somewhere in a corner of his mind, he realised he should stop and take Emily away, but a rage like no other roared in his chest. How dare this thug threaten Emily? Brandon didn't feel the small of his back or his legs anymore, but he didn't stop punching the man. The thug shoved him hard. Brandon fell over, hurting himself again as the attacker ran away, staggering.

Emily crouched next to Brandon, her face scrunched up with

fear. "Darling. Brandon. How are you?" She caressed his hair. Soot dirtied her nose, and her curls were in disarray.

He gritted his teeth, groaning. If he waited for the pain to pass, they'd stay there the whole day.

"You must go." Each word rasped in his throat. "Leave. He might return."

"I'm not leaving you." She gently slid an arm under his. "I know you're in pain, but we must go. I'll help you."

"No, leave!" He swatted her hand away because he would only slow her down.

"Brandon, stop this instant! I'm not leaving you here. You'd be vulnerable and in danger. So help me help you. We must return upstairs."

Tears welling in his eyes, he picked himself up, leaning against her. Each intake of air was a chore. Each exhale reduced him to tears. The only good thing about the situation was that she wasn't hurt.

"You're doing great," Emily said, her voice cracking. "You can lean harder on me. Don't worry."

He couldn't reply. Dragging his feet forwards required all his energy. They slogged up the stairs one step at a time. He gripped the bannister and forced his feet up. Hot tears streamed down his cheeks. He couldn't stop them. The pain consumed him to the point he wanted to throw up.

"I know, love. I know." Emily's voice broke with a sob. "You're doing beautifully."

Tremors shuddered through his body as he pushed himself forwards. He wanted to cast up his accounts, or better yet, to pass out.

When they arrived at the landing, Brandon stopped and leaned against a wall to catch his breath. "So... painful," he said through clenched teeth. His knuckles were red and swollen from the punches he'd thrown. "I'm dizzy."

"I know." Her hand trembled when she brushed a strand of hair from his face.

"Are you hurt?" The words struggled to come out of him.

"I'm fine."

After a breather, they resumed their slow march back up. He wheezed and felt queasy by the time they reached the hallway. Maybe it was the pain, but the smells and sounds hurt his senses.

Emily waved at a passing nurse. "Help! Please help. My husband is injured."

The nurse shouted something he didn't understand before rushing towards them with a doctor. People gathered around him. Anonymous arms helped him up. He could hardly keep his head up.

"What happened?" the doctor asked.

Brandon grimaced when a man and a nurse supported him fully.

"Someone attacked us," Emily said. "My husband has problems with his back from a previous injury. Please help him." Tears glistened in her eyes as Brandon was laid on a stretcher.

Hell, his head spun. The whole room tilted. The pain was worse than after the accident. His legs remained numb and stiff. He couldn't bend them. Emily explained to the doctor about his back injury, but he couldn't answer any of the questions the doctor asked him.

"This way." The nurse led them to a room with blinding white walls. The air was thick with the smell of carbolic acid. "We'll examine you immediately."

"Brandon." Emily caressed his hair with a gentle hand as if she worried he might break, which could be possible.

He gathered his energy to speak. If the attack had been planned and he'd fallen into a trap, then Cowley might be well and fine. "Ho-home," he whispered. "Home."

She leaned closer. "Do you want to go home?"

He gave the slightest shake of his head. "Cowley." His chest hurt from the effort of talking.

Emily raised her eyebrows to her hairline. "You're right. I'll check if Cowley is fine. I'll let you know immediately." She ran out of the room, almost bumping into a white-coated medic.

"Lord Astley?" someone said.

The face of the doctor filled his vision, and that was the last thing he saw before passing out.

twenty-two

FAINTING HAD BEEN the best part of Brandon's day. No pain. No nausea. No head spinning. The pain had returned after the doctor had revived him and applied ice bags to his back. Aside from applying ice and a numbing cream, there wasn't much the doctor could do. Brandon wanted to go home, especially after Emily brought him the welcome news that Cowley was at home, safe and sound, with Matthew.

The trip home seemed to take longer than usual. Unable to sit, Brandon lay on his stomach on the seat while Emily gently rubbed his back. He rested his head on her lap, glad she couldn't see his face contorted with pain.

They hadn't talked since the attack, and he was grateful for that because he didn't have the energy to talk. Her hand trembled though. He hated to see her scared and distraught.

"Lean against me," Emily said when the landau rolled to a stop.

He did as told, gritting his teeth and swallowing his tears.

Cowley's sharp intake of air was the first thing Brandon heard upon arriving home. "Master."

He lifted his gaze, and a wave of relief washed through him at the sight of his oldest friend. Another reason to be glad. A tight smile was the only thing he could manage.

"Hell, mate." Matthew's concerned face swept into view in the hallway. He relieved Emily of Brandon's weight by holding him up. "Cowley, help me, please."

Brandon had to gnash his teeth as Matthew and Cowley almost carried him inside to a guest room on the ground floor to avoid taking the stairs.

"Careful, please." Emily's voice broke with a sob.

He sighed when he touched the soft pillow and bedsheets in the single bed. Emily fussed around him, covering him and checking to see if the stove was hot enough. He didn't miss her wiping her eyes.

"Master." Ashen and agitated, Cowley sagged onto a chair next to the bed. "I'm so sorry."

Brandon waved a hand to say Cowley shouldn't worry.

Cowley dabbed his forehead with a handkerchief. "I was with Mrs. Allen when the attack occurred."

"What?" Emily said at the same time as Matthew said, "She must have sent the thug."

Emily nodded. "I agree. The man hit Brandon's back deliberately. He knew where to strike to cause the most devastating damage."

"I was discussing the absolute necessity of signing the renunciation contract with Mrs. Allen." Cowley's voice sounded lower than usual. His face was paler than ever. "She refused, but I wondered why her answers were so meandering. She talked a lot about random subjects, her financial problems, her daughter's struggles in society, and even offered me tea. I should have known it was a ruse to keep me busy."

"Miss Catherine also kept me busy," Matthew said. "I met her on my way to work. She stopped me and asked me to walk her home. How stupid of me to say yes. I thought she wanted to tell me something about her mother's awful behaviour."

Brandon swallowed hard to clear his dry throat. "I'm glad both of you are fine."

"Master." Cowley's eyes reddened. He clamped a hand over his mouth.

"What a hag," Matthew said.

"Hag is a too-nice word for my aunt." Emily carried a bowl filled with ice.

"I've called your physician," Matthew said. "He should be here shortly."

Sweat glistened on Brandon's forehead as Emily lifted his shirt. A collective gasp sounded around him.

"Bloody hell," Matthew said, running a hand through his hair.

The fact that Cowley didn't scold Matthew was a testament to how shocked the secretary was.

"How bad?" Brandon asked.

"Brandon." She drew in a shaky breath. "Your back is swollen and purple."

He squeezed his eyes shut and didn't reply. Yes, the pain hinted at that description.

She applied a bag of ice to the back, and he grimaced at the shock from the cold. "You can feel your toes, can't you?"

Matthew removed Brandon's boots and socks. "Can you wiggle them?"

The ice brought some degree of relief. If anything, it numbed the flesh but froze him, only to give him a wave of a different type of pain when the blood circulated again. He focused on his legs and moved his toes, ignoring the stabs to his legs and back muscles.

"Good." Matthew covered him with the quilt. "That Allen woman will pay for this. Mark my words."

"I think Master would be more interested in Mrs. Allen signing the renunciation contract," Cowley said. "So Lady Emily will be free to do what she wishes with her parents' legacy without further interference."

"Yes," Brandon said. "Once she signs, Mrs. Allen will be out of our lives."

Emily stroked his hair. "Darling, I'm sorry. This happened because I left my aunt."

"Don't. Just don't." The last thing he wanted was her blaming herself. He tensed when the doorbell rang.

"It must be the physician." Matthew left the room and returned with a man Brandon had never seen.

The man removed his bowler hat. "Lord Astley, Lady Astley, I'm Dr. Stewart."

"Where's Dr. Hopewell?" she asked.

"On a holiday in the Continent. He left me instructions to take care of his practice while he's away. Do not worry, my lady. When he returns, I'm sure he'll want to visit his lordship himself." Dr. Stewart put his bag on the nightstand. "Let me examine the injury. Would the others please clear the room?"

Matthew scowled but obeyed, eyeing the doctor with suspicion. Cowley left on trembling legs, likely in need of a physician himself.

"I'm staying." Emily gripped Brandon's hand.

"As you wish, my lady." Dr. Stewart pushed up his glasses and bent over Brandon to examine his back.

Brandon's muscles contracted painfully, even though Dr. Stewart probed him with light fingers. He clenched a fist over the pillow, sweat dampening his neck.

"Nothing is broken." Dr. Stewart rummaged through his bag. "His lordship needs something to reduce the pain, of course, and a cream that will help with the swelling."

"Not laudanum," Brandon said, breathing heavily. "No opium or morphia."

The doctor stopped rummaging. "We don't have many options left, my lord." He scratched his goatee.

"There must be something else," Emily said, covering Brandon.

Dr. Stewart produced a glass bottle from his bag. "I have a valerian tincture that might help. It's not as powerful as morphia, but then again, nothing is."

Brandon gave a quick nod. He'd rather endure the pain than touch opioids again. If he did, he'd never get rid of them. He didn't pay attention to the rest of the conversation as Emily and Dr. Stewart talked about what Brandon needed to eat and do for a speedy recovery.

"I'm sure you'll feel better soon." The doctor put his hat on before leaving the room without a last glance at him.

Emily sat next to Brandon, caressing his matted hair. "They attacked you because of our wedding."

He closed his fingers around hers, but he lacked the strength to hold her hand properly. "Then I would endure this pain ten times over to marry you." His voice sounded broken to his own ears.

She kissed him. "I'll give you the valerian tincture immediately. Maybe you'll be able to rest."

He swallowed a couple of teaspoons of the potion without complaining. The sugary taste was too intense for his liking, but he'd try anything to feel better. "Thank you."

Emily stroked his hair gently, and finally, darkness claimed him again.

EMILY WASN'T sure she deserved Brandon's gratitude. If she'd tried to understand how her inheritance worked, if she'd asked more questions, her aunt wouldn't have dared to steal a penny. She shouldn't have involved Brandon. But no, she'd worked like a maid in her aunt's house, without doubting her aunt's claims that her parents hadn't left her much, without thinking.

She'd been focused on her own problems and neglected her parents' last wish. Aunt Rose had told her that she'd spent the meagre savings of her parents to feed and clothe her, and Emily had believed her. Grief wasn't an excuse for her lack of sense.

She stared at her husband. Even in his sleep, his face was contorted in pain.

When Brandon's breathing became soft and regular, she covered him and tiptoed out of the room. Matthew's and Cowley's voices came from the sitting room, and she headed there. They showed matching concerned expressions and too-large eyes.

Matthew poured her a cup of tea. "How is he faring?"

She closed her hands around the warm cup. "He must be in great pain, but he doesn't want to show it."

"He's always been like that." Matthew rubbed his forehead.

Cowley sat with his shoulders hunched. "I should have understood the conversation with Mrs. Allen was a decoy. I should have followed my instinct."

Emily patted his arm. "It's not your fault."

He gave a warm smile. "My lady."

"I don't understand what Mrs. Allen wishes to accomplish," Matthew said, scratching his stubble. "She hurt Brandon, not killed him. And then? It's awful, but Brandon will recover. Why didn't the thug stab or shoot Brandon? He had the opportunity and plenty of time."

Emily winced. The thought of Brandon being stabbed or shot made her shiver. "Please don't say that. Perhaps this was only a warning, and Brandon fought valiantly, scaring the man away when he tried to punch me. Maybe that disrupted the thug's plan."

Both Matthew and Cowley hissed at the mention of Emily almost being punched.

"The worst thing," Matthew said, "is that we don't have a shred of evidence that your aunt is behind the attack. If we had, I would drag her to the police station myself."

Cowley shook his head. "The culprit is certainly Mrs. Allen.

The timing of the request for her odd meeting was too convenient, but yes, we don't have any concrete proof."

"I don't understand my aunt's plan either," Emily said. "But I'll make sure to contact our solicitor and exclude my aunt from any chance of inheriting my money."

"Good point, my lady. I'll do it myself immediately." Cowley sprang up, straightening his jacket. "If you'll excuse me, my lady." He bowed but didn't wait for Emily's word to be dismissed. Not that she cared. Poor Cowley likely wanted to do something, anything, to help Brandon.

Matthew leaned back in the armchair, rubbing his eyes. "We must find a way to force your aunt to sign the damn renunciation contract, and pardon my language."

"Consider it pardoned."

He thumped the armrest. "Brandon might be a gentleman, but I'm not above blackmailing people to keep him safe. Does your aunt have any dirty secrets we might use to our advantage? Your cousin? Nothing dirty?"

Emily shrugged. "I can't think of anything that would force Aunt Rose to do what we want. She's worked hard all her life to keep Catherine fed and happy. My father helped her, but I guess she resented him, and their relationship became strained after my father married my mother. Maybe Aunt Rose wanted more money from him." She sighed. "I'm sorry. My father never spoke ill of her, and if there was something he knew about her, he never mentioned it."

"We have to work with what we have," he muttered, his gaze lost to the flames in the hearth. "Hell, I'll fabricate a scandal if I have to."

Hours ago, Emily would have been horrified by such a proposition. Not anymore. Watching her husband broken and writhing in pain had shocked her to a reality where she either attacked or was attacked. Aunt Rose didn't deserve Emily's sympathy. Too many times, she'd underestimated her aunt. Never again.

They remained in silence until quick footfalls echoed from the hallway.

"Madam!" The maid's voice came from the door that was flung open, revealing a furious Lady Robinson.

"You!" Lady Robinson said, pointing a finger at Emily.

Matthew stood up, nearly knocking off the low table. "What's the meaning of this?"

Lady Robinson stopped in the middle of the room. "Lord Astley ignored my messages while I heard some disturbing rumours about him. Thus I'm here to see him immediately. Where is he?"

Emily rose as well. "What disturbing rumours?"

Lady Robinson huffed. "Some nonsense about him having had a red-hot wedding in Gretna Green."

"It was Edinburgh, and it's not nonsense." She jutted out her chin. "Brandon and I are married."

Lady Robinson's cheeks reddened so quickly Emily worried the lady's nose might start bleeding.

"I must see him. Where is he?" Lady Robinson gazed around as if expecting Brandon to be hidden behind the curtains or under the table.

"Madam," Matthew said in a calm tone Emily didn't approve of. "Brandon is currently indisposed."

"What do you mean by that? How can he be married and indisposed at the same time?" The lady stomped a foot on the floor like a petulant child, and Emily had no patience for a tantrum that day.

"He was attacked." Emily raised her voice not to show her fears. "We returned from Edinburgh a few days ago, and the moment we left the house, someone brutally beat him. He's asleep now. In pain."

Lady Robinson tossed her a sceptical look. "How convenient. I don't believe you."

"How dare you?" Matthew hissed. "Lady Astley isn't lying."

"Let me see him, then." Lady Robinson didn't flinch. "If he's really unwell, I won't disturb him. You have my word."

"Not that your word is worth much, but follow me." Emily marched out of the room but slowed her pace close to Brandon's bedroom. She inched the door open and walked in.

Pale and with dark circles around his eyes, Brandon breathed softly, sleeping on his belly. The smell of the cream Dr. Steward had left thickened the air. No one looking at Brandon could believe he wasn't sick.

Lady Robinson took a few tentative steps inside and gasped upon seeing Brandon. "Lord," she whispered.

"Out," Emily mouthed, waving Lady Robinson away. She waited for the lady to leave the room before shutting the door. "Happy?" She clamped a hand over her mouth as a sob threatened to come out. "I wasn't lying. He's in great pain and needs rest. Whatever argument you have with him, you will have to wait."

Lady Robinson's features softened. She fiddled with her reticule. "I'm sorry. Goodness me, he's so pale. Why would anyone do that to dear Brandon?"

Anger caused Emily to shake. "My aunt." Why lie? In fact, the more people knew who her aunt really was, the better. "She wants my inheritance and Brandon's money as well. If something happens to Brandon, now that we're married, my aunt will get everything."

Lady Robinson paled and tottered on her feet as if about to faint. If she did, Emily wouldn't stop her fall. "Your aunt is Mrs. Allen, isn't she?"

"Yes, why?"

"I had a conversation with your aunt last week."

"About what?" Emily balled her fists on her hips, preparing for more bad news.

The lady chewed her bottom lip. "Mrs. Allen asked me a lot of questions about Brandon. I thought her interest came from the fact he was obviously smitten with you, so well..." She gazed everywhere but at Emily. "I told her some nasty things I knew about Brandon to make her agree that he should stay away from you. I just wanted to... I'm sorry."

Heavens. Emily wanted to slap her. "What nasty things?"

"Bloody hell," Matthew whispered.

Lady Robinson shifted her weight. "His addiction to laudanum to start with. The fact he kept it secret for years. That sort of thing."

"How do you know about the laudanum?" Matthew asked.

Lady Robinson waved a hand. "My brother had the same problem as Lord Astley, and well, London has only a few opium dens. People who attend those places know each other. And all those scratches on Lord Astley's arms were clear enough."

"Scratches?" Emily asked.

Lady Robinson flushed. "Laudanum causes chronic itching. People who abuse it can't stop scratching themselves, leaving red and often bleeding marks on their skin."

"Great." Matthew threw a hand up. "Congratulations, Lady R. You ruined one of the best men in all the empire for your own purposes. I hope it was worth it."

Emily leaned against the wall, needing support. She didn't know how her aunt would use that information about Brandon's addiction, but it couldn't be good.

Lady Robinson joined her hands as if in prayer. "I've never meant for any of this to happen. I have never wanted to hurt anyone."

"You blackmailed Brandon by withholding those stupid papers!" Emily scoffed. "Doesn't that mean hurting people?"

Lady Robinson held up her hands in a pacifying gesture Emily didn't care about. "I didn't want to cause him physical pain. Is there anything I can do to make amends?"

"Yes!" Emily hissed and folded her arms over her chest. "Now that you mention it."

twenty-three

SHEER, PURE BLISS.
Finally, the pain disappeared from Brandon's back. Not a trace remained, and it wasn't only the pain that had vanished. He felt weightless, relaxed, and at peace. His body didn't exist. All the little aches that usually tormented him were gone. Vanished. *Poof.*

He blinked his eyes open. An oil lamp and a few candles shed a warm glow in the small room. Emily slept in a cot next to the bed. She frowned even in her sleep as if trying to solve a riddle. He wouldn't wake her up. She needed to rest.

He stretched out in the bed, mentally thanking the doctor for the miraculous potion. The bottle of valerian tincture sat on the nightstand, gleaming invitingly in the candlelight. Instant craving. Surely, it wouldn't hurt if he took another dose or two.

His fingers itched to reach out for it and get him drowned in it because the pain was crawling back to life. His skin tingled with the sensation of thousands piercing of needles. Even the bedsheet chafed his skin hard enough to cause him to wince. His throat tightened as the pain slowly conquered his body again.

Sod it. He'd take the tincture and be done with the pain in a moment. Excitement ignited as he reached out for the magical potion that would make him better. He hadn't experienced such a wonderful sensation since— his next breath scratched his throat raw. It couldn't be.

But it was the only possible explanation. The realisation sent his heart into a frenzy and froze his body. His fingertips were an inch away from the solution to all his problems. Except the promise of bliss was an illusion. For the potion didn't offer any solutions. Only more problems.

There was only one thing so powerfully addictive and blissfully effective against the pain, but he'd explicitly asked not to have laudanum or any other opioids. Still, the call of this particular siren was too familiar.

Had the doctor made a mistake? Panic set in his stomach like a punch. Not again. He couldn't and wouldn't go down that path again. It was a slippery slope. One step, and he would roll down to the bottom. Rolling down was the easy part. Climbing back up wasn't. He would never, ever put Emily on the gruesome path of his addiction.

He knew what he had to do. Get rid of the evil thing before his resolve wavered and he became a slave again. He propped himself up on his forearms, groaning as his body throbbed without mercy. He knocked the pitcher off the nightstand in his clumsy attempt to get rid of the bottle. Glass smashed on the floor with a loud thud, and water soaked the floorboards.

"Brandon!" Emily's lovely face swept into view, a little out of focus. "What is it?"

"The bottle," he croaked out as pain shot up his spine.

"Do you need more tincture? Immediately."

"No, no."

She uncorked the bottle and started to pour the tincture into a spoon. For a moment, he stopped his protest. He yearned for the morphia, craved it, obsessed over it— a type of slavery that had held him prisoner for too many years. But it wasn't only him now.

He had a wife and wanted to start a family with her. He was stronger than before. Emily gave him that strength. She'd faced the Flying Scotsman for him. He could be strong for her. His love was certainly strong enough to help him refuse the potion.

I'm stronger than that.

"Here." When Emily offered him the spoon, he threw it away with a sloppy gesture.

He'd meant to wave his hand to say 'no,' but the aftermath of a good dose of opium had always left him clumsy, uncoordinated, and sleepy.

She gasped. He didn't mean to scare her, but his limbs didn't obey him well.

"No," he said again. Now he smelled the unmistakable pungent aroma of the morphia under the scent of the spices trying to hide it. "Opioids," he croaked out.

"What? It can't be." She took a sniff, then another, took a sip, and recoiled. "Goodness, Brandon." She uncorked the bottle again and breathed in. "Good Lord. The doctor gave you morphia."

He had to lie down and close his eyes not to snatch the bottle and drink the whole thing. "It was not a mistake."

Her chest rose and fell quickly. "Heavens. You're right. It was planned. Lady Robinson told my aunt about your problem with opium. My aunt hired that thug to hurt you and then she sent that strange doctor here to drug you. That monster!" Her nostrils flared as she clenched the bottle hard enough to whiten her knuckles. "Killing you would have been too suspicious, but if you become addicted to morphia again, it's another thing. If you were to be declared unfit to manage your estate, she would—" She let out a loud scoff.

Brandon stared at her, a little worried. She was a frightening sight. Her wrath was palpable; it charged the air between them like the smoke from a bonfire. He'd never seen her so angry. Her whole face transformed into that of a hardened warrior with amber eyes glowing from within.

"This menace ends here." She slid the bottle into her pocket and thrust out her chest. "Don't worry, my love. My aunt isn't going to threaten you ever again. I swear it."

"How?"

Instead of answering him, she marched out of the room with long strides like a woman on a mission.

"Emily?" He propped himself up again, his muscles tightening in protest. She wouldn't do anything reckless, would she? "Emily? Please come back."

"Brandon." Matthew strode in, his chest heaving. He must have slept in a room nearby, given how quickly he came. His nightshirt was all wrinkled, and even his face was bruised with fatigue. "How are you? What is it? Do you need the doctor again?"

Brandon shook his head. "Dr. Stewart works for Mrs. Allen. He gave me morphia, not valerian." He didn't need to add anything else.

"Bloody hell. I'm sorry, mate." Compassion and worry etched Matthew's face. He squeezed Brandon's shoulder lightly. "It was only one dose. We can do it."

The 'we' warmed Brandon's chest.

"We know what to do," Matthew said. "Lots of tea, fresh fruits, cod oil, and a bit of whiskey."

"Fantastic." He massaged his eyes.

Matthew crouched to collect the glass shards. "Emily?"

"I've never seen her so furious. I don't know what she has in mind. I'm worried."

"I'll keep an eye on her. You think about getting better." Matthew mopped the water with a cloth.

"Apologies, Master." Cowley entered as well. "I couldn't help but hear the conversation." He gave him a bottle with a dark liquid. "After the doctor left, I took the liberty of ordering more valerian tincture directly from Gibson's Pharmacy in case you needed it. I believe this is the real valerian tincture."

"You're always one step ahead of us," Matthew said without amusement though.

"It's my job, Mr. Tyrell," Cowley said.

"Thank you, Cowley." Brandon swallowed a spoonful of the tincture, and yes, the bitter, pungent taste had nothing to do with the delicious drug Dr. Stewart had given him. He coughed, trying to keep the potion down. Bugger. It was awful.

"I actually have some good news," Matthew said, finishing cleaning up the floor. "In a moment of unusual mercifulness, Lady Robinson approved our prototype. It's done. We're legal."

If Brandon's body weren't broken, he would cheer. In the pitiful state he was now, he could conjure only a faint smile. "Wonderful. I swear I'm more excited than it looks."

"You rest, Master." Cowley tucked the covers around him. "No more excitement for today."

Matthew smiled. "We'll celebrate once you're better."

Brandon dropped back onto the bed, fatigue shuddering through him. "Emily first. Don't let her do anything hasty."

"I'll personally take care of her." Matthew put a hand on his chest. "Trust me. She's in good hands."

Cowley shot his gaze towards the ceiling.

ANGER SEEMED to be a good motivator for Emily's hands to work properly because she managed to assemble the tiny centrifuge within a few hours. No screw was too small. No gear was too difficult to set. No spring was too tight. Did it work properly? Absolutely not, but she didn't care. Not now. The device twirled and spun. That was all that mattered. She admired her work with a sense of triumph she hadn't experienced in years. The centrifuge wasn't particularly pretty, just a ball of metal the size of an orange with cuts alongside it and mismatched bolts spread through its surface. Its appearance only added to the efficacy of her plan.

"There you are." Matthew entered without knocking. Or maybe he'd knocked and she hadn't heard it.

"Good morning, Matthew." Her voice sounded steely to her own ears.

He pointed a finger in the general direction downstairs. "Brandon is worried you might do something hasty. I swore to help you through this difficult moment."

"Nothing is hasty in my plan. Everything has been carefully planned and calculated." She showed him the centrifuge. The metal surface glinted in the sunlight.

"Er... well done! You assembled the centrifuge." He scrubbed the back of his neck, drawing his eyebrows together.

"It doesn't work, but that's what I want." She twisted the two semi-spheres in opposite directions to allow the internal spring to coil tightly, and a metallic noise similar to a clock's ticking came. Although that was it. No actual spinning happened. The small engine didn't work. But never mind.

Matthew raked a hand through his dishevelled hair. "Great. But I don't understand. What does the device have to do with helping Brandon?"

"Everything." She stashed the device in her reticule. "Where's the renunciation contract?"

"In Cowley's office. Why?"

"I'm going to visit Aunt Rose and I need the documents."

"I'll fetch them and come with you." He stared at her as if she'd gone mad. And maybe she had.

"Quickly though. I want this done and dealt with."

Ten minutes later, Matthew kept staring at her with a concerned stare as they drove to Aunt Rose's house in a closed carriage because Emily was through with fears and doubts. His bloodshot eyes, dishevelled hair, and wrinkled clothes proved he hadn't slept well, and his generally unkempt figure made him look like a madman. Perfect. Exactly what her plan required. She probably looked the same.

"Don't you want to tell me what your plan is?" he asked. "You aren't going to hurt your aunt, are you? I understand and share your anger, but murder tends to be taken rather seriously by the police."

She huffed. "Oh, please. Of course, I'm not going to hurt my aunt. Not physically, at least. Only in the spirit."

He frowned. "With a centrifuge that doesn't work."

She nodded. "With a centrifuge that doesn't work."

"Do you want to throw it against your aunt?"

"No."

He threw up a hand. "Fair enough. Why not? Let's use centrifuges to solve all our problems. The world doesn't make any sense anyway."

She didn't mind his sarcasm. "It will make sense." She needed him to be ignorant of her plan for now. The effect of his surprise would make everything more realistic.

He didn't ask her questions for the rest of the trip, muttering something under his breath.

When the carriage stopped, Emily didn't wait for Matthew to help her out. She knocked on the door to her aunt's house hard enough to hurt her knuckles, but she didn't care. Threatening and mistreating her was one thing. But attacking Brandon was quite another. Her aunt would soon discover the difference.

"Allen Residence— where are you going?" the maid said as Emily rushed past her and into the hallway. "Miss Emily, what are you doing here!"

"It's Lady Astley, Countess of Hastings," Emily said.

Matthew followed, muttering an apology.

"Aunt?" She stomped upstairs to her aunt's study. She flung the door open with a kick, startling her aunt who was sitting at her desk.

"What is the meaning of this?" Her aunt touched her neck, standing up. Goodness. Her nose was still swollen, and a large bruise crossed it.

Matthew clenched his fists. Anger distorted his features. He seemed the one who was about to commit murder. "You hag! You hurt Brandon, and for what? So that you can buy pretty dresses?"

Aunt Rose pressed her lips. "How dare you! I don't know what you're talking about."

"Oh, really?" Matthew shot forwards. "I'll—"

Emily grabbed his arm and stopped him. "Remember what you told me in the carriage. Let me handle this. Please."

Folding his arms over his chest, Matthew gave her a brusque nod.

She showed her aunt the bottle of morphia. "I know what you did. I know about the thug you paid to hurt Brandon and the fake doctor you, or maybe Mr. Payne, hired to give him morphia."

Aunt Rose didn't flinch. Only her brow furrowed.

"Your pathetic attempts to hurt us will end now. Here." She slammed the documents on the table. "Sign the renunciation contract. Now."

Aunt Rose flustered. "I don't know what you're talking about, and I'm not signing anything without consulting my solicitor."

"Hag," Matthew repeated but with more venom.

"Sign," Emily said through clenched teeth. "You sign this deed of renunciation, and I won't tell anyone what you did. You'll keep what little is left of your dignity."

Aunt Rose's face hardened. "No one will believe you or your husband. A hysterical woman, who becomes agitated and panic-stricken when she sees a carriage, and an opium-addict earl." She huffed. "I'm not going to sign anything, and once your new husband is declared insane, I'll take care of your inheritance and even his money. It turned out that your eloping was the right thing to do. For me. Do you have an idea how difficult it was to take care of you without help? You owe me everything."

Emily exhaled theatrically. "Thank goodness I've come prepared." She opened her bag and took out the centrifuge.

Matthew lost some of his composure and shifted his weight. Likely, he didn't trust her.

"What is that?" Aunt Rose said.

Emily put the device on the table and kept her unblinking stare on her aunt. "A bomb so powerful that, if it goes off, it'll burn your house to the ground." She rotated the two semi-spheres, and the clockwork started ticking. "You have ten seconds to sign. If you don't sign, I'll set the bomb off."

"This is absurd." Aunt Rose's gaze flickered over the device.

Matthew croaked out an icy laugh. "Yes, yes! Do you hear that? Boom! Bang! The whole house. Everything. And goodbye, Mrs. Allen!"

Goodness. Emily didn't know if she should be impressed or worried. He did seem deranged.

Aunt Rose's eyes showed too much white. "But you'll die as well."

Emily forced her face to remain deadpan. "If I can't have the life I want and keep the man I love safe, then so be it." It was a bluff, but she was glad her voice didn't betray her.

"Perhaps we're all addicted to laudanum. Perhaps we're all mad." Matthew laughed again, a deep, cavernous laughter that echoed eerily. "Tick. Tock. Tick. Tock," Matthew chanted.

"It's true, dear aunt." Emily tilted her head. "Maybe you are right. Maybe I hit my head too hard during the accident, and now I'm a little deranged."

"Sign, Mrs. Allen. Time is slipping away," Matthew went on.

Smoke rose from the centrifuge. That wasn't part of the plan, and Emily had no idea what was happening inside the device, but the timing was perfect.

Aunt Rose grabbed the pen and scribbled her signature on the document faster than one could say hag. "There. Done. Now leave and never come back, you crazy demons!"

"With pleasure." Emily twisted the spheres again, stopping the ticking noise. "Ouch!" The metal burned.

Matthew came to her rescue, hastily shoving the device in his pocket and collecting the document.

Aunt Rose sagged in her chair. "Out now! Or I'll call the police. Leave!"

Matthew sneered one last time before rushing out of the room.

Emily didn't smile until she was on the pavement. It'd worked, and it'd been magnificent.

Matthew whooped when they were outside. "You brilliant, amazing woman." He hugged her so tightly she gasped. "I will never, ever doubt you. Let's go to give your husband the good news."

BRANDON COULDN'T BELIEVE what Emily had told him. He'd listened speechless to her story about a centrifuge, a bomb, and Matthew becoming deranged.

She waved the deed of renunciation. "... and she signed it! I'm a free woman, and you're safe from other attacks."

"Blimey." He touched the ugly device she'd built. It did look menacing. "And you scared her with this thing."

"Yes." She blushed and lifted her shoulders. "It was a silly idea, but it worked. Matthew helped. You should have seen him. He was out of control. I didn't tell him anything on purpose. When he understood what I wanted to do, his face transformed. He was scary."

He smiled and opened his arms. "You're an amazing woman."

She giggled. "Funny. That's what Matthew said before he hugged me. I think he squeezed me so hard he bruised me."

"Excuse me?" He would have a word with Matthew soon. "He hugged you?"

"In complete friendship." She snuggled next to him with caution. "I couldn't let my aunt hurt you and not force her to face the consequences, and I'd had enough of being bullied by her."

He scattered kisses over her face. "I'm so proud of you."

She kissed him, a deep, lingering kiss that made him forget about his back. "So am I of you. You found the strength to reject the opium. I know how difficult it must have been for you."

"Without you, I wouldn't have been strong at all. It was you who stopped me." He kissed her again, a slow kiss to savour her. That was all he could do at the moment.

She hugged him, and he rested his aching head on her chest.

"Listen, do you really want to cut all ties with your aunt and cousin?" he asked.

"Absolutely." No hesitation.

He winced as he moved on the bed. The valerian tincture worked better than he'd imagined, but the pain never really left him. "They're the only family you have."

She frowned. "My aunt is a horrible person, and Catherine isn't different."

"Yes, but—"

"But?" She arched a brow. The same warrior-like glint as before flickered in her gaze.

"Unless your aunt pays for the expenses she's made since moving here, she'll be thrown in prison, and after that she and Catherine won't have any means to survive. Catherine's life will be ruined. What do you think will happen to a young, pretty woman like Catherine?" He brushed a curl from her face. "We can afford to be generous. We can pay her debts and offer her an allowance to lead a decent life."

She stuck out her bottom lip in an expression that held more determination than cuteness. "She doesn't deserve our generosity. She's the cause of her own suffering."

"It might be in our interest as well. While I think your plan was brilliant, your aunt signed the deed under duress." That was a bit of law he knew well. "There have been cases like that before. A contract signed under duress might be invalidated by the court."

Emily drew in a breath. "She wouldn't win!"

"She might, with a solicitor like Payne. Let's show her some compassion, and she'll be out of our lives for good. Compassion will disarm her, make her feel ashamed of her actions, and she'll owe us a huge favour."

Her shoulders stooped. "You're too kind and with a heart of gold. I wonder what I have done to deserve you."

He kissed her again. "Just being you."

epilogue
Three months later

BRANDON STROKED DIABLO'S muzzle and scratched the spot on his sleek neck the horse loved the most. It'd taken weeks of hard work, tonnes of apples, and moments in which he had to dodge a hoof or two, but finally he and Diablo had forged an agreement. Brandon's pulse stopped spiking whenever Diablo was close, and Diablo stopped shooting glares at Brandon or threatening him with his hooves. Yes, Brandon was convinced the stallion could glare at him.

To be fair, the misunderstanding was all his fault because the moment he'd stopped being afraid of Diablo, the horse had trusted him immediately. He was sorry it'd taken him so long to befriend Diablo. The horse was indeed a gentle giant with a sense of humour although Matthew said it wasn't possible. But Brandon had heard that before.

Healing his back had been faster. The valerian tincture had helped, but Emily's hands had done wonders. He had a massage every evening and morning, and his muscles kept improving. He might ride Diablo one day. Besides, Diablo would become a father soon. The broodmare Matthew had bought, Diablesa, had ignited

Diablo's passion immediately. One glance at her, and the stallion had been thoroughly smitten with the dark beauty.

In the pasture with Emily and Cowley, he smiled at the two magnificent horses.

Emily hooked her arm through his. "I'm so happy you and Diablo are friends now."

"He's going to pull our second wedding carriage. I have to be his friend." He kissed the horse. Yes, he did. He often did.

"Your parents would be—" Cowley couldn't finish the sentence as a sob came out of him. He took out his handkerchief. "Sorry, sir."

"Not at all." Brandon hugged him. "Although you seem prouder of my progress with Diablo than of my progress with controlling my addiction to laudanum."

Cowley wiped his eyes. "You've always been scared of horses. You used to grab my leg and not let me go whenever a horse was close."

"Did he?" Emily asked. Too much astonishment rang in her voice.

"Cowley exaggerates." Brandon caressed Diablo again. "I did let him go eventually."

Cowley laughed behind the handkerchief.

"How's the dress fitting going?" Brandon asked Emily.

She exhaled. "Mrs. Sala is an artist, the best modiste in town, but she keeps changing her mind about what type of fabric and which colour she should use. I've seen dozens of absolutely perfect gowns that I loved, but she refused to listen."

"Only the best for you." He kissed her.

"Thank you, darling, but if she doesn't make a decision, the wedding will arrive, and I won't have a wedding dress. I don't want to postpone it."

"Because your class on chemical engineering starts soon? Or because you really want to marry me again?"

She grinned. "The classes might be one of the reasons. But I do want to marry you again."

Matthew strolled towards them. He walked with jauntiness, and his dreamy air softened his expression. "Good morning, sir, madam, Cowley." He flourished a hand. "Diablo, how's our stallion doing?"

"Diablo and Diablesa are doing well. Did something happen to you?" Brandon asked.

Matthew sighed. "Lady Robinson happened."

"Matthew!" Emily put a hand on her chest. "Have you met that woman?"

Matthew nodded. "For work, mostly. She signed the documents, but there were other little things to take care of."

"But you don't have to deal with her personally," Brandon said.

Matthew lifted a shoulder. "She's truly sorry for how she behaved towards both of you. She's a lovely lady, lonely I have to add. Her husband doesn't pay attention to her. I enjoy her company."

Cowley pinched the bridge of his nose.

"I haven't forgiven her," Emily said. "And I'm not going to."

Oh, well. Did it matter? Brandon hugged Emily, Matthew, and Cowley, happy to have his family around him. Diablo nudged him with his muzzle, and Brandon welcomed him into his trusted circle. Diablesa joined them, nudging him with her head. Now his happiness was complete.

He'd lost his family but found another one.

THE END

about the author

Love stories have always captured my imagination. What's better than two people falling in love with each other? I write steamy romance, usually with a paranormal twist in an historical setting. Add a touch of suspense and mystery and a pinch of darkness. I love stories with strong, sexy heroes and mischievous heroines who pull no punches.

I live in the City of Sails, New Zealand, drinking tea (coffee gives me anxiety) and devouring books.

Join my newsletter for exclusive content and the chance to receive an ARC copy of my books. Just copy and paste this link into your browser:

Barbara's Newsletter

also by barbara russell

If you love steamy paranormal romance set in Victorian London, my Royal Occult Bureau series is for you:

The Royal Occult Bureau Series

Are you into shape-shifter romance? Check out my da Vinci's Beasts series, set in WW2:

da Vinci's Beasts Series

For more Victorian paranormal romance with witches and sexy warriors, see the Knights of the White Blade series:

The White Order Series

Love steampunk? Check out my Auckland Steampunk series:

Auckland Steampunk Series

www.ingramcontent.com/pod-product-compliance
Ingram Content Group UK Ltd.
Pitfield, Milton Keynes, MK11 3LW, UK
UKHW010839260525
6079UKWH00009B/46